Andrew M. Stephenson was born in Venezuela
of British parents in 1946, but was educated in
the United Kingdom. He graduated from
The City University, London in 1969 and went
to work for a large telecommunications
company, where he was employed on circuit
design of data processing and transmission
equipment. Writing and illustrating was just a
hobby, but science fiction writing has now
become a full time career. This is Mr.
Stephenson's first full length novel.

Andrew M. Stephenson

Nightwatch

Liberty means responsibility.
That is why most men dread it.

George Bernard Shaw:
Maxims for Revolutionaries.

Futura Publications Limited
An Orbit Book

An Orbit Book

First published in Great Britain by
Futura Publications Limited in 1977

ISBN 0 8600 7957 0

Printed in Great Britain by
C. Nicholls & Company Ltd
The Philips Park Press
Manchester

Futura Publications Limited
110 Warner Road, Camberwell,
London S.E.5

the first
is for

my mother and father

for more than
the traditional reasons

acknowledgements

this one page is dedicated to
all the writers who have
made science fiction what
it is today

however
a number of other people
who rendered material
assistance also deserve to
be mentioned

I list them
in the order which pleases me
not
that which signifies relative
gratitude;
without the efforts of any
single one I consider the
whole would be the less:

Chris Priest

Coral Clarke

Judy Blish

Rob Holdstock

not mentioned here are some
who might argue that they
were only doing their job;
nevertheless their help also
is appreciated.

Andrew Stephenson
September 1976

PART ONE

CHAPTER ONE

A tall gaunt man sat down on my right.

I nodded to him. He smiled weakly back at me. We said nothing at first; it was not the time for conversation. Like me my new neighbour seemed to have been, in the euphemistic jargon of the medical technicians, 'depilated' all over. I could tell by the way he kept his eyes directed towards the floor that he wished to be alone for the moment.

It was a feeling with which I could sympathise. Seated in the large white departure lounge at Cape Canaveral, freshly clothed in faintly aromatic white coveralls, waiting for the groundcrew to start hustling us into the shuttles, I think we were all suffering from partial disorientation. The new aesthetics of our surroundings, coming so quickly after the humiliating treatment meted out by the space facility medics, were overwhelmingly strange to ordinary citizens for whom science had been more a profession than a way of life.

The public address system chimed softly. *"Group Alpha-One prepare to board in five minutes. Five minutes."*

That meant I had about a quarter of an hour to wait before my group was called. To pass the time I watched the people drifting in from the medical area. It was marvellous, I thought, how wide a selection of types had been caught in the project's net, of all sizes and races, of both sexes in about equal numbers, of almost any age short of fifty albeit most were young; I took that more as an indicator of loss of scientific expertise with age than physical debility, however. One deficiency did strike me after a while: there were no children. It was not immediately apparent in that coldly adult place. The Moon, I realised, might well have been inhabited by mankind for nearly twenty years; but it had

5

yet to be colonised. We were all bound there for some short-term purpose, every one of us to apply his or her freak talent in the cause of some as-yet-secret scheme. In a way it was flattering to have been selected, for I was sure that none of my fellow travellers was in any way of average intelligence or training. An elite of freaks indeed. At that time it did not occur to me to wonder why so many skilled people should be needed so early in what I understood to be an extremely long-term project.

The chimes sounded again. *"Group Alpha-One to Gate 64–B, please."* People began to stand up while the chimes repeated themselves between restatements of the announcement in various languages. Each chime was like a ringing bell, softly persistent

insistent, beating into my subconscious mind, prising me from sleep into wakefulness. Stiffly I rolled over in bed and felt for the unfamiliar instrument. My groping fingers nudged the handset onto the bedside table, where it clattered loudly in the sudden silence. I picked it up and put it to my ear.

"Frome," I sighed.

The operator was faint and indistinct, as required by long and honourable tradition. He seemed to say, "Mister Daniel Frome?"

I thought about it. Outside my room the CIA men were murmuring to each other. One laughed quietly. A lorry rushed past the motel, its headlights turning the window blinds a speckled yellow for a few seconds.

"Yes," I admitted at last.

"A call for you from the United Kingdom. One moment please."

The line became clearer. I heard Helen's voice.

"Dan?"

I wanted to groan; the authorities should have blocked the call. Instead, I yawned, adding: "Did you know it's night over here?" Then, as an afterthought: "Anyway, good morning."

"I'm sorry," she said. "I completely forgot about the five hours."

"You're forgiven," I said. Could I have bawled her out? Hardly; and Helen knew it, for she said drily:

6

"*Mea culpa*." There was a pause. "Dan, I had to speak to you again."

"So?" I said, with my throat tight. My voice did not quite betray me.

I imagined her twisting the telephone cord around her left forefinger. In the background the radio was bleating out some inane lovesong. Breakfast-time, with one end of the table laid : one small plate, with toasted brek-bisk and a pat of vitaminised margarine; a mug of coffee, with its plume of steam –

"Dan, don't go . . . Please."

"Helen, this line will be bugged."

"I don't care. Just don't sign on tomorrow –"

"Today," I interrupted her, angry that she should compromise me so seriously. Again and again I had explained to her the terms of my indenture to the government. Only someone who has been a ward of the State can ever understand how complete is the legal obligation, amounting to slavery, with which I started my professional life. Helen knew the words of my story; she did not care to believe the sense of it. To her I was an unfortunate economic orphan, not someone stolen from his parents by bureaucracy.

"As you say," she replied: "today . . . Dan, until you sign that paper they can't touch you."

"They can and they will," I said. "Goodnight, Helen."

"Dan, listen! You could be killed so easily up there! Two years –"

"Goodnight," I repeated. She fell quiet. I went on, more gently: "Helen, whatever happens, remember: I do care about you."

The click from the phone was loud in the quiet bedroom as I replaced the handset. For some while I lay awake in bed, thinking

about the past with all its twisting false trails that had brought me finally to this sterile room, filled with waiting lines of people, lit by acres of glowing glass, redolent of plastic.

My neighbour roused himself suddenly and looked around at me.

7

"Getting to you too, is it?" he asked. His accent suggested West Coast, perhaps Los Angeles, tainted with another elusive sound quality.

"Yes," I said, wishing I had a moment's privacy in which to recover from the memory of the night before last. Cutting Helen off like that had been a painful act but a necessary one, vital lest she say anything to harm herself.

I saw that we were amongst the last left sitting. For some reason the groundcrew were marshalling all the groups at once preparatory to boarding.

"I'm Frome," I said. "Dan Frome."

"Byron Yale," he replied, adding with a smile: "From Harvard." His face lengthened abruptly. "God, I never guessed it'd be like this, not quite. The lectures didn't mention, well ..." He swept a hand cautiously over his scalp and inspected the palm. "Bald as a coot," he observed. "The kids would love to see me now ... You English?"

"British," I corrected him. When he displayed surprise I explained: "One of those unimportant technicalities that only politicians and hijack insurance forms worry about."

"Oh," he said. "Yes." He looked puzzled, then shook his head as if that would dismiss the illogic of it. "I guess it could matter to some people."

There had once been a time, back during my country days as a child in Somerset, when such distinctions had seemed purely technical to me also.

"Which shuttle are you on?" I asked.

"Second. And you?"

"The same. Want to ride up together?" I was desperate to escape from introspection. Talk might help.

"Suits me," he said, "so long as the loading clerk's scheduled our mass that way."

It transpired that we had both been seated near the middle of the rocket, yet it would hardly have mattered had we been at opposite ends. There turned out to be no way of holding a conversation other than by sign language, a development I should have expected from our training. We were strapped into our seats in turn by brisk groundcrew who made us wear full-face masks through which our fresh breathing air was supplied. Only the most determined of conversationalists could have communicated more than a mumble.

Thus I was alone, amongst so many, whose massed breathing merged with their restless movements and the countless noises of the rocket gathering its strength for the takeoff. Together they subsided into the background of my thoughts.

It was late summer, 2006, and already verging on autumn. September had started cold in Britain; and in Florida they were turning down the air conditioners. Sixteen years earlier there had been another damp chilly summer, one that never failed to spoil the autumn for me ever after. The image of my father, doggedly striding through his own fields, fanning the hot breath of the flame thrower across the deformed crops; the government men watching from the road, unsure whether to defy his will and take over from him so as to finish the job quicker; my mother, dry-eyed, holding me close while we looked on too : these are my September memories.

I believe our farm was one of the last to be taken over by the State. Owing to archaic laws of tenure, Somerset in the late 1980's still harboured its private farms, like field mice amongst the government corn. When ours was caught and killed by the progress of society, I like to think it did not collapse unobserved by history.

My personal history, by contrast, was undistinguished. Governments and boys of nine are unequal adversaries : I followed where I was led. A ward of the State has no choice. In education, practical training, and employment, I was fitted into the national interest. Throughout the process the State's experience in handling human beings ensured all went according to the book. Unfortunately, they failed to allow for Helen Lorraine *and* the Golem project. Naturally the two clashed.

Even through the shuttle's hull we heard the first flight go up on time. We felt it too, as a muted juddering of our seats that unsettled the viscera and made one think of earthquakes. Yale, I noticed, gripped his armrests until the sound and the sensation had ended. Seconds later the earphones in our masks beeped.

"This is Ground Control, Passenger Liaison," announced a

female voice. "*Welcome aboard shuttle flight Ten-Three Oh-Six, Alpha Two. In approximately nine minutes we shall be lifting from Pad 64–D for rendezvous with translunar carrier Pegasus Four in two hours or so. We shall be employing maximum admissible thrust, which in your case will create an acceleration of roughly* –" There was the briefest of pauses as the computer inserted the correct words; the launch control sequencer was taking a few microseconds off to supervise a multi-track tape deck somewhere – "*six gravities.*" Another pause. "*May we remind you that any attempt to loosen your harness could easily result in fatal injuries both to yourself and your co-passengers. As in the training simulator, should you find yourself in need of comfort please press the red button on your face mask. This will summon aid or, when free movement is inadvisable, administer a mild tranquilliser gas mixture. As a last resort, comfort bags are stored in the locker in front of you. Please dispose of these thoughtfully in the same locker and remember to twist-seal them after use. Neighbours are encouraged to assist. We regret that refreshment and sanitary facilities are unavailable at this stage in your journey. We hope you have a pleasant flight. Thank you.*"

This cheering message was repeated in Russian, French, German, Chinese, and a number of other languages. Every broadcast contained the same double pause. I accepted the information without being deluded that this was to be in any way a luxury journey. Ruggedness was still a key concept in the design of all space hardware and passengers were only system components whose critical yield points had been assessed and accommodated.

But there were nine minutes to wait. No, eight. Or maybe less. Far too long, in any event, to be locked up with the recent past.

Swallows had been barnstorming the Space Museum like miniature orange-and-blue kamikaze planes as I mounted the steps to the new entrance. From behind the glass doors the flabby guard eyed them with the same attentive hostility a sedentary cat devotes to birds just beyond its reach; and when I pushed through into the cool lobby to present my credentials he seemed glad of the interruption. Nevertheless he carefully straightened his tie and slipped on his dove-grey jacket with its gold piping and gaudy badges before he would accept my wallet. He peered at the identity card for a long time.

"This supposed to be you?" he said at last, glancing from me to the colour photo. "It sure don't look like you."

"They never do," I said.

"If they can land a man on Mars I don't see why they can't make halfway decent photos," he grumbled. Pointing to the picture of Helen in the opposite panel, he asked pleasantly, "This your girl, Mr. Frome?"

"That's right," I said. I was anxious to escape his chatter. "Is this —"

"Looks mighty like my eldest," he said. "Hair's the same. Don't often see genuine blondes that colour." Folding the wallet he returned it to me. "Going up tomorrow, Mr. Frome?"

"Yes," I said. "Look, is this place open?" Helen was too recent a wound for any discussion of her to be other than painful.

"To you guys, any time." He waved a key at the inner doors and one sprang wide for me. As I left him in the lobby, silhouetted against the midday glare, I observed on his face the same expression as he had used on the birds: hatred vieing with jealousy. Frozen into his union sinecure at Cape Canaveral, one step from space, he would gladly have thrown up his job for the imagined freedom of the Moon, whatever its dangers. But just as surely as the wrong sort of expertise had confined Helen to Earth and the study of its deep oceans, the guard's rudimentary schooling barred him from the Moon and Dvornik Base. Had he known the truth, the man would not have envied me.

Behind me the glass door boomed shut. My heels clicked on the fleck-patterned stone floor, scattering echoes through the cathedral gloom of the Museum like the footsteps of exploring children.

Enough of the stands were incomplete to give the series of boxy exclosures the appearance of a film set. None of the exhibits belonged inside a normal building, relating as they did to advanced space research whose proper backdrop was stars and scenes of alien worlds. Pastel chipboard was all wrong. It made the satellites and probes look like exotic butterflies pinned out for exhibition by a collector.

The section devoted to cybernetic systems was well advertised, as it was expected to draw most of the crowds. I strolled along an avenue of chunky boxes resplendent in gold, silver, and black and found my life's work tucked away in an alcove of their own.

All three three computers were labelled collectively as Project Golem, though in fact only the two most recent versions had been funded by the government. The earliest had been a private venture by Deltrak, my employers in the UK, and I was amused to note that the company came well down the list of credits to the participating firms.

There was, however, no mention of me. Not that it mattered. No bureacratic love of personal anonymity could erase me from the memories each computer held in its store. I was part of them. When the exhibit itself will speak on behalf of its designer, who needs a label?

The power leads, I saw, were already connected, which was a relief. Theoretically the units would speak when running on their internal storage cells but doing so severely debilitated their reserves. I felt along the underside of the oldest for the switch we had installed before shipping it off to the Museum, as protection against casual interrogation by visitors. Robots were not so well established in everyday society that people would not flock to hear one talking, which would annoy the Museum authorities.

The click was nearly inaudible, yet I knew at once that the machine was aware of me, for the loudspeaker rustled softly, the mechanical equivalent of a man preparing to speak.

I stood back from the built-in camera.

"Remember me?" I said.

The response was surprisingly prompt. In its characteristically hoarse croak it said, simply: "Dan."

This cheered me. It was as if I had encountered a long-lost friend.

"How are you?"

It hesitated before answering. Disillusionment followed as it replied:

"Define dimension to be quantified."

I had forgotten how far we had progressed since the early days.

Even the voice box had been improved on. Sadly I switched it off again, reflecting that once this machine had been regarded as a marvel.

I activated the second, which dated from no more than six months after the first.

"Remember me?" I said the words with greater caution; the Mark Two had never really been pleasant company: too cerebral, too clever, too noticeably non-human. Those words had always been the same, the opening phrase of a complex test litany, a mandala of trap-phrases and misleading idioms with which to draw out the robot's nature for analysis. For months I had lived with them, reiterating paragraph and chapter until I could recite them from memory.

The Golem took its time in answering.

"I think so. Daniel Frome?"

"How are you?"

"Operational, if smaller than when we last spoke."

That had been in North Africa, when the multi-purpose robot was being tested in the chassis of a giant earth mover.

"But how are *you*?" – Test PSYCH–TT8902: self awareness/identity resolution.

"Idle. I have nothing to do."

"Are you bored?" – Test VOCAB–WG6494: language extrapolation and usage.

"I still do not understand that word. No meaningful answer."

"Will you be okay here?" – Personal interest. You don't spend several months with a thinking creature without learning to care about its feelings.

"There is power. I should continue to exist for a long time."

And it would be a meaningless existence, I was sure. No-one else would think to come and talk with this machine, except in the cause of further research. Dispassionate caretakers would clean its outer casing. Occasionally some technician would make good any incidental damage to paintwork and power leads. But ultimately there would come a day when the machine would not respond to the special switch and would stay silent. Then, to save the few milliwatts of electricity the robot consumed, its supply would be disconnected; and the dead box of electronics alone would remain to be stared at by people who thought themselves so very clever for being born in an age when robots were taken for granted.

What would they know or care about these early days of struggle?

There was one last favour I could do for the Golem without compromising myself with the Museum authorities.

"Do you want to ... exist?" I asked.

Somehow, that question had never been asked before, I realised. A moment's further thought demonstrated that no intellect as totally self-aware as the Golem could answer it: its mind was constructed to presuppose indefinitely continuous anticipation of the future; death, I was sure, meant nothing to such a machine.

"Please restate the question," it said. And waited.

I wrestled with my conscience. With three instructions I could wipe its mind clean of all thoughts; it was only a machine and could not resist me. At the same time, however, those instructions would wipe out part of my own life, so that no-one but I would know where that time had gone. In the balance was: compassion that might be misplaced; and selfishness that might be something worse, arrogance perhaps. It would not be like the old days in the lab, where reprogramming facilities were available. The decision, once made, was irreversible, for the original tapes had been destroyed, the computers reallocated to new work, and I was off about other business. I had qualms about taking such a step.

Then I saw that there was no choice open. If I cared, I had to close the account cleanly. Quietly, I set about murdering a mind.

"Revert to basic control code," I whispered.

"Basic loaded."

My heart had begun to beat fast.

"Call Program END–DUMP OMEGA –" I had to think; it had been at least a year since I had needed to use this order sequence. The numbers came back to me all of a sudden: "– Zero Nine Two Three."

"Program END–DUMP OMEGA-0923 ready."

I could still pull back. I did not.

"Go," I said.

That was it. To be sure, I said:

"Remember me?"

Silence.

I switched off the voice box and left the Golem to its mindless empty dreams.

I found I was trembling. There was a lump in my throat. Unable to face the last of the three units, I made for the doorway. A pretty girl was standing there. Several seconds passed.

"Remember *me?*" she asked.

With a shock, I recognised her as Helen. Only then did I realise how involved I had become with my past.

She appeared tired. There was dust on her shoes; and her coat, which was far too heavy for the Florida climate, was creased. Nevertheless she had managed to retain her dignity.

I almost opened my mouth to answer her but could think of nothing to say. Words would have lent an uncomfortable precision to my feelings.

"Well?" she said. Her greeting felt like an accusation.

I smiled, a little too automatically. "Of course," I said.

"Is that all?"

"I . . . You shouldn't have come. It was a wasted ticket."

"The Department paid. I traded the ticket to the Woods Hole conference."

"That's not for two weeks. How are you going to afford to live here? Have you seen the prices?"

"I'll stay with friends . . . Dan, I don't give up easily." Then she lowered her eyes. "Anyway, I had to come. An argument is a dreadful way of saying goodbye."

"It's forgotten," I lied, hurting at the remembrance of it.

"You don't forget that quickly." She paused long enough for me to protest, had I been about to; I was too slow. "Neither do I," she added, wistfully. "That proves something, doesn't it?"

"I'm still obliged to go," I said.

We looked at each other. I took hold of her hands and leaned forwards to kiss her but she turned her face away with a jerk, and said:

"Are you sure you mean it?"

"Yes." This time I did not hesitate.

She faced me again. "How much? How sincere are you?"

"About you, absolutely. About the project ... 'Sincere' isn't the right word. Sometimes I couldn't care less; at others I get frightened, just thinking about how important it is. Helen, don't force a choice, please."

She nodded and kissed me. "There," she said, with a smile.

I wasn't convinced that the matter had been settled.

"The guard," I said, to fill the conversational void that developed. "How did he know to let you in?"

"That's the funny thing: he said he recognised me. Strange man."

"The photo in my wallet," I said, recalling his interest in it.

A light frown puckered her forehead. "May I see it?" When I gave her the wallet she cradled it in one hand, studying the photograph.

"It was very different then," she said.

"Yes," I agreed. No more than four years. Her hair had been longer. Otherwise she still looked the same. The changes had occurred around us.

"And in the future, Dan? Two years this time. But the next — how much of you can they take? You said this was a probe to Jupiter; what are the chances you'll be on the first manned mission?"

"Negligible. I'll be too old by then."

"You're not even thirty."

"Damn close, though. By the time they stop using robots I'll be past it."

"And what's to prevent them keeping you on the Moon?"

"With my indenture due to expire in three years? They wouldn't take the risk of having to pay me full lunar rate, or the insurance premiums." I managed a laugh. "Just hang on. You'll see: I'll be back; and with the extra points this'll put on my qualification index —"

"No, Dan," she said. I felt cold. My heart seemed not to beat for a second. "It's the principle that matters. I don't want to see you gobbled up by the space programme, on the Moon or here on Earth. You've chosen. So have I." She folded the wallet and pressed it into my hand gently. "Keep the photo. As a souvenir."

And she was halfway out of the door before I caught her arm. "Helen," I said. "Wait a minute." I found myself gripped by something like panic. "I've changed my mind."

"Oh?" she regarded me sideways.

Far down the corridor I could see the guard standing with his hands in his pockets, peering out at the wheeling swooping swallows.

"I'm not going," I said; and felt free.

I had perceived how poor a substitute the romance of space was for that of real life. To spend the next few years trapped in the company of inhuman intellects was an appalling prospect, one it would be as well to avoid, especially if it meant losing touch with the one person in the world whom I truly valued.

Her reaction, however, was far from what I had anticipated. Glancing at the ceiling, she briefly closed her eyes, then drew a deep breath and turned on me. "You bloody fool!" she said.

I stared at her, numbed.

She went on: "Do you think I don't know you well enough after four years to see you really were prepared to go off and leave me? I can't imagine what this secret work can be; but you wouldn't care so much about it unless it mattered. Dan, I came here to be sure. Don't let me down now."

"They only think they need me up there," I said, adding as I pointed to the third Golem, tiger-striped in gold and black, like two shoe boxes on a pedestal: "*That's* the sort of robot they'll have on the Moon. The others were prototypes, simple things. *They'd* need me. That one, it doesn't. Not really. He's good. Special."

"Oh Dan," she replied, shaking her head. "I caught that sad little sideshow earlier. Until I heard you talking to them I thought you were building robots like the ones on television, that can always take care of themselves. These are helpless."

I was undecided. I could over-rule her argument and march us both out of the Museum or I could risk a demonstration.

Suddenly she said: "I'll make a bet with you: that I can convince you within five minutes, if you'll let me talk to that thing."

So I switched on the third Golem, the justification of six-thousand man-years of effort, the king-pin of my reputation, the same reputation I was willing to discard within the hour if I could convince Helen of my case. There was no real uncertainty as to the outcome. The robot could think rings around many humans; I could depend on it to set her mind to rest.

"Remember me?" I said.

"Yes, Dan," it answered smoothly. "Of course I do. And I remember all those other silly tests too. Don't bother with them. I'm fine; in fact, I'll last a damn sight longer than you will, if what I've overheard of your tryst is any guide. That switch doesn't control my ears, you know. Dan, you want my advice too: don't be an idiot. Go to the Moon."

Trans-shipment from the factory had done the computer no harm whatsoever.

"Helen would like to talk to you."

"I know. But what about you?"

Helen said, "May I . . . please?"

Before I could answer its last remark, the Golem had switched its attention to Helen. "Dear lady, you may talk to me any time."

"Have you a name? I wouldn't like to say 'hey you' all the time."

"*He* does," said the robot. "Officially, I'm GOLEM–30–001. Will that do?"

"It's not terribly friendly."

"Then call me –" It broke off for what I swear was a laugh. "Call me Ishmael."

"For God's sake," I said. "Why *Ishmael*?"

"He was Queequeg's friend."

"So?"

"Queequeg harpooned Moby Dick, the great white whale."

"That's enough," I said harshly. The robot's remarks meant nothing to me then but I sensed trouble. "Whatever you've overheard, keep it to yourself."

"You might prefer to be told."

"I doubt it."

"Three people came here a week ago. One was from the CIA; the other two were foreigners, a Russian and a Japanese. The Japanese kept asking if I was really able to compute real-time strategies applicable to impulse-fire weapons –"

"Don't say another word," I said. There was a moment's silence. "That's an order."

"Make it a request and I'll do as you ask, Dan."

"Okay, it's a request." I took Helen's arm. "This is a waste of time," I said to her. "Let's get out of here."

"Uh-uh," she said. "Stay right where you are. We have a bet, remember?" She addressed the Golem: "Ishmael, will you tell me something?"

"I will try."

"Can you tell lies?"

"No."

I roused myself from thinking over what the Golem had told me. "Yes he can. That's his rotten sense of humour. Epiminedes' Paradox doesn't work either. Lies and other irrational statements have a special set of conceptual filters assigned to them in his input buffer. Likewise in his output language interface. He can lie, with the best of them."

"Dan, I am deeply wounded."

"You'll recover. Now answer the question she should have asked."

"My dear," the Golem said, "what our friend is suggesting is that your question is a prime example of a query with implied conditionals, only he lacks the command of English so to express himself. Certainly I can lie; I can also make mistakes. In order that the distinction between classes of truth may be free of any arbitrary quantisation process, I grade all my internalised information according to veracity, certainty, and importance. In this way I preserve a picture of right and wrong, which can guide the development of any scenarios I may have in hand. At the same time, I am predisposed towards honesty, so any excursions into deceit are purely for constructive purposes. That is, I may lie but only beneficently. I never knowingly generate a false statement except in error or without making it good in the long run."

"What he's trying to say," I remarked, "is that he won't mislead you for the sake of it."

"Must you be so simplistic?" asked Ishmael.

Had I been arguing with a human I might not have taken the objection seriously. As it was, Golems did not operate according

19

to human rules, so if Ishmael felt moved to complain of my summary I felt obliged to respect its feelings.

"I'm sorry," I said. "But you were being longwinded."

"Since when has the truth been simple?"

Helen said, "Suppose you had to lie to someone you expected never to see again and whom you would hurt with your lie, could you, do you think?"

"And? . . ."

"And nothing. That's all."

"But what is the nature of the lie? To what purpose?"

"Generalise the problem. Invent a reason if you must have one."

"Tell me more about this person."

"Does this have to be a special case?" she asked, frowning.

"It's implicit in the question. Before I can lie I must know more. Action without purpose is action wasted. Why should I commit violence on the truth for no good reason? The truth may be more effective unperverted. It may even be kinder."

"Does hurting people bother you?"

"Of course it does. Any careless disruption of order is a bad thing. I think you are trying to confuse me. Dan, I can't answer such vague questions."

Helen's look of satisfaction made my heart sink. There was, as she had guessed by some unknown means, a flaw in the psychology of the Golem. Also, as we had inadvertently learned, there was more to the Golem project than even I had been told. Either fact would have been cause enough to demand my presence on the Moon.

"That's all right, Ishmael," I said. "It's only a game. Helen, I think you've made your point."

"What point, Dan?" asked Ishmael. "It was a fragmentary scenario with too many free variables. How could anyone be expected to define policy given such information?"

"You're right," I said; and found I could not meet Helen's gaze. "Be seeing you, Ishmael."

We left the Museum. Helen sat on the low wall which bordered the steps and I sat next to her. Neither of us spoke for some time. Then Helen said:

"Go on. Ask me."

"Okay," I said. "How did you know?"

"I'm an expert on Dan Frome, remember?"

"Never mind the jokes," I said. "How could you put your finger right on the trouble when you've never seen a Golem in your life, while I couldn't?"

"All I did was pick on your blind spot. You prefer life to be straightforward. You hate senseless lies. The people you dislike are the ones who are false without good reason; the ones you stick with are those who are themselves. Your blind spot is that you haven't learned to be unscrupulous.

"I realised that you'd build your robots the same way without being aware of it; and because you would also write the tests ... *Voila.*" She ran a finger along the brick face of the wall. "Before it can achieve its full potential that poor thing in there has to learn how to be deceitful."

"If that's what's involved," I said, "then I'm not capable of it."

"And what would you do," she asked softly, "if those rockets go up without you tomorrow? Come back to oceanics?"

I nodded.

"If you did, you'd work alone. Or not at all."

Her face lifted. She was relaxed, I thought, until I noticed her hands, clenched tightly about her knees.

"Do principles matter so much to you, Helen?"

"They do to somebody. Whatever it was you stopped Ishmael talking about must be important. You don't often get so angry. And right now you're acting like a man about to hang. Dan, if you cut loose from this job, I can tell : there'll be no peace for you. Someone else, if not yourself, will see to it. The government, who knows? But it's more than just a Jupiter probe, isn't it?"

I almost choked on the single word : *"Yes."*

"A lot more?"

"More than a lot more. Once I was sure; I could have told you that in a way it's as important as your deep sea work. Now I don't know what to say. But we mustn't even speculate in public like this – it's that important."

21

"I don't think we need to talk about it any more, do we?"

I stood up and took her hand. "No," I said quietly. "Let's go and make the best of our time."

A siren wailed out on the launch pad, its voice made faint by the thickness of the shuttle's hull, its message undiminished. As if in reply, our earphones beeped twice, signalling the one-minute mark.

From afar our line of rockets had looked lost, strung out along the salt marshes amongst the tidal lagoon on their separate concrete islands. On my first visit, years earlier, it had seemed to me a landscape without Man, populated only by lonely fenced-in enigmatic structures. It was as if those structures were phantasms risen from the sea spray, too white and clean to be real; and that there was in that place no more than sage green grasses and dark water, rippled by the wind from off the Atlantic, and a sky wider than any in the world. Nor were there silent buildings like cubist mountains, nor Euclidean overlays of pipes and empty roadways, nor any faraway white spires pointing towards the attenuated clouds, waiting, waiting. Shakespeare had a phrase in which to trap the essence of that experience: ... *such stuff as dreams are made on* ... Yes, and in the morning they would be gone, I had thought. Shakespeare managed to be right in so many ways: 'Parting,' his Juliet said, 'is such sweet sorrow.' When the morning came I had the taste of it on my lips; the scent of it was heavy about my head; it was all I had left of Helen; and the medical technicians made me wash it off in the delousing sheds of Canaveral.

They were known jocularly as the 'delousing sheds' but their purpose was more comprehensive than the extermination of body lice. Space was a clean zone. It had to be, or disease, fungal infections, vermin, and pests of all sorts would make it Hell-off-Earth. The first man on extended-EVA in a spacesuit who took a flea on board established the principle; by the twenty-first century it was law : no passengers.

So Helen and I took our leave of each other in the lobby of the Terminus. That was how we had agreed to part: simply, without an extended farewell. I promised to call her when I was established at Dvornik Base and let her have my number, then we kissed and that was that; I went off to be processed with all the other people on my flight.

Technicians took biopsies and blood samples as we shuffled through progressively cleaner decontamination chambers. For about three months I had been fed with pills that included systemic fungicides. Despite my fervent hopes that they had not worked on me, the effects of the treatments satisfied the technicians and I was through.

From that moment in a sense I had left Earth. Isolated from all that made our planet unique as a home of life, save its gravitational pull, I lay in my seat in the shuttle sustained by an artificial environment. Then even gravity seemed to change, as the earphones relayed the last ten seconds of the countdown, the engines growled and bellowed below us, and we were lofted into the upper atmosphere and through it into Earth orbit.

The engines died, after which there was much pressing of red buttons which to nobody's surprise administered only the gas mixture. No help came until we had docked with the translunar carrier; and the first crewman in was pushing a vacuum cleaner ahead of himself to mop up the few gobbets of drifting vomit that had escaped the bags.

CHAPTER TWO

Inside the translunar carrier there was a queue for the toilets. Rather than hang about, clinging to the handrails which crisscrossed the walls, I decided to grit my teeth and went in search of my seat.

We were in free fall for the best part of three hours because a fault developed in the docking mechanism of one of the six shuttle craft in our flight. Eventually they linked successfully, the passengers were offloaded and settled, and we sat doing nothing until the onboard computer decided we were in the right place for the burn that would place us in translunar orbit.

As in the shuttle up to orbit from the Cape, there were no

windows for passengers in the Pegasus. Misers had built it and windows cost money. Consequently the two passenger decks were metal grids to which rows of foldout bucket seats had been bolted, so that when the ship served duty as a cargo carrier the seats could be removed and the cargo put in their place. My seat had a stick-on label which read: "Dismantle according to Handbook NAS–2004–56–00–492; alloy frame AL–H661; plastics padding ORG–P0738; Dvornik, Flight 10–306–A". By the looks of it, the seats were part of this flight's cargo, a convenient means of transporting raw materials.

There were also the basic face masks and again there was an announcement. I was greatly reassured to detect in the casual manner of its delivery the mark of humanity that told us it was the flight commander herself speaking. On cargo hauls they used only computer control, to minimise ship mass; it was good to know the authorities had not confused the flight numbers:

"Are you all tied down? Anyone not, press the blue button on your mask . . . Right, stay that way 'til I give the word. This trip will take longer than the last: about one hundred and sixteen hours according to the books. But don't hold your breath. A word of warning: you might be tempted to use the knockout gas to make the time pass quicker. Don't. Save it. There's enough for two shots in each mask and you might need them both. Another thing: if we leak, and you spot it, use the foam in the green cans clipped to the wall to choke the hole, or one of the larger adhesive pads in the green sachets to cover it. Then start pulsing that blue button. Anyone who puts in a false alarm will answer for it, later. Rations will be issued when the first burn is complete. Out."

The remaining time was spent in conversation between those passengers who had understood the announcement and those who needed to have it clarified for them. All spoke some English but their familiarity with the language varied. The sound was like that of the subdued gossip in the waiting room of a ration station, just before the clerk opens his window for business. I relaxed and tried not to think about the next five days.

About fifteen minutes later, there was a terse, "Burn in ten seconds." Something on the far side of the floor beneath my seat started chugging. There came a hard push on the ship from behind. I found myself staring up a dim shadow-patterned chimney lined with metal mesh one side and human heads on the other. Abruptly, the sensation this produced was superseded by the novel one of spacesickness. It was my first bout. I fought it. After a while the urge to share my lunch with the man in front subsided. I felt terrible.

"Soon be over," groaned Yale from beside me. He sounded no healthier than I was and his face was pale and glistening with sweat. "If it isn't, I swear I'll spew ..." Closing his eyes, he breathed deeply but raggedly.

The same crewman who had used the vacuum cleaner to such good effect came down the line of seats towing a box clipped to a pair of rails on what I saw as the ceiling. "One each," he bellowed. The stubble on his chin must have been at least two days old, and the smell that wafted from him about a week older than that. "One each!"

Yale was immediately next to the box when it came by but was in no condition to distribute the packages of dried food and tubes of water. I leaned across him for six of each and handed them to the other passengers in our row. The crewman inspected Yale.

"See he takes some of the chicken soup," he said to me. "It's got tranquilliser in it. And you look like you could use some." He went on his way, pulling his box behind him.

I learned about space travel on that journey. I learned that there is no such thing as modesty or self-pride but that there is a rough compassion which replaces both. I discovered how rare a pleasure true comfort is. I began to understand what endurance means and how different are perseverance and acclimatisation. The food was tolerable in that it provided some relief from our discomforts, though the first meal left me wishing I had never left Earth when I recalled Helen's cooking – or even my own. But by a process of familiarisation subsequent meals made me feel at home in space. As the crewman had said, there was something in our rations. I suspect, however, that it was more than an innocent tranquilliser.

If food was the high point of our existence, boredom was its nadir. We all slept for unnaturally long hours, a possible effect of the drugged soup; but we exerted ourselves so little that only a sedative could have kept us asleep when the lights came on in the 'morning'. The crew kept to themselves except when they were obliged to mingle with us, such as at meal times and whenever a medical crisis developed. After a day or two I began to understand why: we could hardly have smelled any fresher to them than they did to us; and we outnumbered them. Had it not been for the face masks which supplied unfailingly sweet air I think we should have choked on the fug by the third day.

Yale and I whiled away many hours in conversation. Frequently our immediate neighbours participated: a Polish structural engineer was on our left, beyond Yale, and a Malaysian chemist on my right. The Pole spoke a smattering of English but as I was the only one with any command of his other freewest language, French, he usually listened and confined his contributions to enthusiastic agreement or vigorous disagreement. The Malay was inclined to be mystical and though his English was extremely good he mostly eavesdropped while Yale and I debated between ourselves, with a secretive smile curling his lips as he reclined with his eyes closed.

We soon agreed that some topics were to be avoided. Politics was one.

"Too much damn politics in the world today," said Yale.

"*Doskonale*!" declared the Pole, whose name I never did learn any better than some of his pronouncements.

"Quite so, old chap," murmured the Malay.

"Suits me," I said. "What else?"

"Economics," said Yale. "Any time I open my mouth in foreign company – all respects to you guys – some nut gets hysterical about the Hawaii Oil Field as if it was all my fault. I'd as soon be without that if you don't mind."

The Malay opened one eye. "Quite understandable, though, don't you think?"

"How so?" demanded Yale, leaning across me. He stayed like that, challenging the Malay by eye until the need for another lungful of real air obliged him to clamp the mask over his mouth.

"Simple enough," said the Malay. "You chaps can't go on keeping it all to yourselves. Sooner or later you'll have to tell where it is. Why not do so now? It'll save ever so much unpleasantness." He took another breath.

"Look," said Yale. "I said I'd rather skip it. Okay?"

"As you prefer," said the Malay.

The Pole nodded as if it confirmed some dark suspicion he had long held and sat back in his seat.

Strangely enough, religion was one subject that caused us no difficulties. The Pole was an atheist; Yale claimed to be an Episcopalian; I preferred to mind my own business, and the Malay made it plain, with infinite pains to be polite, that we could never hope to comprehend the subtleties of his beliefs and therefore ought not to exert ourselves. Thereafter we simply made allowances whenever one of us expressed an individual opinion of a religious nature.

Sex was discussed only occasionally, perhaps because of the chicken soup.

The subject that predominated was what we would be doing on the Moon. Prior to boarding the shuttle I had been oppressed by the demands of secrecy, for the M16 representative who briefed me in London had made plain what sort of an attitude was adopted towards those who could not keep their mouths shut. At last that was done with : all at Dvornik were part of the project. I was eager to discover those aspects of it I had not been permitted to know about whilst working to update the Golem.

Nevertheless, I broached the subject cautiously. Nudging Yale on the fourth day, at the end of a long discussion of current space research, I said quietly:

"Have you thought much about the implications of *this* project?"

He cast me a sideways look. "You kidding?" Checking to see whether the Pole was awake, he said confidentially, "I can tell you one thing : soon as we have that vacuum welding problem cracked it'll be every man for himself."

I wondered what he was talking about, then dismissed it as some problem of his speciality, metallurgy. "Oh, I'm sure that'll be important," I said. "But shouldn't we be considering the long

27

view? When there are people living on Jupiter's moons, mining those valuable materials . . ."

I faltered. He was staring at me. "Hey, Dan, you okay?" he asked with apparent concern. "Jupiter? This job's nothing to do with Jupiter. I'm talking about brittle fractures of cold weld joints in free fall. As in space stations."

"Wait a minute," I said. "Let's get this straight: for the past two years you've been studying space assembly?"

"Two-and-a-half years, actually; but yes, mostly these last two . . . And you've been ready to go to Jupiter?" He shook his head. "Dan, some guy's been putting one over on you, and then some."

"I rather think," I said slowly, as it sank in, "that we've both been had."

We ruminated on this development for a minute or two. Then Yale said, "Let's ask old What's-his-name-ski." Turning to the Pole, Yale shook him. The Pole opened his eyes and yawned
"*Oui?*"

Yale said to me, "This one's yours, Dan."

I leaned across and addressed him in French: "Forgive me asking but we have to know: how many years is it since you began preparing for space station assembly, or for a Jupiter mission?"

His reaction was the same as Yale's. "What?" Gaining no encouragement from Yale, he shrugged his shoulders. "I don't follow your meaning."

"What have you been working on these past two years?"

His voice fell to a scared whisper. "Are you mad? The *flics*
. . ."

Yale interrupted him. "Friend, there ain't no cops up here. So give: what's your special kink?"

The Pole's face twitched. Reverting to English, he whispered, "I am working to make – *chemin de fer?*"

"Railway," I said.

"Yes. I make railways. In vacuum. Electric-magnetic railways."

Yale sighed. "Like I told the wife the morning I left home: I shoulda stayed in bed. Dan, this is crazy: you design robots and want to send people to Jupiter; I want to build space stations; this guy wants to play with trains. What about our tame Bhudda?"

The Malay said, "I would appreciate it, Mr. Yale, if you would refer to me otherwise."

"To hell with that," said Yale. "What do you reckon you'll be doing on the Moon?"

"What concern is that of yours?"

I took over. Those two would rather have fought than talked. My mind needed to be set at rest. "Did you hear what we were talking about?"

"I did. It appears there has been a clerical error of some magnitude. It is fortunate that I at least will not have made the journey in vain."

"Don't bet on it," snapped Yale.

The Malay ignored him and addressed himself to me: "As it is you who asks, Mr. Frome, I shall be happy to enlighten you, though we ought to observe a measure of secrecy. What I can tell you is that my principal concern has been complex organic dyes suitable for nuclear-pumped lasers." He smiled modestly. "I like to think that my recent endeavours have not gone unrewarded."

"My God," said Yale. "Now I've heard it all." He subsided into five minutes of speechlessness. None of us seemed inspired to speak, except for the Malay, who finally said,

"Though I must admit it is a trifle odd that of all the two hundred or so people on this one ship, the three who have been sent up in error should happen to be sitting together. Curious. Still, it's statistically possible so perhaps we ought not to draw too many conclusions."

"*Nie*," said the Pole. "Too small chance. Maybe more wrong. Maybe all wrong."

"All two hundred?" I asked.

"Right," said Yale. "Every last one of them. And that I don't believe. There's more than luck involved; someone's set us up and now we're about to find out how the con works."

"Really?" said the Malay. "What kind of confidence trick had you in mind?"

"Hanged if I know," said Yale.

"Maybe all correct," said the Pole. "Maybe we still work but different. *Plus ça change, plus c'est la meme chose,* I think."

"I'm sure there's a lot in what you say," replied Yale. "But maybe it all ties up in something else."

"What, for instance?" enquired the Malay.

Yale scowled at him. "Go get mugged, will you? I don't know, I said. Can't you see that something's wrong?"

The Malay closed his eyes again, effectively withdrawing from the argument. As a final shot, he said, "I really cannot comprehend the totally disproportionate fuss you are making. Such a scheme as you postulate would imply a wholly unrealistic desire for secrecy which I cannot for one moment believe would be appropriate to any conceivable project, however far-fetched. If it troubles you, I would suggest you make enquiries when we arrive tomorrow. In the meantime. I shall be resting."

Little more could be said, for in essence our chemist had summarised the situation. We had all been subjected to stringent security controls for about two years, that much we were sure of; beyond that fact logic failed us. We possessed individual skills that appeared only distantly inter-related. Only waiting would reveal the truth about the projects in hand at Dvornik Base.

But I was now on the lookout for further inconsistencies or peculiarities in my surroundings and it was not long before a minor irritation that had developed during the journey came to obsess my idle mind. It was this: my wrist watch, a reliable electronic device of high quality, had begun to run slow. By the time the lights came on to signal the fifth and last morning, nominally 0700 hours by the ship's chronometer repeater on the forward bulkhead, it was showing 0247.

A few seconds' error per day would have been bad enough but tolerable and understandable, for the walls were covered with cables that might be radiating powerful electric or magnetic fields capable of affecting the electronics of the watch. A regular discrepancy as large as an hour or more was another matter. I almost went so far as to ask Yale for his opinion.

Then there was a beep in our earphones.

"Good morning, campers!" The shuttle commander sounded cheerful. "This is your fifth day. For those of you who've been watching the clock and wondering when it's all going to end, we have a little surprise prepared. At about 0200 hours tomorrow morning we retroburn for lunar orbit. May we suggest that those of you with personal timepieces reset them now in accordance with the wall repeater, which is being adjusted to local standard time, which in Dvornik is GMT. This has been our little joke; hope you enjoyed it." The wall repeater shimmered through to 0747.

That incident proved instructive. In a harmless way it dramatised my departure from Earth and accented the danger inherent in the cosy habits of thought I had fallen into there. The rules by which life was regulated were exposed as artificial and unreliable; and the social mores defining 'right' and 'wrong' were no less inviolate. Only consideration for her passengers had made the commander advance the ship time gradually so that we could readjust with the minimum of discomfort. It had been her space-oriented self who had chosen to jolt us with that salutary joke. We could expect less gentleness in the frontier environment of the Moon.

Half an hour before retroburn we were ordered to our seats and were spun through a sickening series of manoeuvres. The clock reached 0200: there was a booming in the hull which hovered at the limits of audibility and a pressure from behind as the rockets fired. Again I was at the base of the chimney down which pieces of paper and food wrapper tumbled. The experience continued for an indefinite period that seemed the longer for following five days of free fall. At last it was over.

"Rest easy," announced the commander. "In the next few hours we'll be starting to ferry you down; but Dvornik only has two shuttles and they can take only twenty each. The mathematicians will have figured that as five quick journeys. Sorry, but the up-flights are revictualling runs in case we're stranded before you're offloaded. So chat amongst yourselves for a while."

We endured another day, while the ship resounded to the clangs and thuds of docking mechanisms engaging and disengaging. Once there was an orbital correction and twice an air

31

leak alarm, the second of which caused one man to have hysterics. The six of us in my row were next to last.

I was so glad to be free of that malodorous prison I hardly noticed the rough ride to the surface. Similarly, the serene beauty of the lunar landscape by night, aglow beneath a full Earth high overhead, hardly touched me. I remember vivid fragments of scenes loosely linked by tiredness: being herded into a cramped vehicle smelling of socks by someone in a spacesuit coloured an improbable shade of pink; the sensation of riding a small boat on a stormy sea; tunnels; lights flashed in my face by loud-voiced armed men; questions; echoing rooms carved from stone. And the pleasure of snuggling into the comfort of a greasy mattress.

CHAPTER THREE

There was the pungent smell of coffee in the air. I opened my eyes to the sight of a large black man in purple coveralls standing over me with a steaming cup in one hand and a clipboard in the other. Golden block lettering on his shoulders identified him as an interpreter, with subscripts in the appropriate languages indicating his expertise in English, French, German, Spanish, Dutch, Italian, Arabic, Urdu, and Swahili.

I had never met a Swahili-speaking space engineer. I wondered what the demand was for that language up on the Moon.

"Here," he said. "Get this in you."

I took the metal cup gingerly, expecting it to burn my hands, to find it barely lukewarm. "Thanks," I said and meant it. Both my legs hurt as if I had run ten kilometers with a man on my back. The coffee took my mind off the discomfort.

"That's okay," he said. "When you're done with it, put the empty cup by the door and go wash through there." He pointed across the wide low room to an archway through which wisps of steam wafted. He consulted his clipboard. "Daniel Frome, yes?" I nodded and he held out a stubby plastic cylinder. "This is your room key. The number on it tells you where to go. We don't have enough people spare to guide you but if you get lost use a phone. They're everywhere. Okay?"

I said I'd manage somehow, so he went on to rouse the next sleeper, with whom he held what sounded like a racy dialogue in Arabic.

By all the signs, the room in which I had spent my first night at Dvornik Base was a communal sleeping chamber reserved for casual use. Most of the bunks which lined the walls in tiers were still occupied by passengers from the shuttle, sprawled in blissful slumber or snoring like hogs. I realised that soon they would be competing with me for the wash facilities; and much though I disliked hurrying the first decent drink I had tasted for almost a week, I drank the coffee quickly, for at the very promise of a wash my skin crawled beneath its accumulated grime.

The Base, I discovered, was huge and almost entirely subsurface. At first, when only the Russians had occupied it, they had dug into the Mound, the small mountain near the centre of Lansberg Crater. Later the Base had been transplanted a short distance to the west, where from modest beginnings it had grown to its present size. Subdivided into hexagonal cells, within which were groups of rooms and tunnels, and pervaded by major underground highways, it continued to grow through the subsoil of Lansberg like a mechanical fungus, putting up surface bodies such as airlocks and vehicle exits where required but otherwise remaining hidden.

Unfortunately, notwithstanding its essentially repetitive nature, the layout contained a good many irregularities. Newcomers such as myself could easily become confused.

By my watch, now set to local time and apparently behaving itself properly, I had chosen to hunt for my room in mid-morning. It was past midday before I found the green metal door whose stencilled number matched that on my key. In the interim my memory of breakfast became dim, muddled by confused views of grey tubular tunnels and innumerable airlocks. People were on the move wherever I went; but they were preoccupied or spoke no more English than sufficed to misdirect me. I found an interpreter and persuaded her to escort me as far as my residential zone; I immediately took a wrong turning and encountered her half an hour later, at which point she seized my arm and hustled me off to my room. She then lectured me on the rudiments of the coordinate system by which, as she put it, an idiot could not fail to find himself. It seemed the large black-and-white numbers on the walls had a practical purpose.

Chastened, I unlocked the door, slid it aside, and ventured into the darkness of what was to be my home from home.

Immediately I tripped over something hard and low and fell onto what proved to be the bed. When I found the light switches I also found that I had been housed in a broom closet.

I only call it a broom closet so as to convey the sense of dimension that impressed itself upon me; but it is entirely possible that my private domain had once served such a humble purpose. Size apart, it was furnished in a style that can only be described as niggardly. The corridors and what few public rooms I had stumbled into in my travels, if not generous with elbow room, were at least large enough to convince one that they were intended for human occupation. My own room was about two paces wide by five long.

The bed onto which I had collapsed after tripping over my luggage filled most of the floor space. Chiselled from stone, its many-faceted upper surface contained a depression that prevented the air mattress from sliding onto the floor. Bedclothes amounted to a lower sheet, of plastic, and a hybrid of sheet and quilt for the cover. There was also a pillow; but I concluded that this must have been an oversight of generosity by the domestic staff. From this luxurious vantage point I surveyed the amenities: a stone bench by the door; some shelves for socks; and a foldout metal desk on which were a plastic water bottle and a box of emergency dried rations, the sight of which made by stomach cringe.

At the head of the bed were two coat hooks and a single shelf with a booklet titled, in several languages, 'Survival Drill: Dvornik Base'. This helpful document advised me that unless I had a spacesuit of my own I stood precious little chance of surviving a decompression emergency but might get through some of the thousand-and-one other likely disasters if I followed the

34

simple rules it contained. Of more use to me was the map on the back cover, a jungle of coloured lines and dots. I pocketed the booklet and went out into the warren to comply with some of the rules.

The first was that my coveralls should be dyed my departmental colour. My local laundry arranged that within five minutes: my colour was blue, for electronic engineering. The second rule was to register with my corridor committee, who turned out to be one man in a cubbyhole. He noted my existence and gave me a talk on communal solidarity; I had forgotten that technically Dvorik was Russian territory and subject to their laws though they had surrendered a large measure of control to the project managers. Then he winked at me and we shared a few millilitres of vodka. I came away feeling that there was still hope for civilisation.

The third rule, peculiarly, was the one I considered most important: to register with the Safety Committee, the body which regulated all precautionary and remedial actions by the damage control crews. However, I adhered to the sequence laid out in the booklet and in due course arrived at a sombre cavern reminiscent of a storeroom shared between a fire station, a garage, and a coal mine. There, a man in fluorescent orange coveralls greeted me with a wan look and a peremptory, "*Da?*"

I explained my visit. A troubled expression crossed his face and he pushed buttons on a computer terminal. "You are late," he said. "The briefing begins in ten minutes."

"What briefing?" I asked, not unnaturally, for nobody had betrayed the slightest interest in my movements, discounting the lady interpreter.

"Base Commandant Kallekjan will address all newcomers in the Hall of Congress. Quickly, give me your details. I will have you escorted."

We settled our business and he sent one of his men to guide me. I will not dwell on what I saw of the Base that day. I was overwhelmed by a conviction that the colossal effort invested in the kilometers of tunnels, the moving ways, and the vertical personnel hoists, as well as the fittings, was as nothing beside the urgent will that had caused it all to be. Dvornik Base, then as now, was one of the wonders of the early space age. Huge, clumsy, titanic in its architectural aspiration, it was a marvel. Yet such marvels are born for a purpose. I had lost faith in the story given me to explain the secrecy of my work; and seeing the Base I suspected that some far-reaching enterprise was in hand of which that story was only an echo. There might well be plans for the colonisation of Jupiter's moons, for another year; but I no longer saw myself as part of them.

The Hall of Congress was contained beneath a spacious dome and could have held all two thousand of Dvornik's personnel. With two hundred people in it, it seemed empty. My guide left me at one end of the arched doorways and I entered slowly, wary of the volume of open air above me. I had nearly reached the midpoint of the floor when Yale called me over to him.

I joined him and the Pole towards the back of the crowd. There were no seats in the Hall, a negligible inconvenience for though my leg muscles still twinged intermittently I was becoming accustomed to walking again. Besides, the comparatively feeble lunar gravity made standing no more tiring than sitting would have been on Earth.

The crowd had settled into a loose semicircle around the elevated platform which fronted the Hall and frequently broke into temporary smaller conversational groups. I found that my friends had been waiting for about ten minutes, after being herded from their rooms by a bossy woman Yale laconically characterised as 'a female sheepdog – if you know what I mean'.

A man in a green vaguely military uniform rattled the microphone on the platform.

"Base Commandant Boris Kallekjan," he announced.

There was an attentive silence as a small, narrow-faced man replaced him at the microphone. Kallekjan wore the same uniform, devoid of badges of rank, and was bareheaded in the fashion of the Base. The economy of his movements, combined with his brown hair which verged on being grey, suggested his age as around fifty or slightly older. When he spoke his accent was unobtrusive and his manner calm, unhurried, even assured. I suppose he had it all well rehearsed.

"Friends," he said, "on behalf of my Government and the

people of the Union of Soviet Socialist Republics, may I welcome you." More remarkable than his accent or his manner were the pauses during his speech, as if he weighed the value of his phrases and the emphasis each should have. "I would wish that your first day at Dvornik Base could be a pleasant one, unburdened by bad news. Unhappily, we must be serious."

Yale whispered, "Here it comes."

"Yes," said the Pole. "When a Russian says he is to be serious, is serious."

"For most of you," said Kallekjan, "English is a foreign language, as it is for me. I am sorry; translations will be available but I hope that for the moment what I have to say will be understood.

"Allow me to begin with a history lesson, because here at Dvornik we have become involved with history: ancient and modern, as well as future. It is an accident of history that this Base plays host to you; another accident of history has involved each of you in our project. A review of the past is therefore appropriate.

"2001, as you may recall, was not a particularly memorable year: most of the promises the twentieth-century romantics made in its name were not kept. Likewise 2002; if I may quote from *Time Magazine* ..." He read from a piece of flimsy paper.

"The fragmented peoples of the Earth look back on the past year and forward to the next and see only the remorseless onset of economic and social stagnation as their common future. Those who dare to raise their eyes beyond the present do so without enthusiasm. Imperceptibly the years have become numbers for historians to play with. Mankind may as well prepare to sit this millennium out."

Kallekjan folded the paper carefully and put it in an inside pocket. "Such a dystopian outlook was understandable, you will agree, and the marginal improvement since cannot be more than a reprieve.

"The Romans might have sympathised with us: on the death of their emperor Marcus Aurelius they embarked on ninety years of civil instability, in which there were no fewer than eighty emperors. The empire they built was disintegrating; the same decade that saw the death of Aurelius and the end of a century of calm following that of Nero, saw the retreat from Caledonia and the onset of the slow progress towards defeat by barbarism.

"And where do we stand? Do you not see a parallel?

"That, however, is a mere scrap of history, for 180 A.D. and 2002 A.D. were linked by more than historical parallels. In the first of those years, as closely as our scientists can guess, a fire went out, at a distance so remote from Earth that neither the Romans nor many generations following them would have thought it possible. Approximately one thousand eight hundred and twenty-one years later, some three-quarters of a light-year from Earth, that fire was relit."

He allowed the hush to ripen, then asked:

"Who of you has someone important on Earth? Or here?"

A murmur arose in the Hall, and died away.

"What I am saying, my friends, is this: there is a new star in heaven; and we think it represents a spacecraft built by an extraterrestrial civilisation. At about 1406 GMT on Tuesday 26 November 2002, our astronomers at Mare Moscoviensis Observatory detected it, since when it has moved purposefully. Its speed is incredible: about one ninth that of light, not quite towards the Sun. Backward extrapolation of its course points to Beta Crucis, the second brightest star in the constellation of the Southern Cross.

"Since its appearance this object has been watched closely. At 0418 GMT on Monday 17 March 2003 an abrupt increase in brilliance was observed. Light from beyond the object became distorted by forces we have only dreamed of in mathematical fantasies.

"To have seen such a traveller was marvellous enough. But when the astronomers realised that it had actually changed course and was beginning to swing around so as to enter the Solar System in the plane of the ecliptic, the object passed from being a curiosity to a matter of grave concern for all nations.

"Towards the latter end of 2003 this project was begun and because of it I regret to say that you have been brought here under false pretences, in that the stories you were given were designed to hide the truth. News of an event as outstanding as this could not be allowed to become public knowledge until we were ready to reveal the secret."

Not surprisingly, there was uproar. Questions in many languages were shouted at him, while well-meant attempts by calmer individuals to soothe their exasperated neighbours only added to the noise.

I was not reassured by this rare opportunity to see my fellow scientists as human beings: on the surface they were disciplined; inwardly they lacked maturity. All it had taken to expose their inferior aspect was too much novelty.

Kallekjan showed his mettle. He made no effort to calm the storm and in due course it blew itself out. With his arms folded across his chest and his head tilted downwards as though he were considering some detail of the platform, he kept silent until he sensed that the crowd was ready for explanations, when he raised his head. Gradually silence fell.

"You have every right to be angry. Try to forgive the deception. There was great uncertainty and therefore fear: a thing so bright it could be seen across three-quarters of a light-year; fantastical forces that could bend light by an obvious amount; the wherewithal to deduce planetary orbits from so far away ... There was no way of being sure what might be approaching us or what its intentions were. For now, it still follows its curved course, so far as we know; not until next February will we see whether the object chooses to take a straight line in towards the Sun, or prefers to avoid us entirely. We could not wait so long. The project demanded an early start, or interception would be impossible."

A question was shouted from the floor.

"Oh yes," replied Kallekjan, "there will be an interception. This alien visitor has come a long way. So far and with such assurance and skill that we dare not ignore it.

"Some may say: very well, this may be an alien spaceship coming to visit us. Let us welcome it. Let us extend the hand of friendship. Let us be comrades." He smiled; but the smile weakened. "Others have considered the present state of the world and have wondered whether anyone will be here to do any welcoming if and when it arrives. Friends, few of you are politically inclined – this I know from your dossiers – but you are citizens of the world. You must have seen the danger signs. In the next few years there is every likelihood of a major war on Earth, whatever we do, because of the mounting social pressures. And if there is one, and if this visitor from space is unfriendly and does not care to grasp the hand of friendship except to crush it in an iron grip, we would be helpless. That is why you are here: you are to assemble our defence against this possible threat, lest war come. And perhaps you are to bridge the times of barbarism as best you can, as the Romans could not. That is for the future to decide."

There was a long pause. I could tell he was reluctant to finish his speech.

"So far I have been repeating what I have said to each of the nine groups that have preceded you to this Base. However, you are the tenth and last, so our work force is complete and I must make this announcement:

"Henceforth, Dvornik Base is to be isolated from Earth, except for incoming supplies and essential official messages." He raised his voice to be heard: "You are here to stay, all of you, until the emergency is over. This is by direct order of your individual governments."

His very last words were almost inaudible:

"The new codename is Project Nightwatch."

CHAPTER FOUR

"Honest to God," said Yale, "I thought the guys in the front row were going to murder him. And when he stepped off the platform, I couldn't look."

The Pole swished his drink around in its glass and said, reflectively, "My father tell me: a lot of year ago a man comes to his village with four, maybe five, wolfs. And wolf in Poland is big, with teeth: so." He bared his own gold-inlaid set. "And at night, this man make wolfs do lot of silly things, no wolf ever

40

do when proud. My father says this is because wolfs believe the man know best; and because, inside, there is part which look at man like cub to bigger wolf. They never lose this part: is always there. Kallekjan, I think, is like man: he knows where is cubpart of people here."

After the near-riot which had threatened to break out following Kallekjan's internment announcement, we three had slipped out of the Hall. I had suggested to Yale and the Pole that we locate one of the bars which my map mentioned, where we might adopt some of the native customs whilst we came to grips with the new situation.

Much of Dvornik was new as a result of the international project, so my lifelong fascination with complicated buildings ensured that our search kept me amused, though the others began to display impatience when we encountered the same tunnel junction for the third time. My curiosity, I admit, grew partly from concern for my own welfare: I wanted to know what sort of a life the architects had planned for us. My forebodings that the Base might be a dreary barracks, which dated from the time I learned it was run by the Russians, vanished as soon as I saw the extent to which the other nations had impressed their varied personalities upon it. Overall, the atmosphere was not unpleasant by any means.

But my companions were of more philistine clay and would have none of my aesthetics. Yale, as I had guessed on our first encounter, was an Angelino; to him architecture was a science of functional enclosure, not an art form in its own right. The Pole listened politely when I remonstrated with him about the pleasant choice of colours, then he explained it all in terms of Marxist-Leninism, which detracted considerably from its charm.

However, we found a bar which suited our sundry philosophies and settled in for the afternoon. It was a small room, seemingly a length of chopped-off tunnel, lined with four-seat booths such as the Americans favoured then. The decor was a ghastly object lesson in the brash Art Manhattan style: all swathes of metallic spangles and chromatic discord. Perhaps because of this the barman was our sole company. He was a volunteer, as were all barmen, whose reward was to be the masters of their premises. Not until after several months of the enforced communal life of Dvornik did I come to appreciate the value of this privilege.

Only after the third glass of what the barman referred to as 'Riley' did I notice the telephone in its sound-absorbent booth. The sight of it reminded me of my promise to call Helen. Mumbling a word of explanation, I weaved my way over to it.

The Base had been built with the possible total loss of internal air in mind, so all telephones had sockets into which the standard spacesuit phone links could be plugged; otherwise the communal model seemed to be a push button telephone one might find in any public street.

The instruction plate had already been modified. Halfway down the English paragraph were the words: "Dial 9 and ask for Terrestrial Relay. Have personal code number ready." They had been scratched through.

Helen would be waiting, I thought. I decided to hell with regulations and picked up the handset.

A machine was on extension 9. "This service temporarily suspended. In cases of emergency please dial 111 and ask for External Services." The message was repeated. I rang off and tried 111.

"External Services, please," I said.

"Crash, Air, Power, or Heat?"

"None. I want to make a phone call externally."

"If you know the spacesuit code number, please dial it. The prefix code is 112. Otherwise dial 100 for Directory."

"It's a number on Earth. What's the code for that?"

"Dial 9 and ask —"

"I tried that. They referred me to you."

"Dial 102 for English-language operator."

Smartass machine, I thought. *One day I'll make a point of testing how many answers you've got ready for any occasion.*

I dialled 102.

The operator explained sweetly that the service had been discontinued for the duration. After a decent interval I was asked, "Will that be all, sir?"

I could almost hear the logic elements clicking. "Have you a human supervisor?" I asked it.

"One moment, sir." The line fell to murmuring a subdued melody of computer traffic, with cross-chatter from some unidentifiable machinery. Then:

"Supervisor," said a thickly accented male voice. "There is a problem?"

I explained my dilemma, how I understood that all private traffic was barred but that I had to get a message through. He listened patiently, occasionally asking me to explain some word or phrase he had not understood, and said, "Okay, Jack, I talk to my boss. Maybe good. Maybe not. You wait there, okay?"

I waited five minutes or more. My arm was stiff from holding the handset first to one ear then the other when the murmur of conversation from Yale and the Pole died away. There were footsteps behind me. A soldier armed with a chaff pistol took the handset from me, spoke a few phrases of Russian into it, and hung it up.

"Your identity card, please," he said.

The gun was aimed at my chest as I removed the card from my breast pocket, so I moved carefully. Plastic chaff invariably causes ugly wounds; at close range it can chew the flesh off bones. Its advantage is that it does not penetrate cloth or the hulls of spacecraft. Hence its popularity with the security forces within Dvornik.

The soldier inspected the card with a look of disdain on his face. Then he returned the card to me and holstered his gun.

"That was a stupid act, Mr. Frome," he said. "If you have personal problems you should consult your national representative."

"First I've heard of one," I replied. "No-one's told me a thing; I've had to learn for myself."

"That is as it may be. What do you imagine we are doing here, running a holiday camp? Will you next want a dacha of your own? The British representative is on 152; use him and be more careful. Remember, this Base is on a war footing. Behave accordingly."

My ears were burning when I rejoined the others. Yale looked

43

at me over the rim of his glass. His eyebrows rose in question.

"A little trouble," I explained. "I'll sort it out later."

Yale was about to reply when a stranger sauntered up to our table.

"Mind if I join you?" he asked. He slid into the empty seat opposite me, next to Yale, to whom he said, "We Americans should be on the same side always."

Yale's look of outrage turned into one of bewildered irritation.

The newcomer was a stocky man with mid-length glossy black hair. He appeared well muscled under his orange coveralls but added a fluidity to his movements that owed more, I suspected, to his personality than to his stature. Despite the redness of the light, which obscured his true skin colour, he still seemed of a decidedly ruddy tint, which combined with his broad face and slightly hooked nose to give him the appearance of –

"That's right," he said, gazing back at me, "I'm a North American Indian."

"Forgive me," I said. "I didn't mean to stare."

"Ah, it's nothing," he said, dismissing the gaffe with a wave of his hand. His eyes flicked between my two companions and came to rest on me. "You're Dan Frome." He held out his hand, ignoring the others. "Steelyard Jones."

We shook hands. He continued to act as if we were alone. I saw Yale's face darkening and hurriedly introduced him and the Pole. Jones nodded casually to them before returning his attention to me. "We'll be working together, they said, so I looked you up."

"How did you find us?" I asked, gently emphasising the last word.

He tapped the side of his nose with a muscular forefinger. "Tracking ability," he confided, and guffawed. Whilst he laughed, I noted that he looked at the others as if to check whether they were sharing his joke. They were not. Sobering, he said to me:

"I have friends who tell me things." He proferred a pack of chewing gum which I refused. Taking a stick for himself, he dropped the remainder into a pocket. "So far you ain't doing too bad, you know."

"What do you mean?" I asked.

"Scuttlebutt has it you zazzed the cops with that phone call. I'll tip you: it ain't healthy, and I should know."

"They were very helpful," I said defensively. He had an open, plausible manner that might have passed as likeable in the absence of other clues to his nature. He was rather too ready to presume friendship; I felt he would be the sort who attracts trouble and, smiling, steps aside to let others repair the damage.

"Oh sure," he agreed. "And they are. But don't push it. Softly, softly; you want to bend the rules, check with me and I'll set you straight."

I decided to change the subject. There was too strong a smell of subversion in the conversation and I disliked the way he was trying to cut the others out of it. "What do you do?" I asked.

"All sorts, mostly the tricky work Outside. You know: in vacuum. I put up those aerials on the Mound."

"I'm sorry," I said, "I didn't see them." I couldn't recall having seen the Mound either, though I knew it was by far the biggest heap of rocks and soil in those parts, being the lump kicked up in the middle at the time of the impact which created Lansberg Crater.

"Shame. Best damn set of wires on the Moon, including Moscoviensis."

I inclined my head towards Yale and the Pole in turn. "They're in the hardware business too."

"Oh yeah?" he said coolly. "Fancy that." Addressing me again, he said, "I'm Mohawk, you know. My dad was gang chief on the Saint Lawrence Two-Span."

"I'd wondered about the name," I lied. His ego clearly needed frequent polishing. The effort of polishing it might be repaid, however, as it was possible his unofficial contacts might be able to save us all a considerable amount of running around. Also, if we were to work together I thought it preferable to have him as a friend. I was sure a modicum of flattery would be appreciated.

He lapped it up. "It's not strictly traditional but I reckon it's right. My dad thought so too. You can call me Steel if you like. Most of the guys do."

"What are you on now, Steel?"

"Easy stuff. Antenna rigging at the assembly site: VHF and S-band arrays for suit radios and crawlers. Be ready in a week. Have to be, before the dawn. Too damn hot to work 'way up when the Sun's shining."

Carefully, I asked, "What site is that?" Out of the corner of my eye I saw Yale lean forward fractionally.

He answered carelessly, "Oh, fort assembly."

"Of course," I agreed. "The fort."

"Forts, you mean. There's eighteen of them."

There were nineteen Golems waiting in boxes, I remembered. Coincidence?

Suddenly he said enthusiastically, "Hey, you want to come see for yourself? You being new, you'll need a guide first time around."

"Don't you have to work?"

He glanced at his coveralls. "These? Hell, I'm not due on shift until fifteen-hundred. The extra hour won't hurt." Giving the others a shallow smile, he said, "Pleasure meeting you fellows. We must talk again some time."

Yale said, heavily, "Sure. I was thinking of going anyhow."

The Pole said nothing but I could see that he too was unimpressed by Jones.

Jones led me to a brilliantly lit white room lined with metal lockers. Men and women were donning and doffing spacesuits; one runty man, dressed but for his helmet which he held cradled in his arms, was bawling at them to get a move on. We walked through this racket into a workshop where the smallest man I have ever seen was perched on a high stool at a bench mending a suit. He looked up from applying adhesive to a patch.

"Hi, Steel," he said with a squeaky faintly Germanic accent. "Who's this?"

"A new pal, I think." Even I noticed the odd way he said it. The small man paused and gave me a long look, then bent to his work, remarking:

"Good. He has a name?"

"Dan Frome. He's in Denham's group."

"Ooh . . . that's bad. You met Denham yet?" he said to me.

46

"Just arrived," Jones answered for me. "Last lot."

Again I received a speculative stare "Anything . . .?" asked the small man.

Jones too looked at me. "I don't know yet. We'll see."

I said, "I seem to have missed the start of this conversation."

Jones and the small man laughed and Jones said, "It wasn't very interesting. Dan, this is Gustavus Hochmann, our suit mechanic." His face cleared of all expression as he said, "You can trust your suit and your life with him."

Hochmann slowly shook his head. "Steel, you must not be so generous. What you say is pleasant for me to hear but not safe for our friend." To me he said, "Dan, my duty is to make good the damage that is known about. But it is for you to beware of the hidden faults that kill. You understand?"

"It makes sense," I said. He nodded with satisfaction.

"Good. Have you been measured?"

"They did all that at Canaveral months ago."

"So," said Hochmann, "your number will be on file." Consulting a computer terminal on the bench, he rummaged through an old-fashioned card index. "You are size 18-M," he said. "Memorise that number. In an emergency, you may wear any of the standby suits from sizes 17 through to 19. Or, as a last resort, any you can adjust to fit you. 18-M is your safe size."

"And mind you do remember it," said Jones seriously. "Some s-o-b tried palming me off with the wrong size my second time out and I almost got stranded: my left leg went numb on me Outside. It was too tight for the blood circulation."

"However," said Hochmann, "I see that yours is already in store, so if you will sign for this key you may go with Steel and try it on."

"But I tried it at Canaveral," I said. "It fits fine."

"Come on," said Jones. We went and found my suit. As I was holding up the mass of crinkly material, trying to recall how to put it on, Jones tapped the bare metal door of the locker.

"I'll warn you about this stuff now. It's titanium." My eyebrows must have risen, for he said, "Yeah, really. They process so much ilmenite for oxygen the metal's a waste product. The foundry turns out powder and standard sheet by the tonne. It's available, so even though it's tough to work they use it where the fire hazard doesn't matter much. But if you're stuck in a room with a hot fire and this stuff, suit up: burning titanium will suck even the carbon dioxide out of the air. The only sure way to extinguish it quickly is to evacuate the atmosphere. Now, if you're ready, I'll show you some more surprises."

CHAPTER FIVE

outside.

That was the sum of it. *Inside* there was air, and warmth, and enclosure. Protection. Outside was ... Outside was *open*. The only contact with solidity was the loose gritty layer of dust underfoot, whilst above and all around there was vacuum.

Don't tell me vacuum is nothing and can't be touched; that's a materialistic viewpoint that takes no account of the mental walls a medium or a state of matter can erect. Vacuum is as tangible as anything can be, because of that same ultimate nothingness of which it is constituted. It is a barrier to life as we know it. The outer surface of one's pressure suit is the limit of one's world; all that lies beyond it is of another universe, warped and discoloured by two layers of plastic, heard as static in the radio, touched through thick gloves that, no matter how artfully constructed, can never quite convey the proper texture of what is being handled. And never, never, can Outside be smelled or tasted.

The smells of space are those we carry with us: sweat, plastic, renewed air, body odour. The tastes are those of sterile water and perhaps a narrow choice of tablets for one deficiency or another. The sounds of space are a heart beating fast, air hissing, and directionless voices in the headphones. Occasionally there is a thud as some part of that other universe strikes one's helmet.

Lunar transport also assumes strange forms, stripped of the frills that terrestrial vehicles require in order to accommodate Earth's atmosphere, such as streamlining and protective paint and plating. Many of the standard forms were decided years ago, when the first men on the Moon needed to travel fast and far, for simplicity generally resolves a design to a commonplace minimum. A car has four wheels, an engine or engines, an energy store, some means of guiding and controlling it, and seats. Superficial details such as radios and lights may also be added. Jones emerged from the underground garage in the driver's seat of a vehicle that would instantly have been recognised as a lunar buggy back in the early 1970's: it was the quintessence of a car, with those major features already mentioned and little more. Intended to carry two people, it sat up high on balloon mesh tyres and looked as unstable as it subsequently proved to be.

I strapped myself into the righthand seat. For a second I saw the landscape ahead like a frontier, darkening by imperceptible degrees as the dawn approached and the Earth faded from full to gibbous; then Jones applied power to the wheel motors and we surged out into the night away from the lights of the Base.

As my eyes adjusted to the faint Earthlight, the scene became so familiar I had to laugh aloud.

"What's funny?" demanded Jones.

"It's nothing," I said.

He stopped the buggy so violently I would have fallen out but for the safety harness. "Listen," he said, "out here there's no such thing as 'nothing'. If a pal starts laughing you find out why. And if you can't get a good excuse out of him for scaring you like that you whisk him home pronto, because he's either a sick man or a fool. You don't work with either if you can help it. Now, second time of asking : do we go home?"

I was thankful for the silvering on my visor which prevented Jones from seeing my confusion. Another fact to learn about Outside. "It's not so funny now," I said weakly. "It struck me I'd come all this way for a moonlit drive."

"Yeah," Jones said finally. "That's worth a laugh." He started the motors and we drove on without speaking.

"You know," he said in a conversational tone five minutes later, "you're right." And he began laughing. I felt like demanding an explanation. Then I decided that would be rubbing salt into my own wounds. Jones had me at his mercy Outside. He was the one who made the jokes; anyone who tried to compete could look forward to being slapped down.

We halted near a large outcrop of rock. Dismounting, Jones motioned to me to stay seated and began to circle the rock, bending over as if studying the ground, shining a torch into crevices and sweeping the beam across the apparently undisturbed dust around us.

Then he beckoned but raised a hand in clumsy imitation of finger-to-lips. When I reached him he tapped my commset, repeating the sign of silence. Totally mystified, I watched him pull his phone link lead from its pocket and plug the ends into each of our sets. That done, he switched off both our radios.

I heard his undistorted voice: "Let's talk."

We sat down with our backs against the rock.

"Dan," he said, matter-of-factly, "there's a man in Dvornik wants to kill you."

The rules governing the proper response to such conversational gambits are, at best, ill defined. Dale Carnegie might have known what to say; I made do with a strangled, "Oh?" complimented by the afterthought, "who?"

"We think it's your direct supervisor, Commander Terence Denham."

That explained Hochmann's reaction: *Ooh ... that's bad.* "Why should he want to do a thing like that? And what do you know about it anyway?"

His sigh sounded like a gale. "You probably imagine we're all on the same side, after Uncle Boris' bracing pep-talk this morning. We're all comrades-in-arms against the common foe, right? Stop the slimy aliens. Keep Earth human. Be brotherly. Love thy neighbour. That shlock. Well, that's surface politics; there are squads of people on the make at Dvornik and this communication embargo isn't going to stop all of them."

"Such as you," I ventured to suggest. "You don't only erect aerials, do you?"

"Don't you go hurting my feelings, Dan," he replied. "If I'd been one of the bad hats you could be dead right now, so get this straight: we're on the same side."

I wanted to edge away from him but the cable was too short. In any event, he might have taken it badly. "Why should Denham be after me?" I asked. "He and I are fellow countrymen with similar interests."

"What does that prove? Dan, that crazy Brit belongs to nobody's country but his own. Suppose I fill you in on some background, so you'll understand ... And we'll have to be quick. They're worrying about us."

A red light was flashing on the buggy. "That'll be Comm-Con," said Jones. "As soon as we went off the air, alarms started ringing. The crash tender'll be nosing around here if I don't answer." Unplugging me from the circuit, he went and connected himself to the buggy's radio. I was alone with my own noises and the novel sensation of being somebody's target.

He came back. "Okay," he said. "Officially, we broke our antennae when the buggy tipped over. They do it all the time. You were driving, by the way, so we'll give you some practice on the way home. They might ask questions."

He settled himself again.

"Dan, this job is like an onion. It has layers; and the deeper you dig into it the more you want to cry over what you find. On the top, it's disguised as some strange activity that's happening on the Moon. Each of you was fed a different story as a security blind and the same thing is being done right now on Earth where, believe you me, the press agencies are going mad for news.

"The second layer is what you've been told today: an alien ship, or object, is coming in and has to be stopped if hostile. And that, so far as I can discover, is God's Own Truth, so hold fast to that story if to nothing else. It's worth worrying about.

"The third layer, like in an onion, is a little hard to distinguish from the second, because it ties in with this threat of war. See, we may all be keen to keep Earth free; but we're also human and shortsighted. There are fools who think they can do deals with aliens as if they were humans; they can't credit any thinking creature not being reasonable in their own terms. Because of this delusion they're prepared to take advantage of the confusion to steal a march on their rivals, or – far worse – they're prepared

51

to see rivals where there aren't any and take a swipe at them without planning beyond that action. Commander Denham's one of those."

"So he's working alone," I said. "He should be easy to stop."

"No," said Jones. "He's working with the fourth layer: the nuts. By rights he's fourth-layer too but his reasons are logical so we treat him as third. The nuts are those who get hysterical whenever they see a flag. If it's their own they worship it; and if it isn't they either patronise it or foam at the mouth."

"I know the sort," I said. Yale and his antagonist, the Malaysian chemist, were both of that clan, although from different families within it. "Who are his friends?"

"His sort don't have friends. They have allies, which they change like socks."

"And here we all are," I said, "locked up together in this great big looney-bin in the sky. Most reassuring . . . Steel, you've told me about the others but you've hardly said a word about yourself. Who are you in this?"

"I rig masts."

"Don't give me that."

"Okay," he said, "I catch vermin."

"Who for?"

Instead of saying it aloud, he pushed my knee aside to expose a small patch of ground and traced two symbols in the dust. I could barely read them in the poor light.

$E7$

"Don't say it," he warned me. "My group is interested, that's all."

The world has known many encrypted reductions of institutionalised terror and all have passed into the history books. But E7, though it endured for no more than two decades, built a reputation that few could dream of matching. By the brilliant application of management techniques devised since the mid-twentieth century and the wholehearted pursuit of modern methods, it rapidly outgrew the most powerful of the underground organisations, then set about absorbing them. It hired national security agencies as subcontractors, or bought them off; it owned industrial cartels that were worldwide household names;

it maintained two minor governments as fronts for its activities.

I had seriously misjudged Jones, had thought him an ego-centric simpleton, a braggart. Had he too been laughing at me? The visor of his helmet told me nothing and when his fingers erased the two marks in the dust I had only his voice to go by.

"Have I got to prove it?"

"No," I said.

"Then let's get to the point. Denham's politics are a board game, with rules you're not supposed to change once the game starts. He picks his allies and is surprised when they don't want him. He works up grudges. He acts. He's annoyed if people don't behave like he thinks is right. And you, Dan, have over-stepped his limits."

"But I've never met the man!" I protested.

"You think that matters to a third-layer man? He fancies that Britain and the USA are still bosom pals. Well, okay, we're on good terms but let's face it: you guys changed things more than a little when you went in with the continental Europeans. Denham doesn't accept that. He sees national secrets betrayed to foreigners: in his world this alien is an excuse dreamed up by the Soviets and other scum to gain an unfair advantage ... and by God he's going to stop the blighters." He parodied the stereo-typed Pongo as he said the last few words. I had to laugh.

"Tomorrow morning," said Jones reflectively, "is when I expect he'll try to kill you."

The joke suddenly wore thin. Jones went on:

"In Denham's eyes you're a traitor. Because you're an im-portant one, you deserve killing; and he'll do it quickly so you don't have time to make friends or learn your ground. He's strictly a knife-in-the-back merchant. But cunning. You'll have to watch him."

"I'm going straight to the authorities," I said.

"It's been tried," said Jones. "Trouble was, we couldn't give them real proof without saying, ah, too much." He tapped his own chest. "But the fly in the ointment is that Denham's as important as you are. The Russians won't lock him up simply on a tip-off, or your say-so. So he runs free while we tag him."

"Can't I take any precautions?"

"Yeah, you can guard your back. But you won't be entirely alone: me and a few friends'll be around. However, it's mostly up to you. Make sure Denham shares any food or drink he offers you. Be your own security man on spacesuits and machinery. Stay with the crowd. Sooner or later we'll get him, then you'll be safe."

The red light on the buggy started flashing. Jones answered the call. "Time to go home," he said. "They say our air's got an hour to run." We switched on our radios again after breaking the antennae.

I drove on the way back. The buggy's steering was light and the four wheel motors gave it a considerable turn of speed. But the vehicle as a whole exhibited a number of fundamental design flaws resulting from the high ground clearance and it was not long before I had rolled it twice and learned the purpose of the two stout metal hoops that bridged the seats. After the second accident Jones took the sticks; I had the impression he was anxious to avoid a real mishap of the sort he had invented to explain our radio silence.

I think my mind had not been fully on my driving.

CHAPTER SIX

Jones' warning ensured that my second night in Dvornik was wasted in restless speculation rather than invested in the sleep I needed. As if, like the White Queen in *Alice*, I could anticipate impending injuries, my ribs ached most of the night, not until my wrist alarm roused me in the early morning did I allow objectivity to attribute the pain to my previous day's adventures with the buggy rather than to premonition. By then the damage was done and I set off for work feeling jittery and lightheaded.

My place of work was a new warren of offices and laboratories interspersed amongst workshops on the western fringes of the Dvornik complex. I approached it in the company of a body of workmen in many different uniforms. Most wore the dark blue

54

of mechanical engineers; these talked of wiring and ducts, of plumbing and ventilators, and of air seals and thermal insulation. There were also orange-clad building works engineers, some already in pressure suits in preparation for their shift on the outdoor excavations. Dvornik was still growing, and so rapidly that the only practical constructional technique was to dig the holes from the surface with a ditch digger and replace the soil and rock once the tunnels and rooms had been lined with the local version of concrete, a mixture of crushed rock and adhesive.

So pressing was the need for accommodation that the occupiers were barely one step behind the builders: I passed through the last airlock to find rubble on floors that still had the dusty appearance of new cement and constructors dismantling scaffolding and ceiling moulds. I was trying to reconcile this with what was supposed to be a clean area when a middle-aged man of above average height and medium build emerged from the airlock behind me.

"Don't worry," he said languidly. "Soon be cleared up." His accent was British, born of the managerial sub-culture of the new synergetic capitalist State: non-regional, educated without being strangled by the traditional nasally laryngitic noise once cherished as the embodiment of English culture. This had to be my man.

"Terence Denham?" I asked.

He seemed surprised. "Why yes . . . But you have the advantage of me, Mr. . . .?"

"Frome," I said. "Daniel Frome."

His smile seemed almost too sincere. "Oh you *got* here. I was so hoping to meet you informally before the crowd arrived. Shall we get out of this pigsty?" We followed a side tunnel lined with unmarked sliding doors. "The others have been here a goodish while so you'll have to catch up. They're a grand bunch. Except Guy Palmer." Leaning close he lowered his voice. "Poor fellow deeply resents being dragged up here. Blames the rest of us. Still . . ." We stepped into a small but comfortably furnished office. Polished stone and shades of green predominated in the decor. Tossing his document case onto the carved stone desk, he said, "He'll recover. Now, let's have a drink." He stood poised by an alcove in which plastic jars were arrayed as if for inspection.

"I don't think so, thanks," I said hastily.

"No?" He did not seem as disappointed as I had expected. His face brightened. "Tell you what: I've got something special. A fellow I know in the commissary department brews an excellent whisky. I happen to have some with me, with some ice; a tiny pecadillo of mine, actually. We must toast your success."

"Not for me," I insisted; but whilst he had been talking he had removed a flask and cold-box from the document case. In seconds he had poured two measures of whisky and dropped an ice cube into each glass. He indicated that I should take one.

I had the choice. Presumably, therefore, I was safe for the moment. Picking one up, I sniffed it.

"Quite passable, don't you think?" he said between sips. "Well, here's to it." Raising his glass, he drained it and set it on the desk with evident satisfaction. With such an example I could not refuse to drink and took some myself.

It was, as he had said, quite passable. And tasted of whisky, unadulterated. Although, I thought, poison need possess no flavour of its own. Nevertheless a doubt developed in me: I had only Jones' word that this man was against me and what I had seen of Jones hardly commended *him* as a friend. I resolved to compromise by accepting his advice to guard my back.

We talked briefly about who I was, where I had worked, and how the project had gone. I noticed a slight reserve on his part when we happened to touch on the point of all this activity; the briefing, he said, would go into the details. So we discussed the Golem. He was friendly, though slightly patronising, and I suspected he would be a rigidly authoritarian supervisor. I was wondering what his speciality might be, when we broached the subject of tactics.

"Yes," he said thoughtfully. "This Golem of yours has me worried, I must confess. Never have credited a machine with being able to think like a human being. Seems unnatural. Wouldn't have the same reasons for doing things, you follow me?"

I nodded. "That's why we limited the Golem's executive capability. On the original mission, a five-year deep probe of Jupiter's atmosphere, that would have been enough. The Golem would be an observer, its only goals being to move in pursuit of data and to protect its own existence."

"But not now?"

"Who knows?" I said. "I'll need to study the new mission profile. But we've trained the Golems according to human standards of reason. Logic is logic: the rules are the same in almost any situation."

"Really?" He seemed amused. "And who said there are rules?"

"There seem to be. The relationships between states of matter that we call the 'laws of nature', for example. If a problem can be broken down into its fundamental parts, there's an answer somewhere."

"Ah!" he said triumphantly. "But there's that big 'if' : *if* you can break the problem down." Giving me a speculative glance, he added, "And don't you think you've been guilty of semantic ambiguity? There's another, equally big 'if' lurking in there : *if* you know which rules to apply. One may not know all the rules. You appear to regard a problem as a complete set of questions and answers, or questions and an assumption that there are answers. Whereas, there may in fact only be questions, and no answers, When *you* solve a problem, you set out to establish the relationship between the questions and these answers; so if the answers do not exist, either at all or within the limits of your comprehension, you must fail."

"The scientific method –"

"Is a fraud, my friend. Look, this is a practical universe we're stuck with: sometimes goals can only be reached by way of smaller ones; until the groundwork has been done, the ultimate aim will always seem impossible. In practical terms, it will *be* impossible. Same goes for your Golems. I don't believe we'll make a genuinely aware and independent robot intelligence for a long time to come. What you've got is a kind of complicated reaction-box."

I thought of 3c-001 in the Museum. "It passes the Turing Test," I said.

57

Denham gave a tired laugh. "Dan, tests are only a means of eliciting a desired response from a trained organism. In general terms, I doubt whether any human being alive today could pass a lifelong Turing Test: at some point we all give ourselves away as unintelligent by doing some dumb thing or other. Sitting down at a computer terminal and chatting through it for an hour or so to some response-box that acts in a way that convinces you it's a human is, to my mind, only a complicated party game. The acid test is survivability. Can it face the world and win?"

I took another sip of the whisky. "We thought about it," I said. "God, how we thought about it!"

"Any results?"

"Until this moment I'd have said 'yes'. Now I'm not so sure. We threw out the three standard problem solving techniques as being far too simple. Logical progression is all right for automatic doors; heuristic analysis works fine in weather computers; and synthesis can keep a city running. But when the problems are shifting their parameters by the second; and when they come and go without warning; *then* we need something new. Synectic progression."

Denham was sitting straighter in his chair. I watched the reflections of the ceiling lights shimmering in the whisky glass I held in my hands, remembering the weekend when the giant computer simulation at Deltrak had come on-line for the first time. That period of disbelief, as answers came thundering from the printers before we had drawn breath to ask the next question. That tightness in the chest as the programmers and I smiled crookedly at each other, aware of what had been created. "It might have been enough," I whispered. "But someone changed the conditions." I considered gaining time by taking another drink and decided not to. It was too late to evade the issue.

"You've made me think," I said. "And . . ." *Go on.* "And the Golem's not up to the job."

An indefinable mixture of panic, pleasure, curiosity, and several other emotions suffused his face. "It really won't work?"

"No," I said angrily. "No, it won't. We had to invent an artificial intelligence from the ground up, without much assistance from past research. For all the good the reference libraries did us, the word 'robot' might as well be a mumbo-jumbo term; damn near is, judging by the amount of pseudo-literate gibberish we found listed opposite it in the autoindexes. Did you know there are people who still dismiss it as a symbol? With that going for us, we had to create a mechanical mind that actually worked!

"And it was beyond us. You're right: we're still a long way from the final answer. Now, we have a machine that thinks its way from solution to solution, leaving itself as many options as it can. But that's not the whole of it; what's missing, I don't know. I can't guess. More of the same? Greater speed? Or inspiration?

"We knew the robot had to distrust the whole universe because no-one could say what to expect in Jupiter's atmosphere; and anything intended to last five minutes, let alone five years, had to be resourceful. The robot had to be free to invent its own solutions and aim for the most open-ended one. And so on, indefinitely." I put the glass onto the desk. "Unfortunately, if the Golem doesn't know how the variables in the problem are liable to behave, it stalls. A human might just trust to luck; the robot keeps trying to solve the insoluble. Jupiter's atmosphere probably obeys known laws of physics. But an alien . . . an alien's the biggest uncertainty anyone could hope to meet. So it doesn't become a question of how the alien thinks or whether the Golem thinks the same way, it becomes a question of the alien's *assumed* unpredictability: if the Golem believes the alien is unpredictable, that's quite enough to scramble its nerve."

"You should have warned us," said Denham.

"I only learned of it the day before I left Canaveral."

"Harm's done," replied Denham. "Now, how do we put it right?" Restlessly, he fiddled with the fastener of his case. "I had something like this in mind when I tried provoking you earlier, Dan. Strategy is my speciality. In the final analysis I believe it comes down to a matter of puns; situational ambiguities, if you prefer. One side misleads another by giving it enough information, correct in itself, which will be misinterpreted simply because the other side does not possess the same contextual information. I think your Golems would be in difficulties whatever

59

form they took. I think a man could be in difficulties, unless . . ."

"Unless?"

"Unless both sides agreed to play the game of reduction to basic principles. To rid their attempts at contact of all ambiguities. I believe that all intelligent lifeforms develop their societies by degrees from a limited number of prototypes; and if the laws of nature are as universally invariant as we suppose, then their sciences too must grow from common beginnings. A civilisation capable of interstellar travel is surely capable of determining the essentials of emergent technology and of applying them to this game of reduction."

"One plus one equals one-zero," I said. "Yes, agreed; but why can't a robot handle that as well as a human?"

"Because the simplification would be an openly acknowledged self-misrepresentation. *Listen, we'd be saying, to start with, we must use baby talk; but later, when we've worked out a language we both understand, we'll talk as the grown-ups we know we both really are.*"

"I still don't follow you," I said. "Admittedly, the present Golem can't handle aliens, by the looks of it. But I see no reason why a robot couldn't do all that you've described –"

"Could you depend on a robot to develop a friendship for you?" asked Denham. "Dan, simplification can be the most difficult task of all. Any fool can create complications; often only a genius can extract the essence. And I think it would need a human mind, or its equal, to see through the elementary levels of the contact to the complexity behind it – and then steer the relationship towards its optimum culmination."

"So all robots would be blind to what was important?"

"I think they would. They would stick at trying to analyse the surface detail." He laughed. "Unless, of course, they were acting on their own behalf. Are your Golems free agents, Dan?"

"Far from it," I said. My long-deferred failure was catching up with me at last: I had thought to correct the Golems' indecision by careful remotivation programming; but there seemed no cure for the ailment Denham had just diagnosed. "So our robots won't understand the surface and because of that mistake, they'll . . . It's like a shadow in the Golem's mind."

Denham said quietly, "You know, old fellow, I'm really pleased you've seen the way of it in time." He glanced at his watch. "The others will be here in about three min —"

The floor heaved. Objects leaped from shelves. There was a violent explosion in the corridor: I heard, or felt, a subsonic rumble as of falling rock; there came, faintly and fading, the shriek of air escaping through a narrow hole. There was a dying whistle also; and the public address system began intoning, *Pressure loss ... Pressure loss ...* but it too subsided into silence.

Denham jumped to his feet and ran for the inner door of the office. I followed him; at the door he gave me a wild look.

"What's happened?" I shouted at him.

"Vacuum alarm!" he shouted back. My ears popped, once, and again a few seconds later. "Inner rooms are the only refuge." On looking back, I saw the door into the corridor bulging away from us; I tried not to imagine it bursting open, spilling the air from the office. The next door would then be subject to the same enormous differential atmospheric pressure.

How long would it be before we ran out of doors?

The door shut. Denham seized one of the ubiquitous green spray cans from the wall, handed it to me, and took another for himself. "Seal the edges," he commanded as he began to apply the vivid green foam. There were only a few centimeters left uncovered when there was a *boom!* from the outer office and the door bowed sharply. The remainder of the foam was sucked into place by air whistling through the gap. The office telephone, which had been clamouring for some seconds, was silent.

Finished with the door, I looked at Denham. He beckoned and I followed him down a short corridor past an empty office and through another door which we also sealed.

We caught our breath. I felt dizzy and slightly sick, while Denham was sweating profusely. "We'd better get the emergency suits on," he said at last. Opening the suit locker, he paused, then removed the single suit it contained. "There's one in the next lab I can use," he said quickly. "You put this on while I get it."

I accepted the suit, saw it was about my size, and began to

wriggle my legs into the lower half. Denham stopped at the door leading further into the work area to look back at me. "Is it all right?" he asked.

"Fine," I said, preoccupied with shrugging on the upper half without tangling it. I heard the door close. And I heard another sound, that of bolts being slid home stealthily. When I tried the door it was solidly locked. No amount of banging or shouting would elicit a response from Denham.

With considerable trepidation I performed a routine examination of the suit. My sudden abandonment confirmed in my own mind all the ill I had heard spoken of Denham. However, other than an overgenerous air tap setting the suit was in good order so I completed dressing myself and sat down to wait for the door to fail.

About three minutes later it suddenly bowed outwards. It supported the pressure for no more than a minute before it creased, crumpled, and was swept away in a gale that nearly snatched me up and carried me with it. I clung to a desk during the several seconds the air took to escape. Afterwards I stayed on my hands and knees, listening to the silence which had enveloped me.

The door through which Denham had gone was not deformed in any way; therefore the far side was also in vacuum.

When I went through the offices into the main corridor I found it wrapped in a pallid yellow twilight. A few overhead lights had withstood the blast, as had some of the emergency glo-lamps; but over all lay dust which dimmed them to the brilliance of smoky candles. With their aid I could discern hints of the damage: near the side tunnel the walls and ceiling were largely intact; but further along the ceiling had caved in. A jagged slope of collapsed concrete and rock rubble lay below an opening that framed a patch of starry sky. Bodies in orange suits were scattered amongst the debris. Silhouetted against the stars was the wreck of a giant crawler truck whose rear half seemed to have been blown away by the explosion. One of its headlights still gleamed weakly, spilling its light down into the hole; as I tried to think what to do, it went out.

I plugged myself into a public phone and was told to stay put, so for a few minutes I removed what pieces of rubble I could from the bodies that were visible, until the succession of dead faces, blue and swollen, made me give up.

Soon afterwards a light was flashed down the hole. A figure carrying a powerful torch picked its way down the slope and stood on the littered floor shining the light around until it found me. We plugged in the phone line, for emergency suits had no radios, and a woman's voice said: "Did you telephone?"

"Yes," I said. "The others all seem to be . . . well, what else?" She turned to survey the ruined tunnel. I raised an arm towards the side tunnel. "I left someone in there. He went into a room beyond the inner office. Said it was a laboratory. He was searching for a suit, he said."

"Wait." I heard her talking to CommCon on her radio. "Then he's still in there," she told me. "Building plans show only this entrance as yet. They also show only one suit locker filled; the remainder were to be supplied this morning. Think: had he a personal suit?"

I tried to recall Denham's words. "No," I said finally. "He had no suit."

Denham had meant me to survive. I felt small and mean and found I despised Jones for his lies.

"Then he's dead," said the woman. "These offices aren't meant to hold air this long."

"I know," I said, for the sake of breaking the silence which followed. "Can I go?"

CHAPTER SEVEN

The chief investigator called the meeting to order by rapping on the table with his knuckles. When there was silence he consulted his notes and summoned me forward to the witness bar. I waited, still shaky from aftershock, while his assistant, a Captain Lamov from the security department, read from a printed card:

"You are required to bear witness truthfully and impartially. You are reminded that any failure by you to do so may result in your being prosecuted by this court of inquiry or such other court as may be convened for that purpose. State your name."

"Daniel Frome."

"Occupation?"

"Cybernetic design engineer, Project Golem."

There were whispered consultations amongst members of the board of inquiry. Lamov addressed me again:

"Mr Frome, that project is discontinued. The proper name is now Project Nightwatch."

The words still meant nothing: a collection of letters, pretty enough but empty on their own. Still, I experienced a chill.

"Nationality?"

"European-British."

"Now, Mr Frome, you knew the dead man, Terence Denham?"

"Not really. We met for the first time that morning."

"That morning? Do you mean the morning of the explosion in Corridor W-239-J?"

"I'm not sure about the number. It could be."

The chief investigator nodded to Lamov, who faced me. "At what time did you first see the deceased, and where?"

I described our encounter and our conversation in the office, although I ommited the finer details of the Golem's aberration, on the grounds that though all the people present at the inquiry were experts in their own field, none of the officers was at all inclined towards mathematics or systems-philosophy. I also suspected that such details would be a needless cause of confusion.

When I came to the moment of the explosion Lamov interrupted me.

"What was Denham's reaction?"

"To the bang? He seemed surprised."

"Not . . . shocked?"

"I was shaken up myself. I had no time to watch Denham."

"Continue with your account, please."

Lamov made me repeat the very last exchange with Denham and appeared concerned that there should be no uncertainty about the wording.

"He did not speculate on the cause of the explosion? ... Is that correct?"

"So far as I recall."

"Correct or not correct?"

"Correct, I think," I answered testily.

The chief investigator said quietly, "Captain, the witness must not be pressed to say more than he knows."

Lamov bowed stiffly to him. He returned to me: "What happened then, Mr Frome?"

"He told me to put on the suit. There was another in the laboratory, he said."

"But there was not, as we know."

"Right."

"In that case," Lamov said slowly, "is it not curious that he did not return and say as much?"

I nodded.

"What did you say?" asked Lamov. "You must speak up, Mr Frome. This inquiry is being recorded."

"Yes, it's strange," I said. "I thought so at the time. Especially when he locked the door."

"The door?" Lamov half-faced the chief investigator, hesitated, and faced me instead. "The door was not locked."

"Of course it was," I said. "Denham himself locked it from the inside. He wouldn't answer when I called to him."

Sorting through a sheaf of tissue-thin transcripts, Lamov selected one and held it aloft. "Mr Frome, this sworn testimony by two members of the Safety Committee rescue service disagrees with you."

"Then they're wrong," I snapped "Captain, I was *there*. I saw what happened: Denham sacrificed himself for me. Perhaps the lock slipped when the air escaped; I can't guess."

Lamov's discomfiture was obvious. He chewed his lower lip, dropped the transcripts on the table, and sat on them, regarding me with a troubled expression on his face.

He said, suddenly: "Mr Frome, do you know of any reason why anyone should wish to murder Terence Denham?"

Incredulously, I stared at him until I could muster the self-control to address the chief investigator.

"Sir," I said, "am I supposed to have killed Denham?"

The investigator pursed his lips, shot Lamov an angry glance, and shook his head. "No," he said, "you are not." My legs felt weak for a moment. "But you are our prime witness – our only witness – and we are anxious to discover the truth. This inquiry was convened automatically, ostensibly as a routine accident investigation. However, we believe the crawler's fuel cell did not explode by accident. We are in a delicate position, Mr Frome. So many nations are represented in the Base that we cannot be sure of every individual. Most, we hope, are friendly; but a few ... well, sabotage is a dirty crime at best. On the Moon it is unpardonable."

Whilst the chief investigator had been speaking, Lamov evidently had been recovering his composure, for he wasted no time in renewing his attack.

"Well?" he said. "Would anyone you know want to murder Terence Denham?"

My cheeks suddenly felt hot. "No," I said, with Steelyard Jones very much in mind. I was sure my voice betrayed me. To compensate, I adopted an aggressive pose.

"You're so sure it's murder," I said. "Why couldn't it have been an accident – careless maintenance of the crawler, for instance? Or if it was sabotage, why did they have to be after Denham? Don't I qualify?"

"That is being looked into," said Lamov. "But we have our own reasons for supposing that Terence Denham was the target of a murder plot."

"Or me? Why not both of us?"

"That would have been child's play." Lamov smiled secretively. "Had the killer wanted both of you he would have seen to it that the crawler –" The investigator spoke a word of warning. Lamov hesitated, shrugged, and carried on: "– was parked directly above you. As it was, one of you had to survive because there was one emergency suit in that area and all doors in this Base are rated at a one minute minimum yield time. No, the uncertainty lies in which of you was the intended victim; and I favour Denham." Putting his face so close to mine that I could smell a faint odour of garlic as he spoke, Lamov said conversationally : "And I don't share the faith of our comrade investigator in your good nature, Mr Frome."

Before I could reply the investigator spoke to him sharply in Russian. Lamov gave him a hostile look. I sensed a division forming amongst the officials present. Lamov said to me :

"I have been asked to retract that slur on your character, which I do. But we both understand the situation, don't we?"

"No we bloody well do not!" I shouted at him. "Captain Lamov, if you possess information that suggests I'm guilty then you'd better lay it out on the table where I can see it. All you've got is circumstantial evidence, and feeble evidence at that. Sure, I didn't take to Denham; he struck me as being a capable snob and a stuffed shirt of the first order. But kill him? You're –"

"– crazy?" he finished for me. "Mr Frome, Denham's autopsy showed he had taken a heavy dose of oral anticoagulant mixed with powerful soporific. That alone would have killed him, had decompression not done so. In the glasses that you and he drank from was found a dried residue left when the liquid boiled away into the vacuum. The residue and the drugs Denham was filled with were the same. Now, Mr Frome, how was it you felt no ill effects?"

Stunned, I had to support myself by leaning on the witness bar. A chair was brought and I sat gratefully. "But he brought the drink," I managed to say. "Denham insisted. It was in his document case. He said a friend in the commissary makes it."

Lamov scribbled a note in the margin of the transcript. "And how much did you each drink?"

I concentrated on those few frantic minutes. "I only tasted it. A couple of sips. But Denham –" I saw Denham raising his drink and smiling : his lips moved as he proposed the toast; light glittered on the glass as he tipped it and gulped back the whisky. I heard the glass clunk on the stone desk and heard the ice tinkling as it swirled around, slowly to a halt . . . "Denham drank all of his. Every drop."

For a moment Lamov seemed at a loss for words. *"All?"* he asked.

"Yes," I said, nodding, surprised that he should make such an issue of it. I would have thought he would have rejoiced at the strengthening of his case. Instead, he frowned and conferred with the chief investigator in Russian for several minutes. They appeared to reach an amicable agreement, for Lamov began to rearrange his papers and the chief investigator said to me:

"I think we need detain you no longer, Mr Frome."

I was ushered from the room. As I left, Gustavus Hochmann was sitting on a bench outside, kicking his short legs and letting them swing, idly passing the time. He saw me and said, "Hello, Dan. Got a minute?"

I sat next to him, glad of the rest, and discovered I was shaking from the interrogation. Hochmann noticed. Peering at me concernedly, he asked, "Was it bad?"

I laughed. "Bad? No, not really. They think I killed Denham, that's all. Or Lamov thinks it."

Hochmann tut-tutted. "I think friend Steel should be told."

"Tell him nothing," I said. "I want first words with that man."

"What's he done?" asked Hochmann. "My God, Dan, he's a friend to you. Or have you forgotten so soon?"

How close were Jones and Hochmann, I wondered.

"I've forgotten nothing," I said, so calmly the effort it cost me left a choking sensation in my throat. "I want his advice."

"Good," Hochmann said, nodding slowly. "He was most worried when he heard of your difficulties. He would be pleased to help. I also; but I must stay for the inquiry. I am –" A sad smile. "– an expert witness. You know?"

"Yes," I said. It crossed my mind that few people in Dvornik could have had the facts and figures of suit stowage at their disposal; Hochmann was one, yet, of all the people I had met or seen in the Base, he seemed the most harmless. I decided one had to draw the line somewhere: if Hochmann was the one who had arranged Denham's death, he was free to make an attempt on my life also whenever he wished. He had only to induce a fault in my spacesuit when next it came to him for attention. Such thoughts and such uneasy charity did not sit well in the company of their object; I stood up and made my excuses.

In any event, I had to attend a meeting which had been postponed once already.

CHAPTER EIGHT

I found the remainder of the late Terence Denham's group in a makeshift conference room. There were four in all, three men and a girl, sober and quiet, seated around a circular brown glass-fibre table. The girl, an attractive redhead, in her twenties by my estimation, sat to the left of the table between a morose fellow doodling on a glo-pad and a stolid bald man of forty or so whose coveralls were too narrow for his shoulders. Opposite the girl and on my right was a short slim man with black wavy hair and a full somewhat tattered beard. Catching sight of me, the man stood and performed a half-bow reminiscent of traditional Japanese courtliness; in his unhurried welcome was the same calm precision, though there were few traces of his oriental origins in his excellent English.

"You must be Daniel Frome, the fortunate man. Good afternoon." He held out his hand. I shook it and found his grip firm without being excessively hearty. "I am Shijo. No other name you need worry about. On Terry Denham's death I have assumed responsibility. These are your co-workers: from left to right, Werner Ulm, Odette Galfoy, and Guy Palmer."

Ulm and Galfoy smiled, Ulm with correct formality, Galfoy with more warmth. Palmer spared me a moment from his artwork to twitch a corner of his mouth. Shijo ushered me to a chair on his left beside Ulm but remained standing with his hands in his coverall pockets.

"At long last we are together," he said. "The unhappy events of three days ago have robbed us of one of our team; but the final stages of the work can now begin. Our part of Project Nightwatch, possibly the most important, starts as of this moment."

Theatrical his style might have been, yet it was marvellously refreshing. My mind was dusty with solemnity, subterfuge, and an encroaching dull conviction that the fun had gone out of

69

life. Shijo banished the dust in an instant: he was the conjuror who strides onto the stage, all swagger and panache, and brightens the room with his presence.

"As you can see," he said, tugging at his beard, "I have been here much longer than any of you." Even Palmer managed a wan smile. Galfoy, whose red hair was only a centimeter or so long, brushed a hand over it and adopted an air of high indifference, then winked at me. My own fuzzy scalp felt clean shaven by comparison. Ulm looked glum; it mattered little how long he stayed, as his gleaming head testified. "So," said Shijo, "there are still a few tricks I can teach you about this job. Officially, of course, you still have absolutely no idea what all this is about –"

"I haven't," I agreed.

Shijo regarded me with feigned compassion. "Then, my lucky friend, we must tell you." He lifted a plastic box from the floor onto the table. The box, about the right size and shape to hold a crash helmet, was shown to be full of plastic foam when he lifted the hinged lid.

A hole had been cut in the centre of the foam and Shijo reached into it. Gingerly he extracted a scale model of a spacecraft. Spreading a sheet of synthetic rubber on the table, he set the model on it and returned the box to the floor.

"This," he said, "is a Nightwatch robot fort."

There was the sound of five people breathing. A chair creaked.

"So small," murmured Ulm.

"So large," Shijo corrected him. "And so deadly: a laser with a rocket attached; and a mind to guide them both. Your Golem, Dan."

The model might have been spun from metal by a master jeweller. Perhaps it had; amongst the miniscule lettering with which it was adorned might well be the trademark of Garrards or Tiffanys. Or a film maker with a passion for precision in his special effects might have created it as the centrepiece of his space saga. Ulm and Shijo were both wrong; the model possessed no size that scale could convey by itself. The ship might have been as large as it seemed, barely thirty centimeters from bows to stern, or bigger than the greatest ocean liner of the early twentieth century. As deeply as one cared to peer into the lattices of girders there were new details to be seen. One awaited the moment when the cluster of three tail jets would fire and send it on its way like an arrow; or when the attitude thrusters would spit and flash, to wheel the silvery skeletal lozenge about the central grey mass of reactor and propellant tanks; or when the tangle of cables and pipes in the tapering forward half was brought to bear on whatever target had been selected by the mechanical intellect concealed within it and intolerable light winked for an instant, incinerating all in its path.

"Has it been tested?" I asked.

"Piecemeal, yes," said Shijo. "As a whole, no. We must assemble the parts which are being shipped up from Earth. Then we will dry test each fort in a simulator rig. Later, when the launcher has been built, the forts will be catapulted into lunar orbit and fuelled there. Testing is not the right word; the design is sound. The forts will work because they must; we will merely make and adjust them."

Palmer, who had resumed his doodling, remarked, "Lot of confidence you've got there."

Shijo did not respond. Ulm asked, "How big is it, exactly?"

"Ninety-one meters from tip to tip of the frame. The laser aperture projects by one point six meters, the main jets by three point two meters. At the centre, the width across the flats of the hexagonal cross-section is eight meters. And its mass, when loaded with liquid hydrogen propellant, is over two hundred metric tonnes."

"Ah," said Ulm.

"You have doubts, Werner?"

"I was considering whether the attitude jets could handle it."

"Don't concern yourself." Shijo flashed us all a self-satisfied grin. "The critical design parameters were supplied in every case, whatever you thought you were building. Your controls and navigational aids will work; so will Odette's nuclear engines and reactor, Guy's mainframe, and Dan's pet robot."

Had my opinion been asked just then, I would have contradicted him. Only I, and possibly the programmers who had worked most closely with me on the Golem project, could have appreciated the fact; but my design parameters had not been supplied. Unfortunately, Palmer chose that moment to side-track the conversation.

"And the laser?" he asked.

"Mmmm, I must confess to doubts about that,' said Shijo. "Still, it worked when we tried it last year here on the Moon.''

Palmer's eyes narrowed. "Hold it," he said, pointing his scriber at Shijo. "Were you mixed up with the disappearance of those satellites?"

Shijo seemed to search his memory. "Around December the Third? Yes, that was us."

"You bastard," growled Palmer. "I sweated for months to get that series launched. What right did you have to shoot them down?"

"I do not like to tell you this," said Shijo defensively, "but permission to launch was contingent upon us using them as targets once your principal tests were finished."

White-faced, Palmer appeared on the verge of having a fit. I classified him as extremely unstable mentally and wondered where the balance point lay between necessary genius and unacceptable psychosis in Project Nightwatch. He clutched at his scriber so hard the tip drew blood from the palm of his hand, so that Galfoy had to reach over and take it from him. Gradually he sank back in his seat.

"I am sorry," said Shijo. "I did not intend that offence should be given. The only explanation can be the obsession for secrecy we have all had to endure."

"A fat lot you care, so forget it," said Palmer without looking at Shijo. He hunched himself up as if he had decided to withdraw from the group. Shijo was about to speak to him but instead sighed silently and picked up the model.

Ulm had been watching the dispute with interest and asked in a serious tone, "Could one of you explain what is wrong, please?"

"You tell him," said Palmer.

Shijo licked his lips. "We may be faced with a formidable enemy, and have only one opportunity to penetrate his armour.

Since the quality of that armour is also uncertain the weapons carried by the forts have to be of a power hitherto deemed infeasible. No safety margins can be allowed. The laser we developed is such a device." His left forefinger traced a line back from the tip of the model as far as the central mass. "With every pulse it can vaporise over four tonnes of ice almost instantaneously. In trials it shattered blocks of thirty tonnes.

"But power output of this magnitude is not achieved without making certain compromises. I said we discarded the safety margins. The physics of our refined laser process is close cousin to a nuclear explosion: not only heat degrades the lassing medium; some of the constituent atoms undergo transformations also. After about five pulses the laser's useful life is ended. A few we tested vaporised themselves on the fourth pulse. So you see, we had to be sure it would do its job under realistic conditions but without giving the game away or alarming anyone. Guy's satellites were ideal targets. The news media were told that they had been destroyed by remote control, which was not untrue."

Nervously, I asked, "How clearcut is the plan? Have the forts much of an option?"

"Terry Denham was working on that when he died," said Shijo. "As yet I do not know how far he got. But that is not our problem, Dan."

"That's right," said Palmer. "Man, just do like you're told."

"And when does the confrontation happen?" I asked Shijo. "It's planned for late 2011."

There was a hoarse cry from Palmer. "Five years?" he said. "I'm here for five years? My God, Shijo, you better have a bloody fine excuse this time, not that feeble stream of soapsuds you tried on me when . . ." His outburst became an incoherent shuddering gasp. Closing his eyes, he sank back against his seat, with one side of his mouth raised as if in a smile. He laughed, once, then groaned.

Ulm glanced at Shijo. "I did not mean my question to cause trouble."

"Not your fault, Werner," said Galfoy. "Guy, snap out of it."

Palmer opened his eyes wide, staring at her. "You don't care?"

"We're here to do a job," cut in Ulm, "not to enjoy ourselves."

"But five years?" repeated Palmer. "Doesn't that bother you, in the slightest? Growing weaker in this gravity? Hearing the news from Earth?"

"The news is no worse than it has always been," said Ulm, with his hands folded on the table before him. His large heavy-lidded eyes kept flicking between them and Palmer. "The trouble is, we hear only the bad side of it."

"You don't feel cheated?"

"That hardly matters, does it?"

"It does to me," said Palmer. "Dear God, I want to get out of this place – *now*!"

"That is Commandant Kallekjan's decision, not ours," said Shijo sharply. "I am sure he will ease the restrictions once the forts are on their way. That will be no more than two years from now. You can wait that long, can't you?"

"And what if war comes?" asked Palmer. He was shaking with a strange mixture of laughter and tears. His hands made quick jabbing motions as he waved them about.

"Then I think you would be safer here," replied Shijo. "There is no profit in futile rebellion, or in carrying a grudge against us. We are prisoners too."

"To hell with that," said Palmer, lurching to his feet. His chair overturned to clatter on the floor. "You don't need me. You never have, because those plans of yours are nothing but numbers. People? They're slaves of those almighty numbers. The only option you've left us is what to eat and what to drink, so long as it's what's supplied by the machines. Even the bloody cinemas here regurgitate digitised entertainment from the computer data banks. Well, Shijo, I know one way out that's always going to be open. You understand me? But don't worry, that's for later, maybe. Now, I'm going to get drunk; I'm going to conduct an experiment of my own: I'm going to determine the solubility of your blasted numbers in alcohol."

He slammed the door aside into its slot. It absorbed the shock

After a dreadful silence, Shijo raised his eyes towards the rough ceiling as if he could see through it and the green paint masking its stark utilitarianism, to the Earth. "Very clever, Dan," he said. "Now do us all a great favour: keep it to yourself."

"Good God, man, how?" demanded Ulm. "I have a wife and child in Berne. That's one of the first places they'd hit."

"You have to try to forget ... No, I do not mean that, quite." Shijo began to pace the floor. Notices pinned to the wall fluttered in the wind of his passage. "Above all, *remember* those we have left behind, because they are why we are here."

"Platitudes," said Ulm.

"Werner, you begin to sound like Guy. Self-pity does not suit you." Sudden anger had reddened Shijo's face. He marked his words with jabs of his forefinger in Ulm's direction. "We are here, ultimately, because the people we have left have paid for our tickets. They trust us, Werner. The public has always had to trust the leaders, as the leaders have had to trust their specialists: their diplomats, their generals, their messengers, their nameless servants who kept faith with the people who paid for their keep. I am speaking of a sense of responsibility we all must cultivate in ourselves, that love of truth that holds men honest when there may seem no need for it. We are here, yes ; and most of us think the reason for our presence worthy in itself. But you, and you and I, know better; we have seen beyond that reason to one that overshadows it so massively we cannot see the reason itself.

"Look at the Earth as it is now and tell me: can you imagine it totally helpless, open to space? I say you cannot. You cannot because you do not dare to. And because you do not dare to you will cling to the first reason, the comfortable one, and pretend the real one does not matter because it is a bad dream. But it is long past time for you to wake up, Werner. Metaphorically speaking, the day is coming to an end, and with it the political uncertainty of these past sixty years: tonight, not tomorrow, we shall be alone, under siege by hunger, by thirst, and by despair.

" Yet we must go on. We must keep faith with those who

77

sent us, even though they do not know we are their servants in this matter, and even though misguided loyalty seduces us with the lie that there is no purpose in outliving those we love. Werner, what could you do for your family in Berne? I, knowing what I know, would rather be here than in Otaru, my home. Because when I was eighteen I said to myself: first of all, Shijo, you are Ainu and all that that implies; but also first you are Japanese. And later, when I had understood how large the world really is, I added: and, also first, you are a human being.

"There are no boundaries to truth. If I am to stand by my family, it must be the family of Man. Is this not so?"

Ulm scratched his nose, looked at me, and finally let his gaze fall to the table top. The notices rustled in a stray breeze as the door opened soundlessly. Hearing a footstep, I turned. Palmer stood behind me, with Galfoy behind him. I supposed he had been listening outside the door, to have entered so opportunely. He seemed more composed, though his face lacked animation and his voice was a hoarse whisper:

"Werner, you stupid clod, listen to what he says. That's why I stayed alive: hoping. There had to be a purpose; I'm glad to hear it's a better one than some fraud involving aliens."

"You misunderstand me," Shijo said. "The alien ship is real."

"Two for the price of one?" asked Palmer. "That's rather an improbable coincidence."

"They are not unrelated," said Shijo. "The world as a whole is ignorant of the alien. But governments are not; and their hope of gain or of marginal advantage when it arrives is expected to make them act rashly. One event will trigger another."

"It was too much to hope for," said Palmer, as he left us again.

Shijo picked the box off the floor and set it beside the model fort. "This meeting is adjourned until tomorrow, when we've all had a chance to cool off," he said. He sounded upset.

I stayed behind. I had to talk to someone; Shijo's calm assurance had held up well enough during the past few stormy minutes for me to regard him as one who would not treat my problem lightly. I also felt I could trust his discretion.

"Shijo," I said, "that accident three days ago . . ."

He paused in packing the model, to look at me. "That was no accident," he said.

"How did you know?"

"Captain Lamov is a friend who keeps me informed. Also, Terry Denham expected someone to make an attempt on his life. Inevitable, he said."

"Well, what do I do? Lamov thinks I did it . . ."

"No." Shijo shook his head emphatically. "If he thought you guilty you would be in custody. Captain Lamov takes no chances. However, you are right to be concerned. I was going to raise the subject with you: Lamov thinks you may well be a target again."

"They were trying for me as well?"

"Judging by revised forensic evidence, undoubtedly. From now on you must make every effort to minimise the risk to yourself. And since you cannot defend yourself against determined treachery in a place like this, you can reduce the value of an assassination by committing as much as possible to the records. With luck the killers will not think it worth risking themselves if they know your work will not be halted."

"That's half the problem," I said. "What I know about the Golem can't be written down. And there's work that has to be done on it."

"In that case," said Shijo matter-of-factly, "try not to get killed too soon." The lid of the box clicked as he pushed it shut.

CHAPTER NINE

With the surging, wallowing gait of a seal on land, the crawler and its burden nosed up to the receiving bay of the fort assembly site. The rising sun caused men and machine alike to shed long shadows across the lunar surface; searchlight details from the Safety Committee probed the darkness ahead of the huge vehicle for obstacles, while the voice of the Quartermaster came in bursts from my earphones:

"Left! . . . Right a bit! . . . Hold it!"

The crawler rocked to a halt. The gigantic metal framework cradled in its cargo grapples dipped and swayed until the shock absorbers damped out the movements. The crawler's corner beacons were switched off, leaving only the sidelights burning, and the driver climbed down from his cage.

Quartermaster Bouklis waddled over to me in his armoured suit and proferred a receipt pad for my signature. As I signed, I said, "Last one, George?"

"God be my witness it is and I thank Him for it," replied the big man devoutly. I could appreciate his relief, for we had all followed the ferrying down of the fort mainframes with considerable anxiety. Individually they were worth around a billion dollars; collectively they were priceless. They were also as fragile as fine china, the driver of a crawler had discovered on taking a bump too fast: the crawler had tipped too far and dashed the projecting bows of the frame against the ground. The frame had been mangled beyond repair, whereas the crawler only required new forward suspension units. Like the rockets of old, the forts held their shape under the correct stresses but otherwise were flimsy structures.

A pair of mobile cranes lumbered forward with dust sheeting from their treads. They halted so that service crews could clean the worst of the fine grit from their slings, then inched up to the side of the crawler. Men swarmed over the mainframe, threading cables through the alloy lattices and bolting them to preordained lifting eyelets. A general call was broadcast, checking off all personnel, the signal was given to hoist the frame into its storage cradle alongside the first seventeen frames and the wreck no-one could conceive a use for, and we were allowed to disperse. Soon there were only three or four people left; the Sun was well above the horizon and nobody liked staying overlong in the open lest his suit refrigeration fail in the heat.

Bouklis came to me for the final signature and I marked his pad with a flourish.

We walked around the frame a couple of times, admiring its clean lines and marvelling at the expense of it. Almost complete as it stood, it only lacked the delicate peripheral equipment that might have been damaged in transit. There were no VHF omnidirectional butterfly loop antennae or S-band dishes ; nor were there any of the clustered attitude thruster jets which later would project sideways from bows and stern like solid-geometry Maltese crosses on tripods. The three main engines were there; their dark exhaust cones overhung us as we walked beneath the stern. I involuntarily ducked my head, thinking of the nuclear-fired hydrogen plasma that would stream from them one day, scoring a line of light a kilometer long across the sky. As yet the yellow-and-black trefoils warning of radiation hazard had not been uncovered, for the reactor and jets would not be fuelled until the fort sat on the catapult at the launch site itself, to the east of Dvornik where the catapult rails were being laid.

"Big bloody thing, by God," said Bouklis. "I saw the model and didn't believe it."

I too remembered the model and the first occasion on which I had seen it, five weeks earlier. The real thing was far more impressive. A model is a dream removed from the dream, a translation from one conceptual level, that of the designers who plan for full size, to another, that of the observer who wishes to comprehend the whole at a glance. Dwarfed by the glittering jungle-gym of rocketry hardware, so much more subtly textured than the model had been, one was aware of being confronted with the proper perspective on that original vision. I could stand beside the matt black radiator fins of the engine block and observe how the spreading T-beams of the fuselage interlocked with the finer L-beams, how the joints had been welded and polished to remove all signs of seams, and how this mass of metal fanned out to attain a climax at the embrasure enveloping and engaging with the thirty-tonne power reactor, itself a visual puzzle of welded plates, grilles, cable ducts, occasional mechanical linkages, and maker's labels for the guidance of artificers. Just visible beyond the reactor was the distant fore cluster of baseplates where the navigational equipment would be fixed; and beyond them was the white lump of plastic foam capping the laser's snout. From where I stood to the white speck of the cap was almost a hundred meters. Until a man walked beneath the bows I shared Bouklis' sense of disproportion; but, when the man paused briefly and turned towards us and I saw he would have needed the shoulders of a twin brother to stand on before he could have touched the cap, the scale adjusted itself for me. On Earth, the atmosphere would have blurred the remoter details enough for my subconscious mind to understand what my eyes were seeing.

"Take a good look," said Bouklis. "As soon as I get those no-good security slobs to rig an alarm fence, not even Kallekjan gets close without someone watching him ... And that includes that tourist." He gestured towards the bows of the fort where the stranger had been. "Go and shoo him away, will you?" He trudged off in search of his guard detail.

I walked along the line of fort mainframes and found the stranger far down by the bows of the damaged one. Where the crumpled frame had been bent, it came within easy reach of the ground. The man seemed to be testing one of the joints by tapping it with a small hammer. Concerned and curious, I crept up behind him and was surprised to see Yale's name on the backpack of his suit. Every suit bears its owner's name in large fluorescent red letters for ease of identification.

I came around to sunward of him. As my shadow fell across the metal he was examining, Yale jerked and twisted to look at me. My own name on my chest was clearly lit by the sunlight reflected from his suit and from the ground, yet he only waved casually and went back to whatever he was doing.

A search through the radio channels located one with an idle marker blipping steadily. I tried it.

"Byron, what're you up to? You know this is off-limits?"

He turned, displaying irritation in every movement, and waved me away.

Sorely puzzled and not a little hurt, I backed off. Yale and I had eaten breakfast together that morning, when he had seemed friendly. I stayed to see what his game might be. After a few seconds he noticed I was still there and repeated the signal that I should go away, only this time he was quite violent about it.

Now I was worried. Yale was definitely acting irrationally.

I selected Channel O, the distress frequency that was constantly monitored, and was answered immediately: "CommCon Rescue here."

Spacesuits for kilometers around would be flashing distress lights at their wearers, advising them to listen in. I saw Yale's hand move to flick the channel switch on his radio, so I spoke with one eye on him.

"CommCon, this is Frome 18-M. Suspected Rapture case, by Fort frame Zero, bows. Subject is Byron Yale. Symptoms, aggressive non-communication. Possible psycho withdrawal. Cause not known."

"Check. Mobile?"

"Yes." Yale dropped his hammer, reached into his chest tool pouch, and brandished a small automatic. "He's armed," I yelled as I ducked and ran. "Ballistic handgun," I added. The clumsy suit seemed to be doing its utmost to make my legs go in the wrong directions but I made good speed. Ahead of me the frame dwindled to a remote point and I knew I stood little chance of reaching the far end before Yale scored a hit. In every respect my predicament appeared to resemble the classic pursuit nightmare: my enemy could strike at me hard and at his ease; I, confined by my suit and the gentle lunar gravity, could only run in languid bounds.

However, though my paces were slow my speed was soon great. I began to experience some difficulty in keeping my balance and realised that I was risking tripping over, with possible serious consequences. To my left was open ground, to my right the fort, ahead only distance. Of the three the fort alone offered a realistic refuge and then only once I was past the mid-point where it touched the ground. Thereafter, there was a gap which widened as I approached the stern; and, as soon as I felt I could no longer risk being hit and that the gap was great enough, I dug in my heels, skidded to a halt, threw myself prone, and rolled through.

My movements must have been sufficient to throw Yale's aim, for when he fired the dust spurted up well away from me. Scrambling upright I peered through the frame, to see Yale's feet bounding along the far side, away from me.

"CommCon," I panted, "subject armed. Dangerous. Fired at me. Might have meant to miss. Can't say. But I'm playing safe. Will try to follow at a distance."

"Check," said the CommCon. "Switch to Channel 2 and join Security Command net. CommCon out."

I flicked through to Channel 2 and identified myself. The SecCom operator sounded quite unmoved by the excitement. "Frome, a mounted patrol has been detailed to assist you. Will fix on your signal. Advise status of subject."

"Running hard," I said, giving chase. Yale was now a small figure, a bright white splash against the grey waste into which he was headed. As he was well outside reasonable firing range I ran at his pace, until it occurred to me that the Moon's lower gravity and lack of an atmosphere effectively extended the danger zone. A deranged man might think to take advantage of this, offsetting it against the inherent difficulty of aiming a small gun accurately over any significant distance. He might be lucky enough to be right. I fell back some more, still keeping him in sight.

At a steady jog he led me along a nearly straight path northwards as if he knew exactly where he was going. He must have had some kind of a landmark to guide him, for we were crossing virgin ground, yet when I looked back towards the Base we seemed not to have drifted from our original course. His footsteps were crisp and clear, so that I was beginning to feel the game was too easy when he disappeared into a small crater.

I stopped, wary of a trap. We had come about a kilometer, too far for me to run back for help. If Yale planned to shoot at me from cover I would have to fend for myself.

Something white appeared above the crater rim. There was a sudden flash of yellowish light that spilled across the ground towards my right. Then Yale drove out of the crater on a buggy, on which he soon outdistanced me.

I walked the rest of the way to the crater. Pausing there for breath, I decided the USSR Cavalry could catch him; heat prostration would be my most probable reward for any further heroic athletics unless I rested.

Whilst the suit's temperature controller did its work I tried to rationalise Yale's antics and failed utterly. We were friends, notwithstanding his detestable grouchy chauvinism. He had no reason to run unless he had been doing something illicit to the frame; and even then he could have soothed my curiosity with some technical doubletalk, for my knowledge of metallurgy was practically nil and the spare frame was nobody's treasure. And to run as he had after attempting to shoot me, was insane. The hills were no place for a refugee, for to try hiding in them was like jumping from a ship into the sea. In time he was bound to succumb to exposure or some other want. Unless he had a well-provisioned hideout to go to Yale would be forced back to Dvornik before long.

There was no easy way out, either. The ring of mountains which surround Lansberg Crater reach as high as three thousand meters above the enclosed plains, a savage wilderness of peaks and crevasses. I had been told there were only extremes in those hills: stony plateaux roasted to oven temperatures by the Sun; shadows undisturbed by heat for millennia; and little else. Perhaps Yale had accepted death as the way out, intending that we should follow the wheel marks of his buggy and find him slumped in his seat, with his faceplate broken and his tongue hanging out of his mouth, black with coagulating blood.

Or perhaps not. My eye had idly traced the wheel marks back to the crater in which I presently stood and had noted how Yale's footprints joined them. A second set of wheel marks showed the route by which the buggy had been brought to the crater; but no footprints of its driver were visible. Yale had been alone in the buggy when I had last seen him, so whoever had brought the vehicle to this lonely spot had contrived to depart without disturbing the powdery surface of the ground in any detectable way.

This contradiction of common sense perplexed and offended me, so that I set out to discover what traces, if any, might have been left by the elusive chauffeur. For there had to be one: the buggies were not then amenable to remote control. However, though I circled the crater in a widening spiral encompassing an area greater than that which could have been traversed by any conceivable combination of jumping, walking on fingertips, polevaulting, or other means of locomotion short of powered flight, not a single clue was to be found. There were marks aplenty, all of them attributable to meteoric debris. Unless some highly improbable fall of celestial rubbish had obliterated the tracks, I had the classic 'locked room' mystery on my hands – out in the open. Jet packs existed, it was true, yet I could not seriously imagine any clandestine stowage of a presumably stolen buggy being set at risk by the use of one of those ostentatious devices. Nevertheless a jet pack did at least suggest an explanation, so when the militia appeared on the scene I dismissed the puzzle from my mind.

The lunar version of an armoured car was a six-man buggy with an all-enclosing metal-and-plastic layered mesh canopy that transformed the occupants' view of their surroundings into a pointillist nightmare. It arrived at speed with its headlights blazing and halted amid a wave of dust which cascaded ahead of the skidding balloon wheels. Much of the muck enveloped me. Seconds were lost while I beat the grey floury stuff from my suit. The soldiers pulled me aboard, slammed the canopy shut, and we were off before I had my harness fastened.

Though the driver seemed unarmed, each of the four soldiers carried a repeating rifle with telescopic nightsights. I really felt sorry for Yale: alone and leaving a trail that would betray him for millions of years, he was as good as caught. As if that were not enough, the military buggy soon demonstrated its superior handling qualities in a way that made it seem alive. It accepted misuse that would have disabled Yale's vehicle on the first bump or bend. Official policy must have been to ensure that the military were better equipped than civilians, so that the grip of authority might not slacken, even outside the nominal confines of the Base.

For a while the hills maintained their elusive illusory closeness, then suddenly they were upon us: the horizon broke up and vanished as we drove into the first patch of rough ground. Stone chunks the size of upended buses jutted from scrambled bedrock. The driver slowed the buggy while his arms worked like pistons on the steering sticks, skidding us around tight corners barely centimeters from disaster. The soldiers switched on their sights and began to scrutinise every possible place a man might lie in ambush along the trail. Yale had a head start of ten minutes, most of which must have been eaten into by our greater speed, so we expected to come upon him at any moment.

The sides of the narrow defile closed in slowly; the buggy slipped through gaps hardly wide enough for the wheels, which were slamming up and down on their suspension as we encountered rougher ground. Then, creeping out of the darkness ahead, we saw the red rear reflectors of Yale's buggy, abandoned and jammed between two rocks.

The driver braked in time and we dismounted. Equipment was rapidly handed out: the soldiers had their rifles, packs of food, water, air, and medicines, as well as a full-face night visor each. I was given a ration pack and five coils of fine cord to carry. When I asked about the visor, which would be essential if I was to see my way in the sunless valleys ahead, the sergeant, an unsympathetic gorilla by the name of Topravin, told me not to worry. "We do the search. You come," he said offhandedly. Plainly I was to be baggage, a prospect that appealed so little I suggested that the driver might like my company, to which Topravin made some Russian reply that set them all laughing. "You, Frome," he concluded, "with me. You may be wanted when we catch him."

The defile beyond Yale's buggy deepened into a ravine that darkened as the sunlight shining on the western wall high above became progressively remoter from us. Soon the way was too dim for me to walk with any assurance, so that I had to be guided by one of my companions. We talked very little and then only by way of our telephone lines; we had roped ourselves together as a precaution against one of us falling down a crack in the ground, for the going was uneven in the extreme and the pitfalls were many.

After we had gone about a half a kilometer, I wondered aloud whether we might not have lost Yale.

"No," grunted Topravin. "We are slower. He is running, or should be. Soon he will be careless and lose ground. Then we will see the heat of his footsteps. So far there is only one way he could come."

"He could be anywhere," I persisted.

"Be silent, please," answered Topravin. "Soon. I feel it."

The terrain through which we threaded our path of pursuit is worse than the worst of Earth, yet it is typical of many mountainous regions of the Moon. There is, of course, no air to speak of; I once heard it said that if the lunar atmosphere were compressed to terrestrial pressures it could be contained in London's Saint Paul's Cathedral. Effectively, vacuum is a constant threat to the climber. That threat is made more potent by the ubiquitous sharp edges: at some time in the past, perhaps when the first sea creatures on Earth were debating the choice between air and water, that part of the Moon was convulsed by a groundquake. Rocks split into layers, slid and staggered like packs of cards dropped on edge, and settled again. There are crevices in which feet can, and do, become trapped, and razor-sharp cleavage corners to rip suits. Those edges are underfoot also; they erode the climber's boots as he crunches across talus slopes of fragments shed by the overtowering cliffs during millions of years of diurnal thermal battering. Surface temperatures plummet from above one hundred degrees centigrade to below minus one hundred and fifty, and soar up again; the full cycle may be experienced in passing through the shadow of a rock. And, as if the frightful topography of the land itself were insufficient hazard, the inexperienced climber is often prey to one of his own making. This is the Rapture, which seemed to have affected Yale, and which creeps insidiously into the brain through poisoning by waste products of an overloaded air recycling plant.

I was an experienced suit user but was far from being an expert mountaineer, terrestrial or lunar. My ancestors were farmers – lowland farmers – and to me a mountain is a picturesque peak to be admired from a decent distance but avoided by all sane men. When we scrambled to the top of the first grade and I could look back at Lansberg spread out below like a lumpy grey pancake, then set my face towards the stone maze awaiting us, I had doubts. The soldiers too were making half-hearted suggestions to Topravin that this route or that one would be better, or safer.

Topravin spurned all such faintheartedness. He had a hot trail to follow and he was happiest following it. More and more he was resembling a breed I had thought extinct: the man-hunter.

However, he made one small concession: he allowed us to check our safety lines, the coils of cord which I had been given to carry and which had been shared out by now. Each was a three hundred meter length that Topravin claimed would bear the weight of three men, a claim he jovially demonstrated by seizing a loop and miming the strong man with it. His failure to snap the line did not reassure me; I had multiplied an average mass of man-plus-suit of one hundred and twenty kilos by three and had divided by six. A breaking strain of sixty kilos hardly seemed adequate life insurance.

We resumed our march. Smertz, the corporal, was given special charge of me. Before long we encountered fissure-valleys in which the shadows attained a stygian depth and darkness. At any moment I expected to hear a cry from one of the others, or to step out and never touch firm ground. Topravin would not, or could not slow down. "Is safe," he would mutter over the phones; but I still wished he would allow us the use of our helmet lights.

After about an hour we had to stop and decide whether to proceed in the hope of a speedy capture, or to turn back for want of air.

We had come to a valley formed when the highest mountains split, whose sides were cliffs that lost themselves against the stars. Somewhere, so far above us they looked like bands of light in the sky, the peaks glowed in the sun. At the time of the catastrophe, walls of rock had flaked away from those cliffs, tumbling and crashing, splintering into rubble that filled the lowest crevices, since when the slow erosion by insolation had overlaid a gentler mantle of driftrock. This much I guessed from what my feet felt and from what I touched with my gloves as we filed through the darkness between jumbled crags dimly seen by starlight. I recollected anecdotes overheard at meetings of the Dvornik Selenological Society, when professional cartographers had been persuaded to relate their most unsettling travellers' tales: of pinnacles shaken loose by the quake and balanced for millennia, awaiting a minor shock to tip them onto the explorer; of faults in the packing of the scree over which we now picked our way, and men vanishing into mysterious depths; of the innumerable inexplicable but unsettling accidents that might have inspired the outrageous Baron Munchausen and which certainly induced a healthy respect for the great outdoors of the Moon. When we halted I breathed a sigh of relief.

"Yale is close," said Topravin. "His footsteps glow much brighter." He came back to where I was, third in line, the novice position. "Frome, you know this man Yale?"

"Slightly."

"Would he know you?"

"Well enough to shoot at me," I said. "I'm staying here, thanks."

"No," he said, "you come with me."

I felt like a dog whose owner drags it, willy-nilly, all over town. I was going to argue. Then I became conscious of the other men breathing: they were awaiting my agreement. Two facts impressed themselves upon me: I was as much a stranger to them as Yale was; and if it came to a difference of opinion between me and Topravin, they would side with their sergeant.

Hoping to salvage my honour as well as reduce the risks, I said:

"At least give me some means of seeing where I'm going."

"Agreed," said Topravin. "Przekolov, your night visor."

The soldier handed his visor to me without a word. As I clipped it on over my faceplate, suddenly the world was a brighter, weirder place.

I stood with four dark red mottled figures on whose backs were strapped small bright yellow boxes. The ground was splattered with fading blue footprints and here and there on the rocks were blue smears where arms and hands had brushed against them. The stars far above were brilliant white points hemmed in by slabs of bright orange rimmed with yellow fire. Ahead of us along the valley's cool cobalt floor ran a faint track of ultramarine footprints left by the fleeing Yale. They were widely spaced, showing that he had been running, even after so long and tortuous a chase.

Topravin said, "Yale must be near. He would not run unless he expected to rest soon. Frome, we will go ahead and argue him to surrender."

"He tried to shoot me," I reminded him. "Don't I get a gun?"

"I will do any killing that must be done," he said. "Yale is valuable."

"And I'm not?"

"You also. That is why I will be with you."

I gave up. Topravin appeared to await my counter argument; when none came, he turned to Smerz.

"You will return to Dvornik with Przekolov and Fiodorvich. I will take Frome and as much air as you can spare."

"But that is contrary to regulations," protested Smerz.

Topravin said softly, "Smerz, I have decided. That is all."

The air tanks were redistributed and they left us to find Yale.

The valley opened out. To our left an almost vertical cliff continued as far is I could see; about three-quarters of a kilometer ahead of us a colossal stone wedge at least half a kilometer tall leaned against it to form a natural triangular arch. To our right the cliff face sloped away ever more shallowly in a succession of receding angled steps, until it lay at no more than forty-five degrees to the horizontal. Masses of broken rock lay at its foot. Several gigantic splinters stuck up out of the rubble like golf tees for titans.

The footprints bore to the left of this rough ground, towards the archway. We approached it at a half-run, with Topravin urging me on with a, "quick, quick, quick!" I stumbled over slabs of stone buried in fine dry slurries in an effort to keep pace with him and ease the tug on the safety line. Frequently I had

91

to fling out a hand to brace myself against the cool monoliths whose frigid shadows we were entering. The chromatically aberrant world closed in. I think Topravin was conscious that our time was limited by the air we breathed and wished to complete his business before speed was forced to become haste. A suit's recycling plant really only scrubs the air; it cannot salvage much oxygen from the exhaled carbon dioxide it scavenges. In an hour we would have to turn back.

"Walk closer to me," he ordered. The stone wedge towered above us; we passed into its shadow and I seemed to feel its weight also. The ground became more uneven. For millions of years it had been screened from the Sun and rockdrift by the vaulting overhead so that what debris there was dated from the great upheaval. In itself this was considerable; the lefthand wall continued to be moderately smooth and vertical; but the inward-leaning righthand wall had shed fragments of itself. Consequently, though the tunnel approximated to being triangular, there were many inconvenient deviations from that mean. We were following a modest pathway Yale must have prepared for himself but despite his slight improvements by bridging and infilling our feet began to find dangerously obscure holes in the floor. The problem was that the light was going, for we were now so far underground that the night visors were becoming useless; starlight that had seemed brilliant when enhanced by an image intensifier was lost to us and the cold of the surrounding mountain made it look black by infra-red.

Reluctantly Topravin allowed that it might be time to use our helmet lights.

Lit normally, the gargantuan tunnel still had an air of primordial gloom. Its apex was concealed by lofty shadows. The shards of stone that crowded it and across which we picked a zigzag path were as much a threat as ever, with their sharp corners and unstable balance.

I thought of Yale running across this pile of deathtraps. His motive still eluded me; Lamov would only have locked him up for a while. "What do we do when we catch him?" I asked. There was still no doubt in my mind that we would.

"If we can, we take him back to Dvornik," replied Topravin. "If not –"

A spear of rock ahead of us exploded. Splinters rattled on my helmet and pattered against my arms and legs. I waited, tensed, for the leak alarm to buzz. Topravin must have been expecting some attack, or was dead to worry: before the second burst of machine gun fire could find and finish us he had slapped the switch on my helmet and extinguished my light.

"Move," said Topravin in the darkness. "To the right."

Stepping from one foothold to another, I felt my way into a niche, with Topravin close behind me. I saw his helmet silhouetted against the abrupt glare of gunfire.

"Yale's damn close," I breathed.

"Yes, maybe twenty metres ahead. He was waiting for us."

"How could he have missed from such close range?"

"Fired too high. We find out later perhaps, okay? For now, be lucky, and glad."

Of course I should have anticipated an ambush. In retrospect, with hindsight understanding of the man we were chasing and what Topravin was keeping to himself, I would have thought about it. Yet throughout the chase our man had acted the fugitive, not the hunter. Apart from his first halfhearted attack on me beside the wrecked fort frame he had run and never once stopped to fight.

Topravin was busy with his chest pouch. He bumped into me as his left arm swung back; then the pressure of his elbow was gone. He flung himself against me with a hurried apology, before the wall shook and bits of the mountain dribbled onto our heads and shoulders. The tunnel lit up like the lunar noon. I had an impression of flames flaring past our hiding place like scatter patterns in a nuclear bubble chamber. These endured for only a second or two, then a fine smoke or grey dust boiled along the tunnel. The light guttered low after about half a minute. Topravin eased himself away from the wall, and I was able to breathe freely again.

"What the devil was –" I began.

"Distress grenade," he said. "Meant to be visible from an orbiting spacecraft. Let us see if he lives."

But yet again Yale had out-thought us. When his two attempts at murder failed, he must have run. The tunnel floor dropped away precipitously as the amount of fallen debris diminished; but a ledge developed along the lefthand wall at about the original level. It took us to the mouth of the tunnel, then dodged left along the face of a cliff at an altitude that looked halfway between heaven and hell. There was sufficient dust on the ledge to show that Yale had gone along it.

A cautious man would have put his back to the sheer cliff above the ledge and sidled along with his eyes raised to the stars so as not to have to contemplate the precipitous drop the ledge so briefly interrupted. We, like Yale, had time neither for caution nor contemplation and walked quickly after him. In this I took my lead from Topravin who, as I have said, seemed nerveless; and though I was conscious of the vertiginous panorama to my right I managed to ignore it, most of the time.

The ledge bore us around the mountain, back into the shadows. Fortunately enough light was reflected from the nearer peaks to produce a twilight in which Yale's tracks were clearly visible, so we stowed the night visors in our chest pouches.

The ledge narrowed. It was, in any case, no more than a misalignment of two mountain chunks which had been jolted and skewed by the quake. We neared the point where the overlap diminished to nothing and became an overhang. The ledge ended. Yale had vanished.

First, I thought, *no prints. Now, no man.*

The first thing I looked for was a burn mark on the cliff which would have told us a jet pack had been used there. No marks.

I peered over the edge. It was a long way down; one helluva long way down. In the heat of the pursuit I had failed to notice how high we had climbed, so the drop turned my stomach over. It must have been a kilometer or more.

"He can't have gone that way," I said to Topravin who was following my explorations without comment. Up, then? No, that was as bad: a smooth rock face. The ledge was halfway up a cliff that would have looked good on Mount Everest; a major feature, indeed: imagine that mountain split down the middle to a depth of two kilometers and polished.

"Did we miss him somehow?" I asked.

Topravin muttered to himself in Russian and would not translate his remark.

Part of the problem was that our view ahead was obscured by the curvature of the cliff. Out of curiosity, I got down on my stomach and ducked my head so as to see under the overhang.

I had to laugh once I understood what I saw there.

Topravin did not object when I squeezed past him to examine the corner formed by the ledge and the wall. There I found what I had already seen in the overhang: several tiny metal loops were wedged into the corner, with a wire threaded through them. Yale had an escape route prepared; and it was so magnificently, breathtakingly, suicidally simple: he had only to hang from the wire and swing along it, hand over hand, to leave us scratching our heads, far behind him.

CHAPTER TEN

Topravin was not amused when I explained the trick.

"He is mad," he said. "Quite mad."

"But it worked for him," I pointed out. Topravin conceded the truth of that. "And," I added, "it might work for us too."

He swung his visor towards me.

"You are correct," he said suddenly. "Yes, it might. And you will use it."

"Me?" I said. "You're the leader."

"But your idea," he replied; and did his gun drop fractionally, so that its muzzle aimed at my face? "Please."

Hitherto I had attributed my slight unease whilst in Topravin's company to respect for his professional skills as soldier and tracker. His demand stripped away my uncertainty, placing that feeling where it belonged. It was natural antipathy.

Topravin and I were mutually unsympathetic in a way that argued the existence of no sixth sense but an exchange of subliminal signals which, being more honest than the courtesies of verbal communication, had identified him to me. Topravin had signalled his essential nature as that of . . . of what? The killer? He enjoyed the hunt, yes, and he rejoiced in strategic triumphs and for him the perfect day would end in a clean kill. And I? I do not know even now, after all that has happened, what kind of a person I am, nor what signals I had given Topravin. It is entirely possible that he found me as much a mystery as I had found him, for it was luck alone that showed me the layers of his nature as they shed themselves in the course of the hunt. He had been soldier, tracker, hunter, fighter, killer; I had no wish to confront the next one, though hints of it were already detectable. Like those in Steelyard Jones' onion, it would not be pleasant.

"Okay," I said at last, keeping my tone neutral. I untied the rope that joined us, went over to radio communication, and got down on my knees to take hold of the wire.

I heard Topravin draw a deep breath. The pattern of light on the rock wall shifted. I glanced up, saw him raise his rifle by the barrel and swing it down as if to strike my helmet; and without thinking I kicked free of the ledge in time to fall clear of the blow. My elbows took the full force of the drop when they hit the ledge; they and my shoulders suddenly had to carry the weight of my body at rest, as well as exert the forces required to move it, for the cliff below the ledge offered not so much as a toehold. Partly to relieve the strains this abnormal posture imposed on my arms but mainly to dodge Topravin's second assault, I began to pull myself along the narrowing ledge. He would have followed me, I am sure, had he not run out of room, for he leaned out further than I would have dared in his attempt to hit me with the rifle butt.

"Afraid to shoot?" I grunted. A man in a spacesuit possesses considerable inertia, so although my weight of twenty kilos or so was tolerable, my efforts were tiring me.

I had reached the changeover from ledge to overhang when he answered me. A man of action at heart, I suppose he had preferred to demonstrate his plans rather than talk about them; but when violence failed he was prepared to resort to words.

"This, my friend, is so much more fun. A bullet might leave traces that would be hard to explain. A fall would not be unreasonable under the circumstances."

Sadist. That was the next layer.

"You'll have to shoot now," I said, not wishing to put ideas into his head but to keep him talking those few extra seconds it would take for me to escape around the bend.

"True," he said. I looked back. He had reversed the rifle so that the muzzle was aimed at me. I waited for the bullet, dizzy with fear. But instead of firing he lowered the rifle until the muzzle rested on the wire.

"See?" he said.

I did. The wire was secured only at the end loop, so that if he broke it at any point there was that awful drop waiting for me as the wire slipped out through the loops and through my fingers.

Because there was only one thing I could do, short of letting go and saving him a bullet, I did it: I kept going. Swinging along like an obese Tarzan, scrabbling at the successive handholds with my clumsy gloves, I imagined that whenever I came to a new space between the eyelets and the slack shifted from the last, the brief drop was to go on forever.

But Topravin displayed commendable forbearance. Perhaps, deep inside him, he was a sportsman. In earlier ages he might have been a keen follower of bear baiting or fox hunting and believed in letting the quarry enjoy itself for a while, and even fancied he was giving me a fair chance. He restrained himself for at least ten seconds, then I felt the wire give way.

I had no idea how far around the cliff the hangwire extended. A few meters, or a kilometer, I resigned myself to about half a minute of life, as long as it would take me to drop the one kilometer to messy dissolution on the rocks below.

My body had other ideas and hung onto that wire with a determination I, in my detached state of mind, found quite admirable. It gripped the wire with fingers that discovered hitherto unknown strength and managed to twist a bight about the wrists before any weight had to be borne. Then the shock of deceleration almost wrenched my arms from their sockets: again the physics of non-terrestrial environments demonstrated the difference between weight and mass, for once I had come to rest and was swinging gently at the end of three meters of wire my arms had no difficulty in supporting me.

However, I lacked confidence in Topravin's patience. He was still standing on the ledge, gazing down at me, the rifle held negligently in his right hand. I had decided to ignore him as best I could, when it came to me that he must have been able to hear my laboured breathing by way of the radio, for every gasp was easily loud enough to trigger the transmitter.

For a while this awareness sustained me. I swore to myself that I would not yield easily in what was still a contest between him and me; and though he was watching with interest I acted as if he was not there but concentrated on the wire, my life-line in the most literal of senses, in that it upheld not only my person but my pride also. Whilst I held onto the wire, I held onto my own future and defied Topravin.

Laboriously, I stretched out one arm and gripped the wire higher up, then raised myself to the new level. By repeating this procedure I managed to haul myself as high as the eyelet, where I rested.

Topravin seemed impressed by my performance. "Bravo," he remarked. "You show excellent spirit."

Paradoxically, this simple compliment drained my reservoir of self-control more than the apparently impossible situation had until then. By his tone he implied that he was done with me; and that nearly caused me to give up. Suddenly I saw how alone I was, high above the abyss which had made my head spin when I was still in no immediate danger of falling into it.

Oddly, it was also Topravin who saved me.

"What you should do," he said after I had been hanging inactive for a while, "is to hold the next section, let yourself fall, climb to the next and repeat, all the way round."

"What do you care?" I muttered. My hands were becoming cramped.

He made a helpless noise as if I had rebuffed a genuine

attempt to be helpful. "I do not like to see a man surrender so quickly. What should I tell my friends of you? That you were an easy contract?"

"Doesn't it come to the same end? They want me dead; are they fussy too?"

"You misunderstand. My friends do not think ill of you. They admire your talent; they think you a clever man; and they wish only that your cleverness should not be given to Project Nightwatch. For myself, I wish they had paid me to kill someone else."

"The fourth layer," I said. "The nuts."

"What?" he said. "Oh . . . Yes." He chuckled. "You have been talking to that man Jones, have you not? That is what he would call my friends, yes. But I think he exaggerates. You must try to understand, Frome, what we plan for the future."

"I thought they hired you," I said, almost screaming with the ache in my arms and fingers, and the terror of falling. "And what future, anyway?" Shifting my grip, I grasped the next stretch of wire. Topravin may have noticed my sudden resumption of activity but left me alone. I think the overhang prevented him from seeing how I was tying the loose end of the wire around the eyelet. The work was difficult; several times I thought I had overestimated the strength of my wrists as I hung by one hand. Much of what Topravin was saying was so much noise in my earphones, until I had the knot secured and could place my hands on the next loop for a rest, preparatory to the dash I would have to make before Topravin realised what I had done.

"There is a great future," I think he answered; and his ensuing remarks amounted to a eulogy to the good sense of certain men and women on Earth who believed more strongly in a display of determined peacefulness than in provoking an alien visitor who might only be annoyed by our best efforts. He expanded on how the world would be improved; and how it was his mission – suitably funded – to see that the project failed; and how he didn't really hate me; and quite hoped I could be saved, only it was too late now, wasn't it.

"It may be no comfort to you, Frome," he added, in a tone that suggested he had said his piece and was winding up the proceedings, "but there are at most six people in Dvornik who cannot be replaced. Without them the project is seriously delayed. I will not bore you with all their names; Terence Denham was one and you are another."

"You're only saying that to make me feel good," I said.

He missed the sarcasm. "That is my pleasure. Now you must excuse me. My air supply is at a dangerously low level, so I leave you. You too should think about resupply. To make your air last, I suggest most strongly that you avoid strenuous exercise –"

"And take the tablets three times daily. Thank you, doctor."

His only response was a cheery wave as he walked away.

I wasted no time in agonising over why he had not stayed to see me fall. There was no great mystery in that; I could not retrace my only known route to Dvornik and, as he had said, my air supply was almost exhausted. If I gained the far end of the wire, why, I might be found one day: another lone climber come to grief in the mountains.

With these morbid thoughts trudging through my mind I moved along the wire. To my joy the makeshift knot held and since the weight of my body had drawn the wire tighter there was little slack between each eyelet to slow me. My spirits rose; the delight of partial success following apparent defeat sustained them. And then I rounded the bend to see another ledge ahead, with Yale sitting on it, a machine gun across his lap.

I backed up. He gave no sign of having noticed me. His faceplate remained directed towards the vista of peaks and valleys behind me. It was, I realised, entirely possible that he thought me dead, for he could not have overheard my radio conversation with Topravin owing to the interposition of the cliff. He might not be waiting for me but resting.

It was obvious that the chase had been an elaborate contrivance so that Topravin could arrange my elimination without arousing suspicion. Close cooperation by Yale had been required, nonetheless, and in his efforts to stay close enough to us to leave a visible heat trail he must have had to exert himself considerably, especially when sprinting along the valley that led to the tunnel.

He would be tired. No wonder if he had to sit still for a while to recover.

I inched forward, sliding my gloves along the wire, with my body hanging as close to the cliff as the bulk of my suit allowed. Yale's feet came closer. Still he seemed unaware of my approach. I was about to wrench the gun from his grasp when he moved it, almost negligently, so that it was pointing at me. I stayed still. His faceplate swung towards me.

" You're supposed to be dead," said the voice of Terence Denham.

Given the circumstances, I trust I may be forgiven a lapse of memory. The following five seconds are a little hazy in my mind, such was the effect the shock had on me. I recall looking at the column of telltale indicators along the inner righthand edge of my faceplate and noting that the TX : ON lamp was glowing. Whoever this man was, he had heard me coming, filling the air with my marker signals.

Eventually I managed an answer of sorts.

"That's what they said about you."

"About me ? I don't think so," he replied. "But I'm always being mistaken for someone else, so don't fret about it . . . Dan, you are a most tiresome fellow. Must be one of those confounded survivor types, always having lucky breaks. Just as well I had to sit here a while, eh ?"

I could say nothing.

"So," he continued, "old Toppy flunked, did he ? Have to talk to him about it. Couldn't hear you fellows chatting, mind, so you have my word I won't be too hard on him." He stood, then squatted so that his faceplate was close to mine, like a great silver blind eye. "Shall we get this over with ? You have a choice : will you be a gentleman and go graciously ; or must I mash your fingers against that cliff with my gun butt ?"

"Neither," I said, sliding away from him. He got down onto his hands and knees for a better view of me.

"Oh, come on," he said. " Don't be difficult. This is absolutely not the way I wanted it."

"You sound like Topravin," I said from a distance of three or four meters.

"That kulak ?" His anger showed plainly, along with his contempt. "I really must ask you to mind your manners, Frome."

Was he serious ? He displayed no real awareness of what he had involved himself in. It was a grand game to him, I thought, before I recognised the symptoms of the Rapture and began to have hope. Within minutes, if I was lucky, Yale—or Denham, or whoever he was – would become disorientated; if I hoped hard, he might even fall unconscious. I wondered if he was as inexperienced as he seemed.

" Manners be damned," I said. "Who are you, anyway ?"

"Don't you recognise me, Dan ?"

"I thought I did. You sound like the Terence Denham I met, the day his office was vacuumed."

"Then that's who I must be." He giggled and sat down again.

"Denham's dead. The Dvornik authorities identified his body positively."

"My mistake." He began laughing; it was a low, silly laugh. "Or theirs." This he found screamingly funny, for he began whooping loudly. A paroxysm of coughing seized him, so that I thought he was about to choke. He regained his self-control and said, weakly, still on the verge of hysterics :

"What a delicious joke. Dan, you must hear the whole of it, or I'll never forgive myself. We can deal with you later."

"Aren't you afraid of eavesdroppers ?"

He seemed to survey the endless silent mountains.

"Never mind," I said. "You tell me your joke." Our signals would travel twenty miles at most before fading into the background noise of the universe. Any sizeable hill could stop them.

" It was so elegant," he said. "We already had Denham stashed in the lab; all I had to do was dope you to the eyeballs, leave you to fumble around with your suit, and hide in the locked lab until the air was gone. After that I'd sneak out and wait for the rescuers, when I'd help them 'rescue' the two of you."

"But you missed your opportunity to muck about with my drink," I said "Why did you bother to dose those glasses afterwards ?"

"I didn't," he said. "If that ass Topravin hadn't jumped the gun with that bang, we'd have bagged the whole team, not just you and Denham."

"You're lying to save face," I said. "The only chance you had to drug me was with that whisky; and you drank what I drank. It had no effect on you."

"Only because I drank it before the ice melted," he replied. "Another minute and one sip would have left you *non compos mentis* and no two ways about it. Brilliant, eh?"

"Quite," I said. It sounded utterly impractical, until I reminded myself that it had nearly killed me. Still, that oversight was now about to be corrected, if I read the stranger's movements aright : he got to his feet.

"I knew you'd thrill to it," he said. "Now, I'm afraid I'll have to be off, so shall we finish this chat on a friendly basis ? Why don't you simply let go and we'll call it quits?"

"Why don't you simply jump off the edge ?" I countered.

He seemed about to disagree and went so far as to aim the gun at me. Then he let the gun fall to his side, twitched, leaned forward as if examining me, and toppled into the void.

I heard him moaning as he fell. Half a minute later his marker signal ceased.

There was no time for self-congratulation. I had kept him talking; the Rapture had done the rest. I knew I had to hurry; but when I clambered onto the ledge I discovered how deathly weary I was and lay prone for several minutes, relaxing and breathing deeply to allow my system, body and suit combined, to recuperate. When I tried to stand I found I was shaking, my knees felt unsteady, and my hands would hardly close. The symptoms were those of shock, not Rapture, but either could be as deadly as the other to a man alone on the surface of the Moon. I could not afford the prolonged rest I needed; I had to push on in the hope I would not fall by the wayside as the stranger had.

As I prepared to strike out along the ledge and discover where it would take me, I heard a channel marker signal. It did not fade in but clicked on as if someone had activated the transmitter. I could hear breathing. For a second I thought the stranger had survived by some ruse; then the marker was suppressed for a second time as a familiar voice said :

"You okay, Limey?"

"Steel," I gasped. "Where the hell are you?"

"Right above you," he said. When I looked up the cliff, there at the summit, so far away it might have been a star scraped off the sky, was the gleam of a torch. It weaved from side to side. "Got me?"

"That's the best thing I've seen all day," I answered, close to tears of relief.

"Thought you'd say that. Pretty fancy shooting, huh? Not many guys could hit a man at this range."

Whoever-he-was had not fainted. Jones had shot him. "Indeed," I said, more calmly than I felt.

"Yeah, that guy was no good. He and Topravin belong together."

"Topravin . . .?"

"Had an accident, yeah. Anyways, let's get you out of that hole. How much air have you?"

The gauge hovered at thirty minutes. "Long enough," said Jones when I told him. "Hug the cliff, then grab this line." About half a minute later a cord like the one I had tied to my waist snaked past me, to snap and wiggle as it grew taut. "Wrap it round you," said Jones. "When you feel the tension build, walk up the cliff."

"Walk . .?"

"Yeah, I said *walk*. Dan, this is no time for hysterics about heights: you gotta walk it, so forget that drop."

It was all very well for Jones to talk so calmly. His people had a long tradition of discounting the popular notion of 'ground level', which was why the Mohawks owned the steeplejack unions in parts of New England and the Great Lakes states. I had no such advantage. With possibly exaggerated care I knotted the line about my waist and over my shoulders in a four-stranded cradle and clipped it into the equipment buckles on my belt and backpack to minimise the risk of the strands slipping.

"I think I'm ready," I said, eventually.

"Check," said Jones. "You got maybe twenty minutes to walk one kilometer. That's a slow stroll, so if you slip and dangle you'll get no sympathy: we'll just drag you up and forget about the bumps. All clear?"

"Start towing," I said, anxious to find out if the method would work.

I felt the tension build up and adjusted the lines as I leaned back with my head sticking out above empty space. Of course, I was blind to the view behind and below me but my imagination amply supplied that deficit; and as I began to walk the first few meters of that vertical wall I was waiting for the fall to start.

I will not say that my imagination lied to me, or in any way failed to anticipate the consequences of an accident; but that its gleefully direful prognostications totally overlooked the delight of achievement. My fears were soon discarded as I scaled the heights. Though my mouth remained dry and my hands, by contrast, remained sticky in their gloves despite the dehydrators, the ascent rapidly evolved into an exhilarating once-in-a-lifetime undertaking, one of the sort that enthralls grandchildren, if successful. Indeed, my greatest discomfort was the monotony. My outlook comprised an ordinary sky full of ordinary stars and a dull rocky plain marred with a few cracks and shallow depressions whence scabs of rock had broken free in ages past. Jones' torch guided me in the early stages of the walk when the direction of the pull on the rope was not obvious; and later its apparent size gave me a measure of how much further I had to go.

The air alarm was winking a blue ten-minute warning light as I attained the summit. Pulling myself over the brink, I rolled onto level sunlit ground and luxuriated in the sense of security. All was bright and beautiful. I was alive again. The blue light was so pretty; and so was the red one. And I wanted to laugh. When Jones stood over me I waved at him; but my arm was too heavy; and anyway I was feeling jittery and my breathing was getting shallow and hurried and my scalp was prickling and sweat was breaking out all over me . . .

Jones and someone else rolled me onto my front. They fumbled at my backpack. For a while the air was thick and stale, then with a pop the pressure increased. The purer air hit me like a fizzy drink on a thirsty day.

They gave me time to rest. Jones dragged me into some shade

and sat with me. The men with him were the same three soldiers Topravin had ordered back to Dvornik. These coiled up the four lengths of line they had knotted together to make the hoisting-rope, then came to sit with us, talking amongst themselves in low voices on our channel.

When I felt well enough to move I thanked them individually, ending with Jones. He dismissed my thanks. "All part of the service," he said gruffly.

On the way home I learned what had happened. Corporal Smerz had been unhappy about his new orders, which contravened both general instructions and their specific orders regarding the man we had thought of as Yale. Unfortunately they had been in the radio shadow of the mountain valleys until they reached the hill overlooking Lansberg Crater, so had not known that the real Yale had been discovered at work within the Base. Jones had come out with fresh air tanks and met them; together the four of them had returned to the valley of the fallen cliffs and thence through the tunnel to the ledge.

Jones was reticent about the details of Topravin's accident. He had heard enough of our conversation not to feel any compunction over it. The official story would be that the sergeant had taken fright and slipped.

With the aid of a photographic map they had ascended the peak in time to prevent my own demise. Jones concluded the resumé by saying casually:

"I said Denham was a slippery fish. If an official inquiry decides that a man like that's dead, ask to see the body."

I halted and he almost bumped into me. "But that wasn't Denham," I said. "Didn't you hear him?"

"All I heard was him inviting you to take a dive and you giving him the same."

"Oh," I said. "It was as close as that... He told me he wasn't Denham. They faked the death of the real one."

Jones was quiet.

"What's wrong?" I asked.

"I spent four months before you arrived watching that guy without realising I could've pinned him by slipping Uncle Boris the word, that's all. I thought he was Denham and untouchable.

Side by side, with labels on, I could've told them apart. Only, in a place as big as Dvornik people can disappear for long periods. I caught onto his scheming when I overheard him with Topravin, oh, back in July: he must have been rehearsing his part as Denham, so naturally..." His voice subsided. His marker came up, blipping gently like a metronome. "Dan, you gotta understand, we aren't perfect."

"That's okay," I said. "So long as you win through in the end."

"We intend to," he said.

CHAPTER ELEVEN

That I have so far tended to describe Dvornik Base as a collection of buildings and hardware is no more than a reflection of the extent to which things, rather than people, predominated during my early days there. It was, of course, a community, with all the human idiosyncrasies that a variegated staff of two thousand people could contrive to bring with them from their homelands on Earth.

And there were a good many such idiosyncrasies. There was friction between ethnic factions whose customs clashed; there were weddings; there were accidents and funerals; there were outbreaks of one malaise after another. Intermittently there was grumbling about conditions of work, or food, or the cleanliness of the public corridors; and one humorist even circulated a petition for better weather.

But the community was not as rich in newsworthy events as might be supposed, for alarms and excursions of the sort inspired by Sergeant Topravin and his ambiguous friend were the exception, not the rule. Our principal diversion was work; and while we worked the months passed: October became November, which became December, in seven-day chunks separated by flurries of social activity. A tradition of weekend festivity established itself, to the disgust of the Safety Committee crews who disliked having to double their patrols of drunk-snatchers on rest days; and by the close of 2006 'multi-culture' parties were commonplace.

Jammed into common rooms or, if the extra space seemed warranted, into the Hall of Congress, these flamboyant dis-orderly events were open to anyone who did not mind making a fool of himself in public. They became a unifying force in our society; soon they were the premier extrovert activity, whilst intellectual pursuits were crowded into evenings preceding work days. The dances were a means whereby individuality could be expressed, even inside the prison of Dvornik Base. By com-parison, the Wednesday wrestling bouts were nothing, even when the Koreans enlivened them accidentally one week by introducing their style of boxing.

It was at one of these weekend gatherings that I almost made an enemy of Shijo.

Within Dvornik the closest early friendships naturally developed amongst the members of individual work groups. Given time, the diasporic process of acquaintance would have rearranged the social map of the Base; but in late 2006 we were still a young and artificial community. Shijo's group, being especially small, was also notably cohesive and approximated to a family in many ways, although Shijo was altogether too young to be the father figure this analogy suggests. We five muddled along, helping each other. Even Guy Palmer settled down after a while. It was all very pleasant. Naturally it had to be man-woman-man trouble which almost wrecked the arrange-ment.

I arrived at Dvornik just as Shijo and Odette seemed to have established a mutually satisfactory liaison, so I tried to stay out of their way. In any event I would have held back, doubtful about the ethics of involving myself with Odette when I already owed Helen Lorraine a measure of fidelity. At first I knew Odette as a colleague; then, when the initial self-conscious friendliness had passed quickly into cameraderie, I discovered her to be an extraordinarily companionable girl, charming and easygoing, apparently as carefree as anyone in our situation could be.

She was fun to be with, so much so that occasionally I envied Shijo his good luck. Later, as we settled into each others' lives, I recognised that either my first impressions had been wrong or that some new factor had intervened.

I suspect, although she never said as much, that the factor arrived by way of Odette. There was a morning in mid-November when I entered the clangorous workshop where the engines of the forts were being stripped for cleaning. Odette was leaning on a blueprint projection table with a ball of paper clutched in her right hand. The colour of the paper was white, so in theory it had to be a recyclable document of least importance, yet her tight grip on it and the anguished expression on her face suggested it meant a great deal to her. Only slowly did she relax enough to reveal that it was an official telegram from Earth, notifying her, in the coldest of sympathetic language, of her parents' divorce.

We left the workshop on an aimless walk that lasted a couple of hours, while we talked the numbness out of her. She described the years of domestic uncertainty, seen from afar as her career advanced; I did my best to make useful comments, for my own parents were no more than a fragmentary memory, idealised no doubt, with the same emotional associations I had formed as a child. But I listened: that, I like to believe, was what helped her.

She seemed to recover her good humour, though I noticed she remained intermittently subdued for days afterwards and that her despondency deepened whenever Shijo came near her.

At about that time, or possibly slightly afterwards, her friendliness towards me increased unmistakably; and since the attentions of a pretty girl flatter a man's ego, not to mention his libido, I accepted her interest with pleasure, although I tried to maintain a decent distance so as not to antagonise Shijo.

By the end of December, however, she was becoming hard to ignore; what made it worse was that my wish to ignore her was also weakening. Shijo's even temper developed irregularities over which I stumbled more frequently as the New Year approached; my work, he complained, was behind schedule or of inferior quality, so would I mind concentrating myself on it rather than on my hobbies? Were it not for the superbly diplomatic language in which his criticisms were phrased I might have picked an argument with him and so forestalled the ill-feeling that ensued.

The party to celebrate New Year's Eve 2006-2007 marked the end of a year most of us had begun on Earth. Accordingly it was planned as a special event, a kind of punctuation mark in what we regarded as a sentence of indefinite length. The Hall of Congress and the many rooms near it which had been reserved for activities peripheral to the dancing filled early in the Sunday evening. Kallekjan had bowed to pressure from the social committees and declared New Year's Day itself, a Monday as it happened, a holiday. In this I think he also listened to the Safety Committee, whose accident statistics were never healthy after a normal weekend and whose armour-suited crews were out in force that night, though they kept to themselves most of the time.

The usual small talk and laughter was under way as I strolled into the Hall carrying a tumbler of my Corridor Committee's vodka, obtained from him by stealth and flattery that same afternoon; I sipped it quietly and watched others downing their drink by the glass, while the early-evening dancers slow-stepped around the floor in time with a synthesiser quartet. I have yet to get used to the effect the Moon has on a traditional Viennese waltz.

Odette and Shijo were there, pacing out the twists and turns at arms' length. Neither seemed especially happy and Shijo's smile was more correct than it had been of late. I shrugged mentally and went off to one of the buffet lounges.

Midnight drew on. The festival furore heightened. For a while I danced in a relatively languid fashion with one woman, then somehow misplaced her, so borrowed another until her self-appointed guardian hustled her away.

There were minutes left. The music, stripped to a solitary one-per-second beat, was counting out the old year, the lights were dimming, and I was scouting the heads in my vicinity when someone female flung her arms around me. Surprised, I looked down. Odette's bright-eyed gaze met my alcohol-fuzzed inspection.

"Odette," I ventured, "aren't you with Shijo?"

Just then I caught sight of him coming our way. It looked as if his further progress was going to be prevented by the crowd and the impending darkness.

"He doesn't own me,' Odette replied offhandly.

Uncomfortably aware of Shijo only paces away from us, held back by no more than a dozen closely packed bodies, I said, "Even so, don't you think . . .?"

"I've given up thinking for tonight," she said. The drumbeats stopped; distorted and delayed by their journey from Earth, the Greenwich time pips issued from the public address system like a coda to the old year. I felt Odette's arms around me but could not respond. My thoughts were far away.

"It's midnight, Dan," she whispered.

"Happy New Year," I said, without looking at her. I was watching the dark shape of Shijo's head. There was enough light left. He would be able to see my face; I wished there were some clear sign for apology. Then I saw him turn away.

"Dan ?"

Odette was still there, so for a couple of minutes I pretended she was Helen; but I was not convinced.

Later I took her back to her room and left her there, singing to herself. For the next hour or two I wandered through tunnels grown quiet with the coming morning, feeling myself totally inadequate to handling the problem Odette had created for Shijo and me.

There was a man, a good man, earnest in his loyalty to humankind, whom I had been forced to hurt. Why Odette had contrived that confrontation I hoped never to discover; or, if I did learn her reason, I hoped it would be powerless against me. Expertise has its price, as the legendary Faustus learned, but all too often the price has already been paid before the search for knowledge begins. Some years removed into the future, I can now see the clues to her troubles – and mine – and on the whole I think it best not to summarise; let the conclusions remain as incomplete here as they did in life. Evidently a crisis had been reached in Odette's career and she had chosen to resolve it unilaterally. I could not press her to explain herself.

Shijo, sphinx-like, kept his feelings to himself when we next met, as if the incident had been no more than a romantic fancy of mine. I tried to apologise, once; the kind, slightly puzzled, thanks with which he acknowledged my stammered explanation made me resolve never again to raise the issue with him.

2007 was just another year to be eroded by the Dvornik work schedule. January slipped as effortlessly into the past as had all the other months I had spent in the Base. Then February clicked into the windows of the calendar-clocks and the mood tightened.

The star had crept northwards into the constellation of Libra, to lie close upon the ecliptic. Orbital and ground-based telescopes tracked it across the sky, seeking hints of a course alteration. We tried not to wait for the news.

On the evening of Monday the fifth of February our department held a Godot Party, another Dvornik invention, a sort of waiting-for-some-event excuse for drink and discussion. As planned, it would last through to the small hours of the Tuesday morning, by which time the alien ship would have to be seen to change course or risk missing the Sun.

There were about thirty departmental members and their friends present including Shijo's group, so that although it was possible for me to lose sight of Shijo and Odette for minutes on end there was not quite enough cover for me to feel inconspicuous. Consequently I was under double pressure : that from the night's big uncertainty; and that due to the three-way tensions that still existed in our group.

So as to minimise the social discomfort of the occasion I engaged in what was for me abnormally heavy discussion-hopping : in the course of two hours I talked to every stranger in the room about any and every topic, including some which otherwise would have bored me witless. The subject of alien spacecraft quickly died; it was about as popular as a lunch menu would be with condemned men on the day of execution. For an hour thereafter I debated interstellar political theory with a homely woman from the Astrophysics department who unfortunately proved to be less interested in the parameters of heavenly bodies than in those of the terrestrial variety, male preferred. Regretfully I disengaged myself and retreated to a cluster of seats in a remote corner of the room. Inevitably, Odette chose that moment to move in for the kill.

Calmly, she settled herself in the armchair next to mine, set her glass on the low table before us, straightened the creases of her coveralls – the patterned green set, the ones she reserved for off-duty occasions – and said:

"How's it going?"

"Bit dull," I replied. Involuntarily I glanced in the direction of the astrophysicist and noticed Shijo glowering at us.

Odette said, casually, "You've been avoiding me all evening, haven't you?" She tipped her head on one side as she said it and watched me from beneath lowered eyelashes.

"Not especially," I said indifferently, "Odette, why don't you like Shijo anymore?"

She appeared surprised, though I think she had been expecting the question, or one like it.

"But I do," she said evenly. "He's sweet."

"Then why are you making a play for me these days?"

Her face froze momentarily, before she released an uncertain nervous laugh. "Am I?" she said "I hadn't noticed."

"We've spent the last seven weeks building up to this," I said. "Don't duck out now. We two can speak frankly. And we care about what's happening to our group. There've been ructions between Shijo and you; what's so special about me that . . ." I couldn't finish.

"That I had to involve you?" she asked, saying it for me. "God knows. Dan, can we talk about something else?"

"I don't believe we can afford to," I said, "unless you want to smash this group at the moment it's needed most. There's an alien spacecraft headed for us; all we're waiting for tonight is confirmation of its ETA. We've got to have unanimity or we're crippled as a defence force."

"So what can I say about us?" she asked. "I stopped wanting to sleep with him. Is that a crime?"

"No," I admitted, embarrassed by her open response to my challenge and the hint of hysteria in her voice. "Couldn't you have been more diplomatic about telling him? A fair amount of mud splashed onto me, I hope you realise."

"Then I'll go and tell him not to blame you," she said, rising to her feet.

"Oh, sit down!" I said. She did so. "The damage is done. Patting his hand will only irritate him."

"Then let's discuss the weather," she said. This was Base slang for *I'd rather talk about nothing than this subject;* but I refused to be discouraged so easily.

"No," I said. "Let's discuss the two of us. Why me, Odette? Why not say, Werner, or Guy?"

"*Guy?*" She giggled. Then, because the man himself stood not far away, she reduced her voice to a near-whisper: "Guy hates women . . . Not that he's a mysogenist. He just hates people. And as for Werner . . . Since you ask, yes, he does have something. But he also has his ladyfriend in South-side, not to mention his wife in Berne."

"And I have Helen Lorraine," I said.

"*Ah.*" Odette gave me one of her thoughtful stares, as if I was an engineering drawing with a mistake in it, whose rectification she was pondering. It made me uneasy. "We *are* engaged," I said.

"Yes," she said at last, "you told me." Her tone increased my unease. "Dan, do you really expect to see her again?"

"When this is over," I said. "When we all go home."

"Ah," she repeated, more softly, like a sigh.

"Go on," I said.

Shaking her head slowly, not in negation but in sadness, she said: "Poor Shijo: he used to give me twitches with his gloomy stories. He's been here years too long. Could be he's scared to lose the security this place has given him."

"Say it," I reminded her.

"He thinks we'll never go home."

"Has he any reason to say that?"

"I suppose not. He's as likely to be wrong as anyone."

". . . Unless his theory about Dvornik being a colony is right."

"*His* theory?" she said, raising an eyebrow. "I seem to recall —"

"Okay," I agreed. "I have thought that way too. But that doesn't mean I've dropped Helen." I nudged my glass around the table top for a few seconds, letting it coast on a small pool of spilled drink. "Odette, I . . . I wish I'd met you first. Really I do. But I owe her."

She was silent for a moment. Then, "That doesn't sound much like unfailing devotion," she remarked. "Dan, pardon my saying so, but sticking with her out of a sense of duty is no guarantee she'll love you for it. Or that you'll end up loving her. Believe me, people can rationalise the cruellest ingratitude, given long enough."

"I can't change how I feel," I said.

Odette looked sceptical. "That's what I believed once."

"And life taught you otherwise?"

"Something like that."

"Well," I said, "until the day comes when I'm forced to change my outlook, I'm going to keep hoping that each of us has some say in his personality. And so long as I'm in charge of mine, house rules say you stick with the other person. Otherwise it's a bent game."

"Wow!" she said. "You *are* an optimist. Who's that perfect?"

An excellent question. I had never dared put it so simply.

"One tries," I said.

She laughed but attempted to disguise her laughter as coughing, with the result that some of her drink spilled onto the stone floor. "Do forgive me," she said. "Dan, if I hadn't met you, I wouldn't have thought you were real. You're all wrong, you know that?"

"I'm not the world's expert on personal relations," I admitted. Out of my depth, I regretted letting the conversation go so far. Machines have simpler problems; it could be that is why frequently I have preferred their company. They are relatively predictable.

"How wonderful it must be," she said, "to see it all in black-and-white: good and bad, like a child's bedtime book."

"Look," I said, "do you mind if we try another topic?"

"Yes I do." Odette pointed a slender finger at me. "You, Dan, are about to hear a few home truths. Then maybe you'll be able to reappraise us rationally."

"Then let's go somewhere else," I said, tilting my head towards the crowd.

Without another word Odette picked up her glass and led the way out of the door. As I passed Shijo I gave him a wary smile. Everyone in the room seemed to be watching.

Along the corridor from the party was what we called a 'branch library,' a reading room with televiewer cubicles connected to the main data store. At that time of night it was unoccupied, so we went in there. Inside the air was cool and smelled of mountaintops. There was one of the few carpets in Dvornik and that atmosphere, so conducive to clear thought, which good libraries possess.

I slid the door shut behind us. Odette paced around the small circular room, trailing a hand across the false reed matting on the walls. Her slippered feet made whispering sounds on the pile of the carpet. Pausing to drag a chair from a telereader cubicle, she sat and regarded me seriously.

"I don't want to be lectured," I warned her.

She closed her eyes momentarily and nodded. "Agreed. I want your opinions too. This is for both of us."

I leaned back against the wall with my arms folded and waited for her to begin. She, by contrast, leaned forwards, her elbows on her knees.

"Do you believe in precognition?" she asked suddenly.

"I've no strong feelings," I answered. "It's always struck me as being not worth the study. It contradicts Heisenberg's Uncertainty Principle, just as matter transmitters and time machines would."

"Does Heisenberg have to be right?"

"No; but he predicts a lot more accurately than the crystal-gazers do."

"And what about the traditional means of divination? The I-Ching, the Tarot, and so forth?"

"I tried the Tarot once. It annoyed me."

"Why?"

"Too vague. Its answers could be bent to fit any situation. In the end I ignored it."

"Did it seem to work for you?"

116

I shrugged my shoulders. "If I thought about it hard enough . . . what has this to do with us?"

She appeared to ignore my question. "Do you ever wonder about the future? About what will happen to you and the people you know?"

"Often."

"Don't you wish there were some way of being sure?"

"If it was real," I said after some thought. "Oracles always tell you half-truths, so you can never prove them wrong. If I could be sure about the future, maybe . . ." I bit my lip, thinking. "Maybe," I said finally.

"You," Odette said decisively, "are an explorer." I raised my eyebrows. "If you'd lived four hundred years ago, you'd have been off into those white areas on the map, checking for yourself just how many dragons were there, and how big."

"Well, okay," I said. "So where does that get us? Don't you take that appoach? You're a researcher too."

"A different sort," she said.

"How many kinds are there? The scientific method –" I stopped, hearing a mental echo from my discussion with the false Denham: . . . *is a fraud, my friend*.

She regarded me quizzically, clearly anticipating more.

"Nothing," I said lamely. "But if those dragons are there, or might be, we have to know."

"So we send people like you to look for them," Odette said. "Or, if we don't send you, you go by yourself. Me, I'm one of those who pokes around in puddles on the off-chance that there's a useful bug waiting to be discovered."

I had a vision of Odette prodding a muddy pool with a stick. Smiling I said, "Isn't that what research is all about? Every time we conduct an experiment we're hoping some useful effect will show its face."

"And why ever do we bother?"

"That's what they asked the man who climbed Mount Everest. You know what he said?–*Because it's there*."

Odette shook her head. "He was wrong. I think we do it because we're scared of the *status quo*; we're afraid to trust things as they are; there always has to be a better place over the next hill." She looked up at me "You've been very patient with me, Dan; but this is what it amounts to: I can't stay with Shijo because . . . I can't. I'm scared."

"And I won't let you down?" I asked. "Odette, if I'm the sort of person who goes dragon-hunting, I'm the last one you should trust."

In a flash she was back at me.

"Do you have any idea what the word means? *Trust?*"

"Whatever you want it to, I suppose."

"Dear Shijo preaches about trust and how much we owe to the people on Earth, yet he couldn't escape from his idealism to save his life; it's a habit with him, not a conscious decision. I'll tell you how I see it. It's when two people can be sure that what they share won't hurt them."

"Are you serious?" I said. "I can pick so many holes in that –"

"It's figurative."

"Oh." I frowned. "Not very useful as a definition, then, is it?"

"It has to be taken as a two-way thing. One-way, it's faith, the way you feel about Heisenberg's principle. That can be beautiful too, in a doggy-loves-its-master fashion, but it's not enough, not really."

"Does the distinction matter?"

"It makes all the difference in the world, Dan. And you've got to learn that, or one day you'll find you're alone, or worse. When you said, earlier, that you couldn't change the way you felt, I recognised it: you trust Helen; and that, believe it or not, is why you're an explorer, while I'm only a pond-poker. You're able to throw out anchors. I've got nothing. You said we were part of a group. I agree. I'm sorry about Shijo; I couldn't help myself. That's why I thought you could do . . . something. But you're too tied up in your own problems, aren't you."

Dear God, a small voice within me said, *what a hell of a can of worms we've opened here.* Odette had been one of my ideals of what a level-headed person could be. It was frightening to discover that she envied me. And that I could offer her no real help at all.

I learned self-doubt.

The door slid open. Werner Ulm's face confronted me.

"Oh," he said, apparently surprised by something he saw. He glanced around the room. "No-one else?"

We considered this remark carefully.

Finally Odette said, flatly, "No."

Werner's grin dwindled to a blank look verging on embarrassment. "When you two are finished," he said awkwardly, "would you come along to Indexing?"

"Who's working there at this time of night?" I asked.

"Never mind," said Werner in a low voice. "Just be there by two-thirty hours."

Odette said, "I'd planned to be in bed by then."

I restrained myself from glancing at her.

"This is more important," Werner said with some asperity.

"We'll try to be there," I said.

Werner seemed content to leave it at that. The door slid shut.

"So," said Odette, "after all that, what about us?"

"It's all been said."

"You should broaden your mind, Dan."

"Thank you," I said, "but the answer is still 'no'."

"How old-fashioned you are," she remarked; and she pointed to the old paintings that hung in reproduction on the walls between the cubicles. "The rules have changed since their day. Forget her, Dan. I mean it."

I knew she did and her reasons made sense, in a way. But I shook my head. "Not until I have to."

"There's dedication," she said, "and there's stupidity." The large silver figures on the wall clock changed from 23:59 to 00:00 as she spoke. "Tell her today. Don't let it fester. You'll get hurt otherwise."

Patiently I asked: "And how do I word it? I've grown tired of her and won't be back? Or, instead of lying, do I risk the censors and tell her I'm being held against my will by that ogre Kallekjan and that she'd best go find another man because she's not got so long?"

"That sort of thing," Odette said. "Why try so hard when nothing can come of it?"

As coldly as I could, I said. "Because of that trust you so

119

recently recommended to me." Walking to the door, I placed my hand on the locking lever and pressed. I heard the bolts around the rim click open. But I could not pull the door aside; the strength had gone from my arm.

"Tired of life?" she asked.

I turned. She smiled and tipped her head on one side so that her hair swayed, half of it hanging free, half eclipsing her cheek. Her eyes were nearly closed.

"We don't have to be serious about it," she added.

There was a painting on the wall behind her, of a group of men in dark seventeenth-century Dutch clothes, strapped about with burnished armour. On their heads were awkward angular helmets; in their hands were halberds like surrealist can-openers. For the present they were resting, posing for the artist; but in a moment, one felt, they would be off about their duties.

Odette observed where my attention was directed, twisted about, then turned back.

"I seem to know it," I said.

"Rembrandt," she replied. "The Night Watch."

"Who thought of giving the project that name?"

"Shijo. But –"

"Yes," I said. "It would be someone like him. He's a great humanist, don't you agree?"

"Please, Dan –"

"And who's the little girl in the picture?" She stood amongst the armed men, young and clear-eyed innocent.

Odette's face tilted forwards and her hair swung to hide it from me. But when her shoulders drooped, that was as good as an explanation of her silence: she accepted her defeat.

I knew that painting well. By a coincidence, a torn postcard reproduction of it had been pinned above my desk all the time I was working on the Golem.

Odette's eyes met mine.

"For now. You understand? She's one reason for all that armour. I need my anchor."

Odette's eye met mine.

I said: "When it's all over?"

She smiled. "Perhaps."

I think we both realised there might never be another time. There was no diminution of the warmth of feeling between us. But we were both closer and more distant. Closer, we were more than friends. More distant, we had established a truce on principles neither of us would readily violate.

CHAPTER TWELVE

Deep below the cellars of Dvornik was the cubbyhole known as Indexing. Few people had heard of it but its influence was all-pervasive. Anything that entered Dvornik, be it material such as hardware destined for George Bouklis' quartermaster stores, or intangibles such as facts to be filed in the library computers, was 'indexed': measured, identified, tagged, counted. Even people were classified by the clerks who reigned there. Everything had its place and that place was defined by Indexing.

The importance of the department did not stop me from punching the calling plate harder than was strictly necessary, for after leaving the reading room Odette and I had found the one bar which was not relaying the commentary from CommCon, where we had succeeded in achieving a state of trouble-free euphoria. Then the barman had waved the phone at me: Shijo wanted me in Indexing, the order said, and the barman was determined to oblige.

"Dammit, Shijo," I said as he opened the door. "What could be so important . . ." Words failed me as I heard the harsh voice of CommCon blurting facts and figures about the alien ship's movements. "Must we listen to that?"

"Not if it doesn't interest you," he said. "I thought you and Odette – where is she, by the may?"

"In bed," I said. "She took exception to being hounded. I feel much the same. Incidentally . . ." Shijo paused before a small metal door within the office and turned his head towards me.

"Yes?" he said.

I lowered my eyes. "You don't need to worry any more . . .

About us, I mean." CommCon blatted on. There was an interval of silence, Shijo said:

"Thank you. Your hasty departure and Werner's subsequent report had led me to speculate on what was afoot. However, you need feel no remorse; she is a capricious girl; I should have known better than to undertake her therapy myself."

"You were not close?"

"Under different circumstances we might have been." He smiled. "Odette is the sister I never had –"

"More than that, surely?"

"I speak figuratively," he said, with a dismissive gesture. "I tried to cure her of this insecurity that plagues her; if you can succeed where I failed, then good luck."

"No ill feelings?"

He frowned momentarily. "Of course there are. But if I cannot cure myself of them, I do not deserve to be your group leader. I have wished you luck, Dan; don't let's kick the dog after its dead, okay?"

"Fine," I said. "So what's this meeting for?"

"I fancied that the filtered eyewash these space commentaries consist of might leave you dissatisfied."

"Damn right."

"Would you care for a one hundred per cent solution of facts?"

"It sounds too good to be legal," I said. "Where? How?"

"In Communications Control – down those stairs." The door swung open; he pointed down a cramped spiral staircase, lit by glaring fluorescent panels.

"We just walk in?"

"You'll have to be explained, but that shouldn't be difficult."

"Then lead on," I said.

We descended the steps with warm air funnelling past us from below. About twenty meters lower the stairs ended at another door, which was shut, and a large metal grille from which the air rushed. Shijo pressed the calling plate and a minute later we were admitted to CommCon by a shirtsleeved technician who debated me with Shijo but finally nodded and left him to shut the door and find us seats at the back of the room.

My first overwhelming and enduring impression was of a low-ceilinged octagonal room choked with electronics: the walls and ceiling were encrusted with controls and associated displays. Phosphorescent dots, circles, and rectangles marked out the blocks of equipment ranked around us and overhead. I found myself ducking my head repeatedly as Shijo led me to a pair of foldout seats; the three technicians who flitted to and fro in this rainbow spattered twilight were slightly shorter than I was but even they seemed to walk with a permanent stoop.

Four of the walls were equipped as operator bays with armchairs. Above one of these bays was a wide-screen television display in constant motion, simulating the information channels of the inner solar system communications network, such as it was then. There were astrological planetary symbols enclosed in white circles, amongst which coloured lines blinked and shimmered. Boxed legends appeared too briefly for me to read them properly. Winking dots underlined rows of fugitive figures.

Three of the seats were occupied, intermittently. The man on the left seemed to be the public network commentator and muttered steadily into the boom microphone of his headset, while the one in the middle was holding an animated conversation with what sounded like several people at once. By the sound of it, the climax was approaching.

"Ascension," he said, "do you have lock from Relay?" . . . Check. Coordinates follow on Datex Channel Beta." His hand flashed out and depressed switches, paused, and wiped them back their original settings. "Orbiters Nine and Three, confirm doppler correct on hydrogen alpha . . . Stabilised? . . . Roger, Three: one minute . . . Check . . ." It went on like this for a while, as if three technical discussions were somehow mixed up together. Suddenly: "Orbiter Three, we have lock on video carrier. Processing now." The big screen blanked and filled with coloured flecks. A new picture rolled down and settled into the frame; it was a star-field, computer-enhanced. Cross-hairs formed : zeroed on a bright star near the centre of the picture. Shijo drew in his breath.

"That's it," he whispered to me.

"Quiet, please," said the third operator.

The middle man was speaking again: "–iter Nine, image is clear . . . Please confirm left is Alpha Librae and right is Gamma Virginis . . . Thank you Orbiter Three. He turned to the man on his right. "Raoul, time for your spectrometer analysis program."

Raoul slipped off his headset and hung it on a ceiling hook as he stood up. He gave us an incurious glance, set some switches on the wall to my right, and returned to his seat. Consulting a small screen thick with words, he said, "Image dated as one hundred and four days ago . . . Estimated optimal time for manoeuvre, local time, five seconds from . . . now."

A clock face appeared, inset into the larger picture on the screen. The seconds dissolved into each other, dwindling towards zero, and passed into negative values.

"Nothing," said Raoul.

We all made some sound; collectively it resembled a shuddering sigh.

The clock showed minus three seconds when the image of the alien ship abruptly bloomed. In a moment it drowned the stars in the picture with its brilliance. Only gradually did they reappear; by then the middle man was talking again:

"Orbiters Three and Eight, I want that data time-tagged and back here *fast* !"

Shijo left me and went to stand beside Raoul who, to my surprise, made way for him. A motor whined, gnat-like; a square of photochromic plastic fell from a slot into a hopper. Raoul looked at the figures on it, then handed it to Shijo, who pursed his lips and said, quietly:

"So it is coming." He raised his voice slightly. "Dan, the first day we met, you accused me of being party to a conspiracy. It's time you were told: I *am* the conspiracy. Five years ago, as a graduate from Wellington University, I was stationed at the Mare Moscoviensis Observatory. Fortune contrived that I should discover the new star, compute its course, and guess its origins and possible nature; by another mischance I did so first. Since then this discovery has trapped me here on the Moon. You and Guy Palmer and the rest think yourselves hard done by. Think again, because now–" And he rattled the sheet of plastic, "—now the waiting really begins."

CHAPTER THIRTEEN

With the resolution of the uncertainty over the alien's intentions, my life became more straightforward than it had been. I discovered that sense of direction which I had been lacking; but whether this was a consequence of the alien's behaviour, or of my confrontation with Odette, or of some conjunction of these two crises, I cannot say; the upshot was that I no longer hesitated to speak my mind about the miserable performance I expected from the Golem, once I saw that my semi-secretive experiments to improve our one spare unit were going nowhere. Also, or perhaps as a result of these events, time became telescoped for me. Work I expected would fill months was complete before I was ready; within too short a time the ship fitters were asking for the Golems and I was forced to take a stand. The job stopped. There was much talk. Finally Shijo, Werner, and I marched off to see Kallekjan.

Whenever I think of Boris Kallekjan, I try to remember him as I saw him that day: as the Administrator, keeping things going. As the door to his office slid open, there he was, behind his wide stone desk amid the detritus of his responsibilities.

"Gentlemen," he said, "please come in."

He wore his customary casual uniform, an affected informality that muted his military image; his clothes were no more than coveralls of the correct field green with sufficient badges to identify his rank and function. However, there were details which betrayed his continual readiness for action: the braid stitched to his shoulders was active-service red, not the gold of peacetime; a small embroidered gold star above his left breast pocket emphasised his status as honorary Hero of the Soviet Union; and his hair was clipped short in an uncompromisingly martial style. Neither his clothes, which could be changed in minutes, nor the calculated disarray of papers and empty coffee cups on his desk disguised his essential nature. He was an officer and the apex of authority at Dvornik. One tempered friendliness with discretion in his presence.

When we were seated Kallekjan looked to Shijo to start.

Shijo came to the point.

"Daniel Frome —" A nod towards me, which Kallekjan imitated politely. "— says the Golem brains for the forts are faulty. I do not understand the whole of his argument, which seems to be more subjective than objective, but he is sufficiently worried to insist on your being informed."

"I see," said Kallekjan without a trace of concern. "Mr Frome?"

Odette had rehearsed me for hours. She had also warned me to take my time and not to get flustered. I failed on all counts: the elegant summary evaporated from my mind and I gabbled. Nervous logorrhoea, I think they call it.

In conclusion, I said: "It's not subjective but philosophical. Shijo's all wrong there. Proof can't be arranged, now that the Golems have been put through their training; the fault is subtle. On the other hand, the results will certainly be disastrous for the project unless we take countermeasures."

"What would those results be?" asked Kallekjan, sipping his coffee and watching me over the rim of his cup.

"Typically ... No, I can't say. Anything could happen. Bad shooting. Hesitation. Amnesia. Perhaps complete irrationality."

"All arising from uncertainty?"

"Yes."

"Mr Ulm?"

Werner looked at me apologetically. "The simulator reveals no such flaws."

"But Werner," I protested, "I've tried explaining: they won't show up under our test conditions. The Golem has to be in a situation where it's fully responsible for its own actions. If anyone's there to supervise it the syndrome won't develop. Set it problems and it'll know and will produce an acceptable answer. It's not stupid; it can see you'll catch any mistakes. But put the full load on it and the Golem will crack up with the strain. It has ... well, it has a conscience about mistakes."

Shijo was unhappy and showed it. "Boris, I have talked this

over with Dan for a long time. I am sorry; I think *he* is mistaken."

I was helpless. For days I had argued with Shijo. He was being polite in saying we had talked; we had shared several flaming rows. Werner had partaken of them too and I could see he also was uncomfortable. No display of anger would help. It would lessen me in Kallekjan's eyes and it was his esteem that might tip the balance in my favour at the last minute, another time. So when Kallekjan invited me to comment, I shook my head and left them to agree amongst themselves to keep alert for any signs of the faults. They quietly shelved the matter.

Thereafter Shijo was painfully considerate. He ensured that I was free to supervise the installation of the Golems, though in practice I left that work entirely to the ship fitters and electronics artificers; and when I requested extra time on the simulator he quietly cajoled Werner and the irascible Guy Palmer into volunteering some of theirs. As a result, Odette was the only member of the group who did not make me feel acutely self-conscious. She was sympathetic and whenever the subject of the Golems arose in conversation she either took my part or steered us away from it.

The anniversary of my landing on the Moon was past before I noticed it had arrived. My life was collapsing into sequences of activity and the moments bridging their loose ends became the only meaningful milestones.

I remember: the Pole, building his railway, the most expensive one in the solar system. Its sintered titanium rails climbed straight through the eastern crater wall of Lansberg; they remain with me as an after-image, with plated surfaces polished and shining in the sun like kilometers of light stretched taut across shattered rocks blasted from the mountains by nuclear charges ...

I remember: the Malay, loftily friendly as ever, testing the forts' lasers on low power, knocking holes in sheets of titanium and arguing with Shijo about chemistry and nuclear physics ...

I remember: his antagonist, Byron Yale, whom I had once chased in intent if not in fact. He seemed a quieter man than I had once known, going about his work with an uninspired precision I found disquieting. He had withdrawn into his professional self; and when I tried to discuss terrestrial topics he simply walked away from me . . .

I remember : . . .

Most of all, I remember how much we lost of innocence. In the beginning, anger at their abduction to the Moon had sustained some people and helped them to ignore the possibility that the alien might be a threat. In the beginning, some had seen Project Nightwatch as comparable to the early space programmes. Open-ended, it might succeed and they could return to civilian life with impressive credentials. There was almost a plot to stop anyone thinking of the project as the last great act of a doomed species.

But like most plots that are shared by too many people, it failed. One saw with increasing frequency the silent groups in restaurants and snack bars; and one knew what they were thinking because it was a common thought.

The word 'Project' disappeared; it became, simply, 'Nightwatch'.

PART TWO

Towards the end of 2010 a joke began to circulate in Dvornik Base. I suspect it was put about by the Israelis of the staff, for it held much of the acidity of their humour when taken in the context of Nightwatch. However, it is not easy to keep track of who says what to whom in a population of two thousand when they are spread out through four hundred and fifty kilometers of straggling tunnels and buried rooms, so those who saw the thinly veiled point of the joke either grinned or kept their disapproval to themselves.

Old Father Isaac is dying, so he calls his relatives to his bed-side to take his leave of them. As the solemn crowd presses close about him he calls on them individually by name, giving his blessing to each as he answers. At last he has checked off every one who could possibly be present. There is a moment of peace; then he cries out in a wrathful voice, *"So if you're all here staring at me, who the Hell's minding the shop?"*

Notwithstanding the importance of Nightwatch, it was easy to forget why we were on the Moon. Above us, day in, day out, was the Earth; and no-one could avoid wondering when the day would come on which the klaxons would call us out to watch its immolation in the fires of hysterical nationalism.

Once the novelty of the lunar landscape had worn off, few people bothered to go far from the Base unless they had to. There were occasional scientific journeys, or visits to the now abandoned American base near crater Maskelyne, over in Mare Tranquillitatis; and every so often the shuttles would rise to meet the baggage carriers and bring down the loads into south Lansberg, where the rudimentary spaceport was.

By and large, the Moon is a scattering of spectacular vistas interspersed with monotony; but there was always the Earth to be stared at and the beauty of its dazzling white-streaked disc of blue-green-brown was all the more striking for the contrast it made with the arid lunar landscape. Sometimes full, sometimes dark, usually crescent, it was a constant reminder of why we had to be there. Hence, I suppose, the joke: we were so preoccupied with Old Father Isaac we tended to forget about the shop.

Of course, that was after the forts were launched in mid-2008. Once they had been catapulted into lunar orbit and were given the order to fire their engines for the long journey out to their post beyond Jupiter's orbit, they were out of sight and largely out of mind.

I watched them go with mixed feelings. Each represented a threat to Nightwatch that I now did my utmost to advertise, whatever Shijo might say or do, for I was now only nominally under his command. However, since I still hoped for eventual repatriation to Earth, my campaign took the form of cautious verbal canvassing of opinion amongst influential personnel, rather than any soapbox oratory, which might have irritated Kallekjan enough for him to order my detention. As it was, I rapidly accumulated a good track record of official rebukes. Eventually I found myself under observation by one or another of Captain Lamov's men.

This made me reconsider whether what I was doing was right, not so much for fear of imprisonment, but out of respect for the considerable alarm my subversive activities were causing in official circles. My decision to stop was prompted by the realisation that my message had got across, the day I was waylaid by half a dozen Europeans and lectured, with threats of physical violence, on the merits of loyalty to one's country. It seemed there were people who felt that my public condemnation of the Golem was tantamount to treason and would diminish Europe in the eyes of those nations whose contributions to the programme were not in question. In a community that ostensibly did not distinguish between nationalities there remained only the law of tongue and fist for the jingoist to turn to.

Fortunately there were few who felt their nationality so

keenly and Odette at least remained friendly, though I sometimes found her regarding me sadly. The years of continuous tension brought all of us in Dvornik into a new social grouping that transcended those we had been reared to regard as paramount. We were well aware of our isolation, vulnerability, and interdependence.

Strangely, even the loss of Helen Lorraine was eased by this repolarisation of allegiance, for as my attention was turned away from Earth I discovered that four years was too long a time for which to nurse a clear regret. Eventually, though I clung to the notion that I ought to do nothing that might preclude eventual reunion, I managed to accept that she was beyond my reach. Thereafter the occasions when I would suit up for the sake of being able to stand on the surface staring at the Earth became progressively rarer, until they ceased. I did not forget her but forgot the pain instead.

2008 was forgotten too and after it 2009 and 2010. 2011 was heralded by storm clouds: the overlong and fretful summer was coming to an end on Earth; and as autumn led on towards the winter of ultimate discontent the aerials of Dvornik Base were turned to catch the first hint of lightning and the worldwide thunder that would follow it.

May Day that year was a flop, which left the community more despondent than ever. Oddly, it failed mainly due to the apathy of the CommCon nationals: my friend the Pole, I recall, chose that particular Sunday to attend church for the first time in his life. The customary concerts were thinly attended, the applause was sincere but weak; only the Safety Committee seemed to notice it was a weekend and continued to pull in the drunks and amateur pugilists until well into the Monday morning.

In the early hours of the following Friday I awoke to hear running feet in the corridor outside my room. On looking out, I saw Steelyard Jones leading a group of spacesuited soldiers towards the surface airlock exit at the end of the corridor. They were armed and acted in a manner that made me afraid to be seen spying on them. I would have ducked back into my room had Jones not turned to address his group and seen me at the same time.

Motioning to them to go through the airlock and up the steps to the surface, he came back to me. Bareheaded but bulky in his suit, he stopped a few paces from me.

" Couldn't sleep, Dan?"

I let my eyes stray to the armed men.

"What's up, Steel?"

"Nothing for you to worry about. Only a patrol."

"Since when have we needed armed patrols on the Moon?" I asked.

He studied my face intently. "Dan, this hunch of mine says you're a guy knows how to keep his mouth shut. Am I wrong?"

"Probably not," I said. "It depends. Is this legal?"

"Is this legal?" he laughed. "Dan, don't you recognise Lamov's boys?"

I did. "But with an antenna rigger leading them?"

"We all have several jobs here," he said, turning away. "Dan," he added before he left me, "for your own sake, you've not seen us. Understand me?"

All night I worried about our encounter. At breakfast there was a rumour going the rounds of the canteen that a shuttle craft had landed during the night, several kilometers to the northeast of Dvornik, and that everyone on board had perished of asphyxiation before help could reach them. It seemed they had been a party of politicians and high-ranking military gentlemen interested in joining us in our exile.

Thinking it over, I concluded that perhaps Jones had the best of the argument. What he had done might not be moral, or even legal in the strictest sense of the word. But it was practical. Dvornik had few resources to spare.

Once the novelty of the incident had worn off the Base relapsed into gloom. Conversations became erratic and liable to break off for no apparent reason. People walked quietly, talking with one ear listening to the public address system. Evacuation drills were held more often lest any missiles should be launched at us. Airlock seals were inspected several times a week. A team of engineers was sent over to Maskelyne Base to refurbish it for occupation at short notice. And we were taught how to take mercy pills whilst wearing spacesuits.

Gradually the Nightwatch Committee assumed the rôle of government within the Base; and the community accepted their rule, referring to the authorities on Earth more and more as 'the Syndicate'. This was a polite allusion to the considerable amount of horsetrading that had prefaced the establishment of Nightwatch at Dvornik and the theoretical lien the various contributory nations still had on the hardware that the additions to the Base and the forts themselves represented. It was a lip-courtesy only, for nobody anticipated there would ever be a meeting of creditors.

Then, on the fourteenth of June, I was summoned to a meeting with Kallekjan and Joel Phom, Chairman of the Nightwatch Committee. We gathered in Kallekjan's office and it was he who broke the brittle silence.

"Mr Frome," he said, "we owe you an apology."

"Oh?" I said. Phom's face gave no clues to what the Russian meant so I ignored him and concentrated on Kallekjan. "You do?"

The Commandant shifted in his seat. I have already described him as a small man, quite unlike the stereotype image of his nation. In his late middle age, he might have been a gamekeeper, or some such frequenter of the open country, certainly not the bureaucrat he had so brilliantly proved himself to be in a long and productive career. Now he appeared unsure of himself, so consequently I felt apprehensive.

"For some time now," he said, "you have questioned the advisability of relying on the Golem to control our forts. I wish you to know you were correct to do so."

I felt no pleasure at the news. As evenly as I could, I asked: "What has happened?"

Kallekjan made a sign to Phom, who said: "We have been using the spare unit as a traffic analyser in the radio message monitoring programme. At first there was no difficulty. But lately, with the worsening situation on Earth and the onset of the propaganda war, the information conflict within the messages has begun to exceed the Golem's capacity to reconcile inconsistency. It has already issued several false alarms. We anticipate further trouble." He stopped.

I asked, "Any sign of this in the forts?"

"Not yet. The alien is still about five months from Yellow Range, so the forts will not begin to construct strategic scenarios for another four months. They are semi-dormant. In any case, they have not arrived on-station."

"There may be time," I said quietly, though the last thing I wanted to bother with just then was Nightwatch. The spare Golem was failing, which would happen only if there was a significant probability of its worst-case scenario coming true. And I was sure Phom would have had it programmed to consider total war on Earth as the climax of its worst-case scenario.

Kallekjan leaned forward on his elbows, seemingly poised above his reflection in the polished stone of the desk top. "Now," he said, "disregard the past, Mr Frome. What have you in mind?"

"We send a man out there to take charge."

Phom jerked. "Oh, now!" he exclaimed. "You cannot be serious. It has taken three years to move those forts into position. How can you reach them in time?"

"Chairman Phom," I said, "when you shift the best part of two hundred tonnes of mass out to five-and-a-bit astronomical units from the Sun, you use a lot of propellant, with or without nuclear engines. The only way we could get those forts out there without giving the accountants fits was to put them through a Hohmann transfer: an ellipse with one end at the Moon and the other at the destination, with engine burns at beginning and end, and free fall in between. Finesse tactics like that take time, about three years in this case. What I propose is this: strip that mangled frame that's lying out there on the surface; remove all the useful bits like engines and reactors and build them into a skeleton ship that carries just enough to keep a man alive for the round trip. Then send someone out there as hard as you can – *straight* out. It'll mean a hyperbolic orbit, with heavy acceleration at start and finish. Check with the orbital maths men to see if it's possible. I think it is."

Kallekjan got up from the desk without a word and went to the wall phone.

"And one more thing,'" I said. "Contact the Space Museum at Canaveral. Beg, borrow, steal, or commandeer that Golem they have on display. It's the only one that's free right now."

Phom said, "But we have one."

"You have a few kilos of malfunctioning electronics," I corrected him. "That Golem's worthless without extensive rebuilding, now that you've mistreated it. And those eighteen others out there waiting for the alien will be worthless too if you don't get that prototype to interface between them and the man."

Kallekjan nodded. For several minutes he was issuing orders to CommCon. Someone appeared to be telling him it was impossible; he ended by ordering them to use every rule in the book to get that Golem and to cheat too if necessary. Then there was a relatively peaceful discussion with the Astrophysics department, after which he came and sat down. He was sweating slightly. " They're working on it," he said, "only . . ."

"Only what?"

"CommCon report intermittent communications with Canaveral and Baikonur. Christmas Island closed down yesterday. It seems that DSIF-Houston is off the air; and Parkes is not responding either. They're trying to access a relay satellite directly, to attempt an all-stations call. Not much hope, they say."

He fell into an introspective silence. After a while, Phom said: "We might as well do what we can. Mr Frome, are you sure you want this other Golem?"

"Supervised, it's no risk," I answered, then his words sank in. "Hey *I'm* staying out of this."

Phom looked up from the notes he was making. Kallekjan glanced at him and back at me. "Would you ask anyone else to go?" he said.

"There are others far better qualified than I am."

"Perhaps there are better cosmonauts, better astromechanics, better strategists, better survivors . . . But who knows the Golem better?"

"That's not the point!" I snapped. "It's not my problem! You wanted the Golem in those forts, so you clear up any messes they make."

"Do you feel no responsibility for your own creation?" asked Kallekjan. "If a child of yours failed you, would you disown it?"

"I wouldn't know," I said. "I have no children."

He sighed. "Let me rephrase it, then. Do you have no interest in seeing your project through to a successful conclusion?"

"Of course I damn well do!" I was becoming angry with him. Some part of me with more honesty than the rest wondered if it was not guilt that made me react so strongly. I suppressed this thought. "This mess is as much your making as mine. If I'd been told, right back at the beginning, what the Golem was to be used for, instead of being given some cock-and-bull story about probes to Jupiter, I might have caught the mistake early enough. Since then I've been hijacked to the Moon and imprisoned here. Commandant, I asked for no part of this. I'm an innocent bystander. There's someone on Earth I had hoped I might see again; all I want is to get back to her."

All ... Time hesitated for me, backtracked, ran forward again. Like an echo of itself, that word *all* came back to me subtly restated, drained of emotion, and suddenly I knew why: my loyalties had become divided by the years of separation without my noticing. Sure, I loved Helen, as one loves good friends: there was much I would have suffered on her behalf, willingly and without expecting reward. But there was little of that easy feeling of identification I had discovered in Odette, because the half of me that understood this feeling had not awoken until I met her: it knew nothing of Helen and had no interest in her. That added shade of significance was like a flame against my emotions, melting the icy indifference I had encouraged in myself as a defence against despair. The pain of that despair's revival mingled with the anger and the newer insight, sharpening the dying syllables of my outburst so that both Kallekjan and Phom looked startled.

At last Kallekjan breathed out slowly. "Very well," he said.

Phom sounded doubtful as he asked, "Boris, didn't the announcement —"

"Be quiet," said Kallekjan. "If Mr Frome wants to go home, he may."

"But it may start at any time!"

"Let it, Mr Frome is going home." He made it rhyme and watched me as he said it. I felt the way I had on my second morning at Dvornik, when I sat discussing not totally dissimilar matters with the false Denham, just before the blowout.

"All right," I said. "Tell me."

Phom said, "There is talk of ultimatum, of pre-emptive strikes, and worse. Already there exists a state of maximum alert throughout the world. It will not be long before . . . before . . ." His eyes dropped to regard the desk.

"Before . .?"

Kallekjan's manner changed to one of gentleness. "What he finds so hard to tell you, Daniel, is that you should learn to live without Helen Lorraine. All too soon she will not exist."

I said nothing. Standing, I went out of that room and wandered through the sterile corridors until I came to the workshops where so much of my time had once been spent. There is comfort in the familiar; even the familiarity of the harsh lights and rough-cast concrete was welcome, the way I felt then. Hours of leaden semi-sensibility somehow passed for me, with the lights unchanging in their brilliance, the numbness as constant in its cruel insufficiency. I longed for unconsciousness but lacked the will to move and seek it in drink or pills. Rather, I let time leach the shock from me until I found I could raise my eyes to look around at the world again.

Kallekjan was sitting on a nearby stool. He smiled. His smile held more of sadness than mirth. "I too had loved ones on Earth," he said.

I averted my eyes. He said: "My wife. My children. And others."

I closed my eyes. He went on: "Events of such monstrous proportions are beyond intellectual comprehension, Daniel. Now the heart must encompass the tragedy that has occurred;

the emotions must understand what the brain cannot. If it will help, then cry." He paused. "No? You of the western nations are too tightly bound by your self-image; we Georgians are not afraid to be honest about our feelings. Take no account of what I might think. I have lost both family and country also."

When I looked at him I saw the faint marks of tears on his cheeks and a puffiness in his eyes. A horror grew in me; he must have seen it in my face, for he nodded.

"It has begun," he said.

Half running, half bounding in the low lunar gravity, I raced to the spacesuit locker and scrabbled at the catch. It sprang open and the door slid aside. I grabbed at my own suit and began to put it on; but Kallekjan stopped me.

"Wait," he said. "You must not go alone. I will go with you."

Some sense returned to me. "No," I said, "you'll be needed. I'm okay."

"There is nothing I can do for now," he answered me. He had brought his own suit with him and now picked it up from where it lay draped over a seat. "I may as well come and watch."

The lunar day was about two days short of noon, the Earth was three-quarters in shadow, and India lay towards us, glittering with fires. The Arabian Peninsula was almost totally dark but up the east coast of India and around into Malaysia the sullen glow extended with hardly a break.

"Firestorm bombs," said Kallekjan's voice in my headphones. He appeared to be ignoring Russia, which was pocked with livid blotches, for he remarked. "China is in trouble. And look, that must be Japan!"

Far around towards the eastern rim of the Earth a yellow-white glare lived for a few seconds and died away through the colours of fading heat into darkness. "Big," said Kallekjan. I heard him mutter something in Russian. It sounded like a prayer.

After perhaps ten minutes I found my neck muscles were aching, so I looked away from the Earth. The view had begun to seem unreal in any case, as if it were all some detailed simulation. My credulity was becoming as strained as my neck. Both needed a rest.

Many hundreds of other people had felt as I had, that only

138

their eyes could be trusted at a time like this. At first, when Kallekjan and I reached the surface, there had been people all over the crater floor. One or two had even climbed the slopes of the Mound as far as the lower fringes of the antenna farm. Some, as far away as ten kilometers, were visible by the sunlight glinting on their suit fittings. But the numbers dwindled; within an hour Kallekjan suggested that we should return underground. I shook his hand off: I was waiting for something. When I pointed towards the Earth he desisted with an apology.

The clouds were thick over Europe; their summer had been a wet one but the fires were burning fiercely from one end of the continent to the other, turning the clouds orange and red. Only the mountainous regions seemed dark by comparison: Switzerland was a ragged hole in the furnace. High up, coming over the horizon, would be the British Isles. I stayed until I could be sure they had not escaped the holocaust; and, in time, that dubious reassurance was granted me.

I searched for Kallekjan and found him sitting in the shade of a nearby rock. Together we walked towards the airlock pillar.

For a minute I stopped to look up at the Earth again. I saw it as a stranger, an alien planet. There were clouds in frozen whorls and streaks, as I had come to know them those past four years; and the shapes of the continents were those my childhood's self had learned so laboriously at school. The Earth was as large, as massive, and as remote as it had always been. The difference lay in the mind: now, forced by the fate of war, I accepted my exile. The Moon had become my home world.

I gazed at its sun-bright rocks, at the rounded hills so deceptively close, at the dust-mantled kilometers, grey and white with gradations of other colours according to how the light fell on them. I picked up a stone and threw it towards the crater ringwall rimming the horizon: it flew fast along its flattened trajectory, emphasising by its strangely slow descent to a soundless dust-flaring impact that this was not the Earth. Then I turned my back on that planet and walked the rest of the way to the airlock while Kallekjan followed me.

As I came up to the pillar I found myself staring at my own reflection in the polished metal door.

A stranger in a spacesuit looked back at me. He too stood in an arid landscape; but he seemed to belong there, whereas I did not. I wanted, so *wanted* to belong; yet my heart was elsewhere, in a place I had only just rejected, so that the 'I' was the stranger here. It was behind me, on the turning world where it and this stranger had been born.

The man looked away. The airlock responded to a touch on the calling plate : CYCLING. Reflection and original regarded each other again in the moments that remained before the door opened. Regret had gone. There was a purpose to life still, a visitor to be met properly. In any event, the road lay to the front.

The airlock door opened smoothly, sliding aside into its slot; the reflection disappeared behind the sharp transiting edge; and Daniel Frome stepped forwards into the empty chamber.

PART THREE

CHAPTER ONE

One road to the stars was a railway track.

For fully fifteen kilometers its ten sintered titanium rails confounded the pessimism of the planners who had said it could never be built; and as for the metallurgists who had declined to attempt cladding it in superconducting alloy, why, they too now held their tongues. It had been built and it worked: eighteen forts had been hurled into the lunar sky by its magnetically levitated traction blocks.,

Daniel Frome sat on the buffers at the railhead waiting for the dawn of early July 2011. Nearby a crane blocked out the stars; further away in the darkness a cloud of motionless lights hung above the earthlit Mound. He waited, watching the slot in the eastern ringwall mountains where the railway cut through them and where the Sun would rise.

Although the fourteenth of June was well past and its immediate impact had been absorbed, he felt numb. At times, like a spectator of his own life, he unconsciously withdrew from the immediacy of full involvement in it and allowed it to happen to his external self, as if he could achieve thereby a leisurely examination of it at one remove. His was not the lofty posture of the megalomaniac who delights in the panoramic overview; nor, voyeur-like, did he sample only the pleasures which chance provided. His mental state seemed to alternate between disinterested observation, a condition he abstractedly characterised as faintly schizophrenic, and a diametric desperation to involve himself in reality. Between these limits he swung, never quite seizing the moment when he might settle into a condition of tranquillity, or even one of determined concern. The staff doctors made light of it; they were preoccupied with more extreme cases of depression and attempted suicide amongst personnel upon whose skills the continuance of life within Dvornik Base depended. Frome was left to work out his own problems.

That is not to say he was ignored by the authorities. Kallekjan had convened an engineering conference in the computer centre three days after the war had petered out . . .

Sternly Kallekjan said: "I want no discussion of how useful the proposed project is. We cannot afford the time. Is that clear?" He surveyed the seated ranks of the departmental representatives who had been crammed into the small room against the wishes of the Safety Committee. No-one so much as blinked. "Good," he said. "Dan, come here."

When he joined Kallekjan beside the wall display screen Frome was conscious of the mixed reaction he elicited from the group. Some begrudged him the triumph of his stand over the Golems; and of those who knew him at all more than a few also associated him with some dimly-recalled unsavoury business of a few years earlier. Only Shijo and Werner Ulm seemed not to be frowning; he wished there had been room for Odette.

Kallekjan flicked the power switch on the display and a polar grid appeared, marked out in simulation of the solar system seen from celestial north, with coloured dots to represent the planets which raced around their orbits as the date ate up the months and years. By pressing a few keys Kallekjan caused the display to settle on 17.0 JUNE 2011 E.T.

"By November the fifth," he said, addressing the group, "Daniel Frome – here – has to be transported out to the orbital forts. The purpose of this briefing is to acquaint you with the operational requirements and to assign tasks and areas of responsibility.

"According to Astrophysics Department, we are attempting to achieve with our limited resources what would have been dismissed as a lunatic undertaking only a few years ago. And we must do it perfectly the first time, or all of Nightwatch will be at risk." Kallekjan tapped the display with a forefinger. "The alien is still well outside the solar system, so imagine him as somewhere off the bottom left-hand corner of this picture. At present the Earth – and hence the Moon – is down here also but by the time we are ready to launch our ship we will have moved around anticlockwise into this bottom right-hand quadrant. I call Raoul Lobos of Astrophysics."

The thin young man who took charge of the display was not the Raoul Lobos whom Frome recalled seeing in CommCon. The new man walked unsteadily, had a grey pallor to his skin, was dull-eyed, and when he worked the controls his fingers trembled.

"Mr Lobos," said Kallekjan gently, "would you rather your partner . . .?"

"No," said Lobos. "Just tired. Been on stimulants for two days. Get some sleep after this . . . is over." Resting one hand on the display, he wiped the other across his forehead. Beads of sweat reappeared at once. "I've come this far; I'll finish . . ." His voice was weak and he frequently paused for breath. "Summary. Numbers later. Okay?" This last to Frome. "You're a lucky man, you know that? . . . Well, you are. I'd give a packet to fly this mission instead of you. Because it's one-in-a-thousand you'll live through it . . ."

"Details," Kallekjan reminded him.

"Okay: details . . . The Earth is *this* far from the Sun; where you want to get is about five-and-a-half times further out. It's also behind the Earth in its orbit. Not necessarily a bad thing, except that the Earth's moving into a sort of blind spot: the closer we are to it when we launch you, the more propellant – the more hydrogen – you'll need. The amount rises steeply towards infinity, if we are to get you there in time for the showdown. Because of this blind spot we have to rush the assembly of the ship; then we have to put you through a damn dangerous orbit. And I hope you can forgive me for even suggesting you try it.

"If we can launch by August the first we can make the deadline. But only at the expense of fantastic amounts of propellant, so it'll be back to the days of spendthrift rocketry, I'm afraid: most of all we need *speed*; and that means heavy acceleration and heavy deceleration at the target. And, in the middle, a close transit of the Sun's face that leaves Mercury out in the cold by comparison."

"How close, exactly?" asked Frome.

Lobos closed his eyes. "One fiftieth of an astronomical unit."

Someone gasped. Lobos reopened his eyes and stared at Frome unblinking. "We tried all sorts of orbits. This was the only one. I'm sorry. At least this will get you there in eighty-five days. Perhaps we can relax it a little: there are ninety-six available."

"And do I come home?"

"That's taken care of. A slow return but a cooler one."

"Thank you," said Frome.

Lobos was replaced by Simon Dien of Spacecraft Engineering, a small dry stick of a man whose forefathers had lived in South-East Asia but whose accent placed him as western American.

"So," said Dien, "we have forty-four days in which to design and build a spacecraft." Punching buttons on the display, he called up from the computer memory a series of sketches. Disproportionately large tanks of liquid hydrogen featured in all of them, whereas the pilot's compartment was uniformly miniscule. "As you can see," Dien remarked, "the possibilities are nothing if not unusual."

While Dien discoursed on mass ratios, exhaust velocities, plasma jets, fusion reactors, and orbital velocities, Frome regretted his hasty glib talk of full acceleration and hyperbolic orbits. Kallekjan had turned the tables on him neatly by handing the problem to experts who had demonstrated how unforgiving the universe could be.

Dien was interrupted by a woman in the uniform of Kallekjan's staff who edged through to the front of the audience. Kallekjan took the message block she carried and read what was on it.

"It seems," he announced, "that Cape Canaveral was untouched in the recent outbreak of hostilities although Patrick Air Force Base nearby was obliterated. A single shuttle craft has been launched; Pegasus Six is expected to arrive here in about five days. By good fortune the vital element of this enterprise is aboard her: your Golem, Dan." Folding the cover over the block, he returned it to the messenger. "Otherwise there is no news. Ground control is still off the air."

From the crowd, *sotto voce*, came the comment, "More mouths to feed."

Kallekjan slowly raised his head, saying: "If I hear any more talk like that, there will be one less mouth."

The excitement died. Kallekjan continued:

"Such thoughtless remarks endanger our solidarity. Rationing is now part of our way of life, so it is true that newcomers are an added burden on our resources. But it is equally true that these fugitives have demonstrated their allegiance to our interests. No-one forced them to bring the Golem. By this gesture . . ."

"Commandant." An Australian in Life-Systems-green coveralls had got to his feet and seemed to tower over the crowd. "With respect, you're talking like a galah. These characters want to buy their way in. They'll be crawling with everything nasty you can name; why the bloody hell should we let them infect us?"

"Mister Dien," said Kallekjan with an icy reserve, "would you continue with what you were saying?" The Australian sat down, awkwardly, glancing around him for the moral support no-one dared express, while Dien coughed and moved to the display.

"I have almost nothing to add," he said stiffly. "From the designs you have seen my department has selected the one which best conforms to what Quartermaster Bouklis tells us is surplus from the fort-building programme. And, frankly, I am not happy with it."

"Is it unworkable?" asked Kallekjan.

"Theoretically, it fits the requirements defined by Astrophysics but –"

"Can it be built in time?"

"Given total cooperation –"

"You have it. What is the difficulty?"

Dien's composure broke. "The thing's ridiculous! A nine tonne spacecraft carrying a hundred tonnes of hydrogen? Take a look for yourself."

The display blinked several times. A sketch condensed from grey fuzz.

"There," said Dien. "Would you trust that spacegoing mulberry?"

"Interesting," said Kallekjan. "Why are there so many tanks? And is that a net?"

"The size of the tanks was set originally by the need to fit three inside a fort frame in line astern; twelve of the surplus stock will just hold all the hydrogen that has to be carried. The most practical means of keeping them in position was to pack them in threes around the core of the ship and throw a net around the whole lot. The engine sticks out of the back; the sun shield radiates from the engine to form a protective solar umbrella over the tanks and the rest of the ship; and the teardrop at the bows is the cockpit. Ship's equipment is carried inside the core, of diameter one meter, and immediately aft of the cockpit. Overall length is about seventy meters."

"I see nothing risible in that," said Kallekjan.

"You don't think it strange that we should throw away half our hydrogen stock . . .?"

"Mr Dien, please. And the rest of you: Nature is not afraid of large numbers; nor should we be." Kallekjan smiled wanly at Dien. "But, yes, by all means let us show them respect."

"Nobody could respect this," said Dien.

Frome said, "Will it get me there? If it will, I'll fly it. I'm not proud."

Dien regarded the sketch for a moment. He smiled at Frome. "Then neither am I," he said.

. . . and they were still building the ship.

Frome had christened it *Rosinante*, thereby confusing the engineers; but when Dien queried his choice of name he had been reluctant to explain it fully.

"Are you an admirer of Cervantes?" asked Dien as they watched welders assembling the geodesic structure of the core.

"More an admirer of Don Quixote, I think," replied Frome. "I hoped some of his persistence might rub off on me if I borrowed the name of his horse."

"Very laudable," said Dien. "I imagined it might have been a commentary on the, ah, pedigree of the beast."

Other qualities, such as courage and idealism, had also been in Frome's mind. He had not liked to mention them; Dien would not have sympathised, whereas he understood persistence well.

Since the meeting thirteen hydrogen tanks had been lofted into lunar orbit by the catapult and were being herded into a cluster sixty kilometers above the Moon's surface. In slightly over twenty days the core of the ship would be launched by the same method; and if orbital assembly went to plan Frome would go up in one of the shuttles to join his new command.

He had made a point of coming to greet his last dawn. He did not expect to see another, however often Lobos and Dien assured him that all pains had been taken to ensure him a return passage. Lobos had admitted privately that theory and practice could easily part company on the journey; one could assume ten-figure accuracy in calculations but a solar flare during the time of near-approach, or a hot spot in the single engine, or even a pinhole in the mirror-surfaced sunshield would cripple the mission.

"And me," Frome had said, to which Lobos had replied: "You might be lucky; you might die quickly."

The highest peaks were suddenly ablaze with the dawn and the high mast of the Mound shone silver. The half-Earth, unnaturally brown where it should have been green, grew dim in comparison though its light still picked out the ten rails of the catapult from the bleak landscape which they bisected. Greyness spilled across the crater floor, unevenly, favouring isolated rocks and humps, shunning the pools brimming with night shadows still. The rails took on the warmer hues of sunrise; and, like a flood from the east, a spark poured through the distant cleft in the hills and shimmered down the rails, splitting into ten equal lines of fire that swept to Frome's feet.

The hot edge of the Sun came into sight. He averted his eyes.

Odette was standing by the crane. Her transmitter awoke as he turned.

"I didn't like to disturb you," she said. "You looked like Zarathustra up there, all thoughtful."

"Then I feel like him," he said. "Did he make out in the end?"

"Don't talk like that. You'll get back."

"Lobos doesn't seem to think so."

"He's jealous. He wants to scare you into giving up your seat."

"It's his for the asking."

"Uncle Boris wouldn't agree."

"Uncle Boris can go . . . Never mind." Lately, he suspected his radio messages were being monitored. The events of the twenty-second of June had seen to that . . .

The shuttle craft fell steeply, glinting in the sunlight as its pilot searched for the point of balance. The moment of compromise between fuel economy and the risk of deceleration blackout arrived; the main jet flared white in a tentative burst. The shuttle slowed noticeably and resumed its free fall towards the landing field.

Frome heard Ulm say, "He'll have to make his long burn soon."

Jones answered, "Gamil knows his job."

Further radio talk was impossible for abruptly the plasma jet threw out a cone of incandescent ionised gas which swamped the spacesuit radios in static. Atop its fiery pillar the shuttle settled towards the bubbled metallic surface of the landing field. The exhaust touched ground and turned it white fringed with bright orange as the flame pressed closer and fanned outwards. Then, as if the Sun had set, all was dark.

Frome's faceplate cleared. The shuttle sat safely on the ground at the centre of a rapidly shrinking area of cherry red rock. When the all-clear signal came from Field Control he stood up in the trench where the three of them had taken refuge and awaited Jones' lead.

As arranged, Jones was the first to climb the short ladder for a talk with the pilot through the phone link.

"Trouble," he reported. "Gamil says one of the passengers has flipped. Two others have terminal radiation sickness but are demanding our agreement to quarantine before they'll surrender the Golem."

"What kind of sickness?" asked Ulm.

"Brain damage, with gut trouble."

"Are they armed?"

"So Gamil says. The guy in charge is Colonel Joseph Menby. I knew him when I was at Kodiak Island: he's tough but fair and he'll expect the same from us. If we cheat him, he'll put a bullet through that robot without a thought."

"Damn the Golem," said Ulm. "Gamil matters more. And so do doctors. Can we expose a doctor to what's in there?"

"He can stay in a suit." Jones went back to argue with the occupants of the shuttle. On his return he linked the three of them in a private phone circuit.

"They're waiting for us to call a doctor. That gives us about fifteen minutes before they get edgy about the delay. Dan, I want you to take the carrier box up the ladder and load the Golem from inside the airlock. Then take cover in the trench. Werner, you help me with the gas."

Apprehension made Frome's forearms tingle. Sweat broke out on his neck and face. "Gas, Steel?"

"Do as I say, Dan."

"Is it so much, what they ask?"

"Yeah, it is," said Jones. "This place is thick with aerials. Why don't they talk direct with Uncle Boris instead of dickering with us? Because Menby knows — because Gamil will have told him — that no-one with sickness gets in alive. Gamil volunteered, expecting to fail the quarantine afterwards. Menby hopes we'll let him through too."

"So you're going to gas them? That'll get Gamil too, if you feed it into the breathing air tanks . . . No, what am I saying . . . Steel, you can't simply . . . It's murder!"

"Mercy-killing, Dan," said Ulm.

"Werner? You too?"

Ulm said in a strange voice: "They were in the wrong place at the wrong time. They'll die anyhow. We're making it easier for them."

"Enough talk," said Jones. "Dan, you keep this to yourself. Go get that robot of yours."

"No," said Frome. "I won't have any part of it."

So Jones climbed the ladder and brought back the Golem in its padded box. They gave Frome the choice between complicity and participation; but when he allowed them a reluctant assurance that he would keep the secret, Jones, detecting in his tone a sign of his plan to abort the crime, disconnected his radio antenna and ordered Ulm to guard him. Ulm produced a gun from his chest pouch and used it to signify that Frome should remain where he was.

Unprepared for this development, Frome complied. Confined to a stony seat near Ulm, he hoped that the affair would miraculously resolve itself for the good of all concerned. Instead, he saw Jones plug the hose of a small gas cylinder into the breathing air refill socket on the shuttle. A few minutes later the hose was disconnected.

"For the sake of your conscience," Frome said, when he had been readmitted to the conversation, "I hope that was worth it."

"That," answered Jones, "is up to you, Dan."

And he handed Frome the case containing the Golem.

... Evidently the strain had been too great for Werner Ulm's conscience: a day later he swallowed three grammes of powdered antimony stolen from the foundry stores. Frome never learned why Ulm, the placid, knowledgable family man, should choose to commit suicide with the aid of one of the most painful of poisons available in the Base; a misguided sense of fitness, or of penance, seemed most likely. At any rate, after three days of vomiting, convulsions, cramps, and delirium, he died, bringing their losses from the group to two, for Guy Palmer had finally given up his struggle the night the war broke out. Thus diminished, the group broke up, with Shijo going on to new work, so that Frome and Odette found their natural affinity for each other reinforced by their isolation.

"How's the *Rosinante?*" asked Frome as they walked across the brightening ground with their shadows stretching far ahead of them into the west.

"Yale and Dien are arguing over how many attachment lugs are needed for the fuel tank nets."

"They had that fixed ages ago, didn't they?"

"Yale recalculated the effect of irradiation on the plastic netting. Dien says more holes will weaken the forward collar too much. I left them to settle it between them."

"And the engine?"

"It came out of the fort frame without too much trouble. It's a good one."

"And the other two?"

"We're keeping them handy. You never can tell, they may be useful some time."

"Yes," Frome thought about that faraway future that never seemed to include him whenever he tried to envisage it. "I'll miss you," he said.

"Same here," she answered.

"That's why I asked you to join me here." He switched them from radio to telephone.

Odette said: "That's against regulations, Dan! The new orders . . ."

"They can do without us for a while," Frome said. "This is personal, between us. Odette, if I tried to back out of this job, Kallekjan would have Lamov execute me. As a disciplinary measure. He warned me himself."

"Dan, no . . ."

"So I'm going, because there's still a chance, whatever Lobos says. And if I show willing, we're safe. But I do *not* go willingly, whatever I say or do to please that pocket dictator of ours; and if I don't get back alive you're the one I'm relying on to remember the truth. I'm no hero. I wouldn't want people to think I was."

And because no other words were necessary Frome switched on the radios again.

CHAPTER TWO

Thirteen days before the scheduled departure of the emer-emergency mission Frome was at last allowed to visit Golem 3c-001. Since its arrival at Dvornik it had been in the hands of specialists: the doctors, who were anxious to decontaminate it properly; the cyberneticists, who were more interested in its thought processes and any foreign matter which might have infiltrated *them;* and the engineers, who cared only that the wires be connected correctly. Frome, as user, had been kept at a distance by earnest requests not to interrupt the work.

But as the long lunar afternoon set in and the sun began to decline towards the west and the night he was dreading, the invitation arrived.

Simon Dien questioned him while they were putting on the simplified and flimsy pressure suits that would furnish breathing air in the inert atmosphere of the clean room where the Golem had been tested. Previously Dien had only sought Frome's advice on the robot's physical constitution but on this occasion he concentrated on its behaviour.

" This was a prototype, wasn't it?"

"Right. Made for field trials back in 2005."

"Apart from the peculiarity you've since detected, were there ever any aberrations?"

"It never broke down. Is that what you mean?"

"Not quite. Did it fall into unusual or unpredictable operational modes?"

Frome lowered his helmet and opened his air tap. While he activated the telephone headset he puzzled over Dien's question.

"The Golem's complicated in several respects," he answered finally. "Sometimes it gave us funny answers, usually because we'd asked funny questions. The tests weren't foolproof."

"And the rest of the time?"

"It was amusing itself at our expense. It seemed to enjoy finding the logical holes in the questions."

"That's not what I had in mind. But it's a help."

"Care to explain the trouble?"

"Later. After you've examined it without prejudice."

The Golem was fixed to an antivibration mounting on a dais in the clean room, which otherwise was empty. Marks on the floor hinted that the room had been specially cleared for it. The robot's single lens eye seemed to watch Frome he he approached, shuffling slightly in the baggy suit. He halted and the constant rustling of plastic stopped too.

"Hi," the Golem said before he could speak. "Remember me?"

Was it yesterday?

152

"Of course I do," he answered. "Hi yourself – Ishmael."

The robot burred softly. Dien jabbed a finger towards it. "There! That's one of the oddities."

Frome sighed. "It's only laughter," he said. "Ishmael, have you been tormenting these poor people?"

"No more than they deserve," said the robot. "They ask so many daft questions it's a miracle they haven't tried Epiminedes on me more than once."

Frome looked at Dien, who scowled.

"Ishmael, you mustn't make a nuisance of yourself. This project matters a lot. They want to be sure you're working right. And so do I."

"They should have said," complained the robot. "They treat me as furniture. It's like the Museum here: strangers asking cretinous questions about infantile logical conundrums. All I'm missing is some scruffy brat jabbing a popsicle stick in my eye."

"Did that happen?"

"Plenty of times. The same brat each time. Dan, you've no idea what it's like to be a thinking person locked up with idiots. Sometimes I . . . Forgive me, I actually hated you for not giving me a suicide subroutine, or at least one for total amnesia. I envied that second unit after your visit! The scientists who looked at me were the worst: they knew my capabilities but still they treated me like some *idiot savant*. If it was you who got me out of there, war or no war, thanks."

Frome said to Dien: "Simon, you mustn't underestimate Ishmael. Don't patronise him, or he'll patronise you. And don't think he can't."

"None of the others was this way," said Dien. His usually pleasant expression had warped into one of distaste. "Why's this one got to be a prima donna?"

"Ishmael's different."

"But when I asked, you said –"

"Yes, I said they came off the same production line. But didn't you ever read the standard child psychology texts? The mind is the product of heredity *and* environment. Ishmael's programming has been fuller than any of the rest. He's more aware of life. Right, Ishmael?"

"Right . . . Hey, Dan, you ever see that ladyfriend of yours?"

Loss came upon Frome as a physical thing. Stricken by it, he could only shake his head. Ishmael innocently failed to understand the enormity of its mistake.

"She gave you the push, huh?"

Frome nodded. "That's right, Ishmael. She gave me the push. Excuse me."

He left the clean room. He stripped the suit from himself savagely. When a fold of fabric caught in a buckle he wrenched it free and tore it. The experience felt fine: it was good, sharp, real. He wanted to repeat it, or to smash something so the destruction might purge his soul of the cloying horror that had re-enveloped it. Lashing out at a microscope on a nearby bench, he hurled it to the floor but it only drifted downwards and bounced. It had been designed to withstand minor accidents. The failure angered him still more and Dien's shouts only registered as a noise, an annoying one at that. Frome yelled at him to shut his mouth. Shortly afterwards he was restrained by three men in grey uniforms who came in response to Dien's urgent calls.

CHAPTER THREE

He was lying on a bed, fully clothed, and his forehead was being stroked. The room sounded like his own: he recognised the purr of the faulty ventilator above the door. On opening his eyes he saw Odette sitting beside him, studying his face.

"Don't ask if I feel better," he mumbled and found that his tongue was sticky. "*Gah!* What did they feed me?" He struggled onto his elbows.

"Birdcage waste," she answered, fetching him a drink of water from the bottle on the desk. He swallowed it gratefully.

"I remember shouting at someone."

Odette raised an eyebrow. "More than that. There's a security man going around with a black eye because of you."

"Oh God," he muttered unenthusiastically. "Anyone I'm likely to meet again?"

"Don't worry, he's forgiven you. You're a national hero, you realise?'

"I am? Is that why I'm in my own room instead of languishing in Captain Lamov's dungeons?"

"Major Lamov, you mean."

"Oh yes, I forgot," Frome said acidly. "There's a shortage of generals these days. We all get to move up one."

Momentarily her face showed pain. "Please, Dan, don't make jokes about it."

"Sorry." He meant it; but his apology sounded flat even in his own ears because he had been reminded of the cause of his outburst. "Do you suppose she's still alive?"

Odette returned the empty cup to the desk. The side light was the only one burning, so he could see no more than half of her face; and that was partially shadowed. He thought her lips trembled, moments before she said, "If the person you meant is Helen Lorraine, yes, I think she is."

"Ishmael must have told you."

The secret he had kept hidden from himself was being revealed to the one person he had most hoped would not discover it.

Odette sat down on the foot of the bed. "I went to see Ishmael after you were brought here. Kallekjan said I should . . . do what I could for you." Her unsteady smile brightened. "Ishmael's a nice sort, isn't he?"

"He's a child," said Frome. "Tell me what he said."

"That Helen visited him four months ago. They talked for quite a while: about what she was doing, about her, about you. She asked to be remembered to you and sent her love." Though she must have hated the words she spoke them calmly. "Finally she said she was joining a deep sea research station in the Pacific, where she'd be continuously for a year –" She looked up, directly at Frome. "– isolated from the surface, as Dvornik is."

"Then there is the possibility of hope," said Frome, caught between relief and renewed anxiety. "But what can we do?"

"We?" asked Odette. "She's your problem. I'm only a go-between." She went to the door but stopped with her head tilted forward so her forehead rested against the cold surface. "That's all I can be until you've sorted yourself out." She turned to lean against the door.

"We went over this four years ago," said Frome. "The answer hasn't changed. Maybe it never will."

Thoughtfully, she said, "I'm not sure I believe in you any more."

"Because I stick to my principles? Yes, I suppose that might make me unusual." He waited for a reaction; none came. "As soon as we heard they'd launched a shuttle from Canaveral it was obvious things couldn't be as bad as we'd supposed. Perhaps Baikonur and Christmas Island are still in good shape, ready to be used. There could be towns that missed the worst; ships and submarines that were at sea when the war came, and aircraft, all of which made it to safety. I knew Helen's long-term plans. Because of them I couldn't make you any promises. I still can't. If I was so sure, I might have copied Guy Palmer and taken an overdose.

"Guy was always unstable."

"Aren't we all, in our separate ways, just that little bit crazy? His bad luck was too much pressure. My good luck was uncertainty."

Odette sighed and placed her hand on the door locking lever. "I'll be waiting for you when you get back."

CHAPTER FOUR

On the twenty-sixth of July, when the night temperature of the open surface had fallen below the superconductive critical point of the catapult rails, the *Rosinante*'s core was flung into lunar orbit, piloted by the robot Ishmael.

And on the thirty-first of July 2011, Daniel Frome followed in the shuttle.

He was glad to have made his peace with Odette because the purpose-built suit he put on in the medical centre on his last morning blocked not only chance germs but also all save the clumsiest gestures of affection. As he went in procession through the tunnels of the Base, accompanied by specialists, he met others he would have wished to bid farewell to with more than a wave of a gloved hand. Strangers and friends waited for him along his route; some, like Gustavus Hochmann, spoke to him.

"Remember Terence Denham," said Hochmann. "Know your enemies."

Jones was less oracular: "Don't let them through, Dan."

Kallekjan confined himself to a gruff, "Goodbye."

Frome could not resist trying to upset the commandant's poise, so he slapped Kallekjan on the back and said, "Be seeing you, tovarishch." The results were entirely satisfactory; the Commandant's expression of stunned outrage kept him grinning all the way to rendezvous with the *Rosinante*.

Byron Yale's mechanics had spent four days transforming the ship from swan to ugly duckling. Frome could not deny that the completed structure was, in Dien's terms, like a spacegoing mulberry with a long stalk. As it and the shuttle drifted across the daylit face of the Moon with mountains and pockmarked plains sliding by below, he made the transfer by way of a towline. He met Yale on the netting which enveloped the twelve fuel tanks, as the mechanics were disconnecting the thirteenth tank which had been used to top up the ship's supply. Yale held out his armoured hand.

"On your way, huh?" he said. He used the phone for a minute: "Dan, thanks for saving my sanity ... No, really; this screwball scheme of yours came when I was set to crack up completely. It gave me something concrete to think about. I know a lot of the others feel that way too, only, well, they're a tough independent bunch; they like to pretend that's not how it is." He reverted to radio. "Now see if you can carry it off. Make those robots do their stuff the way they were meant to. Okay?"

"Sure," said Frome, confused but happy.

He pulled himself along the netting, hand-over-hand, and followed the guide rail from the forward collar to the cockpit hatch. Settling himself into the contoured seat within he closed the hatch and sat still for a minute. He was, he realised, totally committed to the trip.

Ishmael mimicked a cough.

"Hello, Ish," said Frome. "Are we ready?"

"When you've fastened your harness."

"Before we go, deploy the shield."

"Are you sure?"

"Yes."

"Screen deploying," said Ishmael. The miniature television display in the control console relayed the view from the ship's ventral camera as it panned towards the stern, where the stars were becoming obscured by a dark disc spreading outwards like an oil stain on the sky.

The radio beeped. "*Rosinante*: your sunshield's opening."

"I know," Frome answered.

"Isn't that out of sequence on your flight plan? You can't retract it."

"Damn the flight plan," said Frome. "I want to know I won't roast. That screen's the only barrier between me and the hottest piece of real estate in the solar system. I don't fancy an early cremation."

"But if it breaks off when you accelerate . . ."

Frome did not care to reply. There was no more than a slight risk that the delicate booms of the shield would snap under the less than one gravity initial acceleration. He preferred to ensure that there were none of the pinholes Lobos had so feared. At perihelion the slightest imperfection in the metallic film mirror might develop into a burnthrough, resulting in the destruction of the ship and him.

The shuttle commenced its descent manoeuvre as the two ships crossed the sunset terminator into the shadow of the Moon. Frome followed its navigation warning lights towards the glow of Dvornik Base, until a rumble warned him their own engine was warming.

"Stand by," said Ishmael. "Go in one minute."

With the dim Moon filling his port viewslit and the full unnaturally brown Earth away to starboard, Frome kept his eyes on the console telltale indicators. The countdown neared the instant of firing and on the mimic diagram hydrogen flowed through pumps and valves from the first tank to the compressors.

Coloured panels blinked; more valves opened; the red line that represented gas at high pressure extended to the exhaust assembly, snaked through preheater coils, and fed back to the reactor. It paused. A light turned green. The red line fanned out: the ship moved.

For the first time in years he experienced a sustained acceleration akin to terrestrial gravity. He was grateful for his doctors' forethought in rebuilding his muscles: the force persisted for hours, holding him to the padded seat gently but inexorably. The pressure became a frustrating encumbrance, for whilst he could move more easily than he could have on Earth, the unfamiliar intangible restraint was an irritation that never eased, like a toothache that hovers on the borderline of pain, inconveniencing the sufferer without disabling him. Ishmael, who had taken the stresses of the catapult in its stride, was of scant comfort; when asked how much longer they would be under acceleration, it responded with a lecture on subjective chronology.

They rounded the Moon, swinging out into an orbit that gradually came to bear on the Sun, as the Earth and its satellite receded from them. Frome appreciated that the impression of a sure collision with the Sun was an illusion, for although the position in space for which they were aiming lay dangerously close to it, in theory they would pass by its fires safely. Even so, he was glad when Ishmael turned off the engine and announced the beginning of his first sleep period.

The Dvornik doctors had convinced themselves by much argument that a drugged sleep would allow worthwhile economies in food and air to be made. Sleep would also spare Frome restless weeks of confinement in the small cabin-cockpit of the ship. They had implanted in him such sensors and intravenous plumbing as was required; and he spent some minutes connecting these to the ship's equipment. Then, as the specialised narcotic invaded his perceptions, dulling and darkening them, he whispered:

"Ish. Wake me before we reach the Sun."

CHAPTER FIVE

He dreamed that Ishmael woke him on the twelfth day of the flight and told him they had come within twelve million kilometers of Mercury, four days earlier. This encounter, a near miss by celestial standards, amused Frome; but when he tried to laugh his throat was so dry he could only cough. He drank some water, then asked if the cabin could be cooled. He complained of the heat: the walls of the cabin were appreciably warm. All Ishmael would do was show him a picture of the Sun, swollen to twenty-five times its familiar diameter and still growing, which struck him as a lousy explanation. He said so.

"It'll get hotter," said Ishmael. "Much hotter."

Oh, well, make hay while the sun shines sonny ... "Ish, did did you ever make hay?"

"No, Dan. Do not try to speak. The narcotic has not worn off yet."

"Oh, fiddlesticks!" There was a big handle above his head. He pulled on it and pushed; then he swung it and the wall opened. Some air rushed out but he was still in his suit so it didn't matter much; and anyway he was more interested in seeing what was outside.

"Dan! Stay in your seat!"

"Ish, you're an old bore, you know that?" Now, this buckle undid like *so,* and that one like *so* – damn clever, these designers ... And this way was up: up and out, and *Oh, God, I feel sick: all that nothing in front of me ...*

There were stars in millions all around him as he clung to the coaming of the cockpit to stop his psyche falling out . . . No, there was one place no stars shone: behind the ship was a dark red disc limned in a fiery glow. Nearer, so close he wanted to touch them, were big shiny spheres held in a net, like beach balls.

"Hey, Ish, how's about a game of football, huh?"

"No, Dan, I don't want one. Please sit down and strap yourself in again. You might be sick if you keep moving about like that."

"Ah, shaddup, Ish." He climbed out. There was a buzzing inside his head that wouldn't go away even when he switched off his radio; so he switched it on again to talk to boring old Ish. "Where's the Sun, huh, Ish?"

"Don't try to look at it, Dan. You'll burn your eyes out and probably die of irradiation. Get back inside; you've already received an unsafe proton dose."

"Ish, old man, you really are the limit. I'm going to find the Sun, so shut your electronic trap, okay?"

The guide rail was almost too small for him to grasp and it persisted in twisting around, but he tricked it and reached the forward net collar safely. He was fascinated to see that one of the cords was frayed and how granular the end appeared. This held his attention for quite a while, before he took hold of the netting and began to climb around the curve of the tanks.

But as he made his way from handhold to handhold he began to wonder what he was doing. Before long he stoped to review his actions. The buzzing had gone and with it the nausea.

"Ish?"

"Dan? Where are you?

"I seem to be on the tanks. What the hell am I doing here?"

"I'll tell you when you're back inside, Dan."

"Okay, okay. I'm coming anyway."

By the time he had refastened the harness he had also remembered all of his temporary insanity. No lecture from Ishmael was needed for him to see that he had courted death most assiduously and had nearly won her. Beyond the frail screen the Sun's silent nuclear thunderstorms came closer by the second, shedding their rain of particles and gamma rays that should have been kept from him by the shielding behind the cabin. Within minutes the ship would be exposed to over two and a half thousand times the intensity of sunlight the hottest desert of Earth received. He had voluntarily forsaken the security of the cabin. He felt faint.

"Ish," he said. "Why do we let ourselves down by being such fools?"

The question had been rhetorical but the robot chose to answer it:

"For good or ill, I do not know. I cannot. But folly opens as many doors as it closes; perhaps you need it to be human . . . Let us hope your suit and the tanks were shielding enough. We have just passed perihelion."

CHAPTER SIX

Towards the end of the thirteenth day of the mission Frome went back to sleep and left Ishmael to radio Dvornik Base once the *Rosinante* was free of the Sun's local atmosphere.

When he awoke, some ten weeks later, it was to the sensation of steady deceleration. Ishmael spared him a cursory greeting which amounted to an explanation that it was attempting to deduce the locations of the forts from the scanty information supplied by the *Rosinante*'s rudimentary radar. Frome was to refrain from spurious conversation, please.

By degrees over the next few hours the deceleration grew fiercer as the ship's mass diminished and the engine's thrust gained progressively greater mastery over what remained. Frome endured it as best he could and reflected ruefully that the forces acting on him were only fractionally higher than those he had grown up with on Earth.

Freed of immediate preoccupations, his thoughts reverted to the dreams that had clung to him in his sleep: apparitions with blistered faces had shown him their roentgen ulcers, seeping sticky fluids; gastro-intestinal degeneration had made him vomit up his own blood; time and again, denied a clean end, he had suffered the wretched progression of decay-in-life. To be free of these consequences was such a blessed anticlimax he laughed aloud, so that Ishmael demanded an explanation; and when From had described his fears, the robot said:

"Yes, for a while I thought I would be alone. Your white blood cell count fell so low you might have died had you not been saturated with antibiotics. I don't want to talk about it."

Ishmael continued with its navigation. Frome found he had discovered a new perspective on the robot. He had been surprised to detect genuine concern in its words.

While he was still adjusting to this development the engine fell silent and the sense of weight vanished.

"I am in contact with Fort Eight," said Ishmael. "Will you talk to it?"

"So soon? Where is it?" There seemed to be only stars in sight when he peered through the viewslits.

"About ninety kilometers ahead."

"How, ah, . . . How are they reacting to our arrival?"

"They resent your presence. They see it as an intrusion. Be very careful."

"Put me through," he said.

He heard a voice that might have been Ishmael's but for the crackle in its consonants. *Less practice,* he thought.

"Zero-Eight to *Rosinante* . . . This is Nightwatch Task Force Unit Zero-Eight."

"Hello Zero-Eight. This is Daniel Frome speaking."

"Welcome Frome." The voice was cool. "You are expected."

In at the deep end, he decided. "Are all of you in communication? Can you speak for all?"

"Yes, to both."

"Do you all accept my authority?"

"Those are our orders, Frome. If we have to do as you say, we will, unwillingly. It seems wasteful, my I say. We have our own plan."

"I will want to hear it," Frome said in an attempt to mollify the forts and because it was possible they had contrived a strategy of their own which improved on the latest thoughts of the Dvornik planners. "Will you accept orders relayed through my own Golem, Ishmael?"

The silence dragged on. At last there came a short, "Yes."

It was a victory, possibly the greatest of the campaign. The Golems had been programmed for independence; they had not been told until a few weeks earlier that they were not their own masters. In their mechanical fashion they must have despised Ishmael, the reject-turned-cornerstone.

"Thank you, Zero-Eight, and all of you." To Ishmael he said, on their private circuit: "Ish, get in there and assert yourself. But for God's sake be diplomatic. None of your jokes. This is a sour lot, more used to sucking lemons by the looks of it."

"I thought they were friends of yours."

"Of mine? I've never seen half of them; the ones I spoke to thought I was the hired help. Their gods are the military strategists who trained them, Ish. They're wild, unlike you: they have no table manners."

"Hah! Thanks!" said Ishmael. "However, I shall be wary."

Frome could hardly imagine the discussion that ensued amongst the nineteen robots. The snappy repartee of which they were capable would be considerably impeded by their wide dispersal; whether this would frustrate their disputatious tendencies or exasperate them beyond the limits of their obedience, he waited to learn. In the meantime he adjusted the telescopic zoom lens of the dorsal camera for a view of Fort Eight.

The image was acceptable, if deficient in some of the detail he had hoped for. Overall, the fort appeared unchanged from when he had last seen it at the catapult railhead, except that the identification number, which had been applied with atmosphere-drying paint to each of the six faces of the amidships section, had blistered and peeled off in patches. This did not concern him unduly. The metalwork was clean and bright; the engines showed no pitting of stressed areas; the microwave antenna which carried inter-fort communications was moving nimbly from setting to setting as the fort addressed its fellows, without any of the jerkiness that signified cold-welding of the joints. With luck the other forts would be in as good condition. They might still comprise a battle-ready force.

"Dan," said Ishmael suddenly, "they want to know if you're a friend of Amrik Chundilar."

"What does that have to do with anything?"

"He designed the gas mixture in the lasers."

"Oh, *him*!" So the Malay had a name at last. Frome had

noticed the small man from time to time but had never felt inclined to strengthen their acquaintance. "If it'll impress them, say we're like brothers."

"They don't want to be impressed. They want to assess your technical competence."

"Then say I helped good old Amrik concoct his original brew. Tell them anything."

"As you wish." Ishmael carried on with the electronic debate. Later: "Dan, they ask: do you know Odette Galfoy."

"Intimately. But that's none of their business."

"Has she discussed the power ratings of the reactor and engine with you?"

"We talk of nothing else . . . Ish."

"Yes, Dan?"

"My knowledge of design detail is totally irrelevant. If it'll settle their doubts, persuade them that I'm omniscient; but convince them, one way or another, to do as I say. Otherwise, invent your own answers to their questions."

Within an hour they held their strategy meeting.

"They are cooperative," Ishmael reported. "They care more that the interception proceeds smoothly than that they should be autonomous."

"Efficiency freaks?"

"What else have they to live for?"

"Okay, that was a joke. Put me through." The sound quality of the circuit sharpened. "Zero-Eight, are you listening?"

"We are."

"I want a summary of your actions to date."

Unemotionally, the fort described the arrival of the armada on-station and their first clear sighting of the alien ship only days before Frome's appearance. It told of the counting sequences which had been flashed at low power at the alien by the laser cannon and of the total lack of response. Some tension entered the machine's voice as it enumerated the challenge routines that had been tried: counting up, counting down, groups of dots and dashes, flashes transferred from fort to fort along straight and curved ranks; and other more complicated combinations of rate, duration, and spacing. None had been answered; and the decision to attack had been made, while the alien ship maintained the steady deceleration it had begun years earlier.

Somewhere out amongst the preternaturally bright stars which surrounded the *Rosinante* was one that did not belong there, Frome thought. Which? Did it matter? All that was important was that it was racing towards them, faster than most comets, yet demonstrating a fine control of prodigious power resources. Why should it bother to respond when candles flickered in the night?

"What then?" asked Frome. "It's ignoring you. What will you do now?"

"Whatever you tell us," said the fort. "We are at your disposal."

The situation was the essence of power fantasy. A despot with eighteen such battleships of space at his command could have overawed the armed forces of Earth were he prepared to accept perpetual exile. One nation could have dominated all others. It was no accident that the forts had been given only enough propellant to carry them on the outward journey, so that they might never return to Earth. Frome was tempted to succumb to the invitation to give orders and have them obeyed; but first he knew he had to humble the forts in a way that allowed them no remnant sense of superiority. The words of the treacherous false Denham came back to him. On them he based his strategy. Whatever else he had been, the man had not been a fool.

Calmly Frome said, "No. First describe your plan."

"It is redundant. We will hear yours instead."

"Describe it."

"If you insist." A brief blank ensued in the channel noise. "Naturally, the plan is expressed as a family of strategies. Do you prefer it as a flow diagram on a video display?"

"No," said Frome. "I do not. I prefer words: simple ones. Convey the primary tactical algorithm embodied. No frills." With cold certainty, he knew he had them, that they were scared of possible ridicule; and in itself that was cause for concern.

"Extrapolation of the target's course yields a solid locus in the form of a cone —"

"Why not a line? Justify this decision."

"Possible evasion uncertainties."

"On what grounds?"

"Hypothesis."

"Indicators leading to formulation of hypothesis?"

"None."

"Justify hypothesis therefore."

A pause. "No justification."

"Continue."

More slowly, the fort said: "Six equally-spaced cross-sections of this cone yield six circular areas, around each of which would be positioned three forts. Their fire, directed inwards, would give total command of the target for intensive attack over a distance –"

"Stop," said Frome. "I've heard enough." Superficially, the plan was not unreasonable, though he was disappointed by its stodginess. *But they're not tactical computers, Dan.* "Re-evaluate your chances of success, given the unjustified nature of your primary hypothesis that the target will behave in a given manner."

So, he thought, *the trap is set. Will they walk into it?*

They did.

"Wait," said the fort.

"Dan," said Ishmael on their private circuit. "What kind of a question is that? As worded, you're asking them, in effect, to solve a problem on the assumption that they have no data. That's a no-solution question."

"I know," said Frome. "I have to muddle them, Ish, or they won't follow my lead absolutely."

"You're taking an awful risk."

"Yes." What Ishmael had not said, what Frome had not dared suggest, was that the forts, in attempting to find a solution, might confuse themselves irreparably.

Suddenly Fort Eight said: "Problem abandoned."

"Why?" asked Frome. Secretly he was proud that the robot's protective mechanisms had worked. Months had been spent in designing-out syllogistic traps.

167

"There is no target."

"*What?*" Frome pulled himself to the window. The alien light was still clearly visible. "Ish, is it, or is it not, there?"

"The target's all there," said Ishmael. "I'm not too sure about the forts, though."

"There is no target," insisted the fort.

"Ish, give it the coordinates ... Zero-Eight, what is that object?"

"That is an alien spacecraft, nature unknown, destination unknown, –"

"That is the target."

"Wait."

"Ish, I want your opinion: what's got into them?"

"If I knew, Dan, I'll tell you. I don't. I'm feeling distinctly confused myself."

"Don't you break down on me too."

"I –"

"Information, please," said the fort. "Define word 'target'."

"Ish, feed them your definition from your vocabulary band."

"Done," said Ishmael a moment later.

"Result follows," said Fort Eight. "Object designated is not a target."

"I'm telling you it is. I have so defined it."

"It cannot be. Vocabulary definition follows: WORD *TARGET* PRIMARY DEFINITION: 'AN OBJECT AIMED AT, WHETHER OR NOT FOR PURPOSE OF DIRECTING INTELLIGENCE AND/OR FIRE THREAT, OR FOR RECEIPT OF INTELLIGENCE AND/OR MATERIEL THEREFROM' – SEE ALSO SUBSIDIARY FILE *TARGET – B*. By this definition the designated object is not a target."

The alien ship drew on. Though as yet many hours distant, it suddenly seemed about to reach the scattered paralysed terrestrial forces. Again Frome tried to understand what had affected the forts and re-experienced the frustration he had known years earlier in the laboratory on Earth.

"Explain your reasoning."

"Syllogism follows. Primary premise: designated object is an alien spacecraft, nature unknown. Secondary premise : a target is as previously defined in vocabulary readout. Conclusion : since nothing is known about the designated object, no evaluation can be made of whether or not intelligence and/or materiel can be exchanged with it; therefore it cannot be defined as a target."

"It has a point there," remarked Ishmael.

"Ish, will you keep out of this," said Frome. "Zero-Eight, your vocabulary definition is too specialised. Does it accord with what you had originally, before transfer from my Golem?"

"Original definition was given in readout."

"Then over-write it with the new one." *Those goddam strategists at Dvornik. They never know when to leave well-enough alone; always have to be mucking about with ...*

"Over-write is forbidden."

"Under all circumstances?"

"Except for direct mechanical input."

"Wait," said Frome calmly. He took off his headset. For a few seconds he played with it, flexing the headband in his fingers. Then he slung it into a corner of the cabin. And swore.

"Dan?" said Ishmael through the console loudspeaker.

"Leave me alone," said Frome. "I have to think. There has to be some means of persuading them to take notice of the alien."

"There is. You must allow me to contrive an artificial machine-code word whose definition is 'target' in the sense you require. I will then translate automatically whenever that word is used in the course of your conversation with the forts."

"It sounds too complicated."

"Not at all. I'm already turning most of what you say into machine code anyhow."

"You take a lot on yourself, don't you? If you don't mind, I'd rather speak to them myself."

"I'd advise against it. They don't understand you as I do, Dan. This way, we can communicate better; wasn't that the reason you brought me?"

"Very well," said Frome. "Have it your own way." Unaccountably he resented the robot's assumption of such an important role in the negotiations. *Dan, be reasonable. He's*

absolutely right – 'He'? IT: that's only a bloody machine ...
He put on the headset again. "Zero-Eight," he snapped.

"Present."

"The designated object is a – " He hesitated, feeling foolish.
"– a target. Do you agree?"

"I confirm: object is a target."

Now we're making progress.

"Good. The previous strategy for dealing with this target is to
be replaced. Do you agree?"

"Wait." *What now, for God's sake?* "There is no previous
strategy. This target is newly defined."

"Ish," said Frome tiredly, "find out just what they imagine
is going on in the world around them. I can't keep discussing
things they think aren't there, or arguing black into white, or
... Oh, *damn* that man Kallekjan ..."

Some minutes later Ishmael made its report: "They agree
that the ship exists and that it is a target, as defined by us. However, they appear to have forgotten that it once existed, or
even that they were sent out here to deal with it ... Dan, I suspect that your trap-question caused more damage than you intended."

"How is it they know what the alien is?"

"The concept happened to be in their short-term working-
memories when the damage occurred, so they associated it with
the ship. The upset is in their main long-term memories: somehow, somewhere, they've developed a massive conceptual block-
age. It varies from fort to fort; but its general effect is to stop
them thinking rationally about certain subjects. Principally, the
alien ship."

Frome took a deep breath, held it, and released a long sigh.

"Dan?"

"I'm still here." *I wish I wasn't; I should be back in primary
school, learning how not to play with matches.* "Ish we're in a
pretty good mess."

"Agreed."

"So where's your bright idea for this occasion?"

"This is beyond my competence, Dan. If I can help, I will –"

"Otherwise it's my game. Thanks." *Roll up! Roll up! See*

Daniel Frome save the world, single-handedly! "Can you list the damage for me, fort by fort?"

The television screen in the console filled with words. Frome scanned it by eye.

"All that on Fort Zero-One alone?"

"The others are not all as badly affected," said Ishmael as it flicked rapidly through the individual summaries. Some of the lists were no more than a dozen lines long; one extended to three screens. Each fault was labelled according to the nature of the damage; and as Frome studied the lists he noticed a pattern, faint but certainly present.

"Ish, most of these seem to be an aversion to thinking about the enemy's reactions to tactical gambits."

"Over ninety-one per cent, yes."

"Of those, how many could be compensated for by blocking off the forethought capability, so they wouldn't even try to foresee the consequences of their actions?"

"There would be a cure rate of about seventy-seven percent of this list."

"Then I'll do that."

"That's dangerous, Dan."

"You think I haven't realised?" he said. "What would you do in my place, Ish? Would you play safe and leave them as they are? I don't care if they shoot each other by mistake, or fire at the wrong part of the target. This is like a rifle range in an amusement park, where the game's rigged all the way: win or lose, it's a waste of ammunition. Ish, these forts are a waste of robots. They ought to be tackling real problems, fighting Jupiter's atmosphere, not an alien enigma. All you need for this is a big enough gun and one man to aim it."

"How were they to know?"

They weren't, Frome realised. Nobody could know. So they made a committee-decision: pour in enough money and the problem would be drowned.

"Let's get down to work," he said.

A psychotherapist might have sympathised with his predicament. The principal obstacle was the remoteness of his patients and the consequent uncertainty over whether they were responding to treatment correctly. Reflexively-generated words and phrases were desperately inadequate indicators of mental condition. Frome knew that if he was unlucky he would have to regress the forts to imbecility, much as he had the Mark Two in the Museum, after which they would obey orders in only the most literal fashion.

"Ish," he said, after several hours' work, "how many forts could you control remotely?"

"At what level?"

"Gross action-programme: stop/start, left/right, that sort of thing. No housekeeping or autonomic processes; there are sub-systems for those."

"I have spare capacity for about six or seven."

"Good. Keep it handy. Stand by to assume command of named units as I deal with them."

For fifteen hours he felt through the forts' minds by question and answer. At first the work went quickly: those he found to be hopelessly damaged he handed over to Ishmael who established command radio links with them. Those which could be salvaged he attempted to reprogramme verbally.

It was a procedure fraught with uncertainties. He felt as if he were trying to thread a needle in the dark whilst wearing spacesuit gloves. Astute questions would disclose concepts from which the robots' thoughts recoiled, as though their inclusion in any reasoning chain triggered distracting associations with no relevance to the topic under consideration.

Whenever he found such a free-association reflex he could only enforce a block, so that the robot became incapable of comprehending the barred concept. Thus, many were deprived of the power of anticipation, so that only learned procedures could be used; innovation became unsafe and therefore, in the robots' eyes, unusable. Others lost their ability to generalise from certain types of input information. With every excision, a part of him felt pain; he had intended no harm with his original question, only that the Golems' dependence on him alone should be reinforced. He had wanted obedience, not mindless subservience. Had he suspected the outcome he would have left them to glory in their arrogance and risked their disobedience.

When he finally abandoned further attempts to repair the forts, he forced sleep on himself. When he awoke it was the day of battle.

CHAPTER SEVEN

Half an hour before the encounter the microsun of the alien ship brightened abruptly. Frome contacted Fort Fifteen, one of the few to have retained most of its mental faculties.

"What's happened?" he demanded.

There was a delay as his message flashed from fort to fort and the answer returned by the same route:

"Variations in brilliance have occurred irregularly since first clear sighting. Appear unrelated to other activity. Advise no reaction."

He recalled the violent fluctuations in brilliance that had accompanied the course change over four years earlier. The variability of the flame thus seemed to be a factor worth bearing in mind but not one to affect the disposition of his forces, now that his freedom of action was so severely limited.

"Ish, what's the condition of the troops?"

"Seven drones: fully on-line, with laser power reactors at critical. Of the remaining eleven, two are on standby circuit, ready for probe assault." Ishmael mimicked a chuckle. "Until now I never really understood what a shepherd did with sheep-dogs."

The forts had been redeployed along a gently curving line wound halfway around the alien's projected path. This allowed for a clear field of fire from any fort, with adequate time for accurate aiming, for by spacing the forts at intervals of ten thousand kilometers along the path, and a hundred kilometers out from it, Frome had ensured that even the alien's phenomenal speed would not save it from at least one severe blow as it ran the gauntlet of the eighteen laser cannon.

The most severely disabled of the independent forts were in the first two positions. These were to be Ishmael's sheepdogs: sacrifices by which the alien's defences might be gauged. The seven controlled units were last in line, so that Frome might have time to direct them personally through Ishmael.

"Ish, any update on the probable outcome?"

"None. The target is unresponsive to radar."

"So all we know is what we can see."

"Correct."

"Well, keep trying. As soon as that damn fireball's out of the way, give me a graduated display of the alien ship, with dimensions overlaid."

There would be twenty seconds' fire per fort: six minutes in all, plus whatever could be gained by tail-end shots as the alien receded. The trouble was, the fireball was like a shield carried ahead of the ship. Still, six minutes ought to be ample time in which to locate weaknesses and concentrate fire on them.

But what are we shooting at? How big? How shaped? How constituted?

No material known to humanity had withstood Shijo's laser tests. Theoretical projections into realms of physical chemistry unexplored owing to difficulties inherent in handling the materials involved revealed no conceivable defence there either. All the alien possessed that defied the attack was the fireball. Once that was out of the way the onslaught would begin in earnest.

"Dan, stand by."

The display screen lit with a diagram of the battlefield: a semi-helix scaled down to fit a rectangle forty centimeters wide by thirty high but all of one hundred and seventy thousand kilometers long nevertheless. A bright red dot moved across the screen from the lefthand side, closing with the first of the yellow dots representing the forts. Numbers changed beside the yellow dot.

"Battle stations," said Ishmael tonelessly. "Unit Alpha engaging – now."

Yellow dot and red merged briefly. The alien ship was upon them, rushing down the line of forts.

The *Rosinante* was well down the line and about a thousand kilometers out from the projected course, so both man and machine relied upon pictures transmitted from ships near the battle focus for information on its progress. The story was incomplete, tending to be episodic: whenever a laser fired the picture dissolved into swathes of static; and the blaze of emitted light illuminated clouds of gas vented after previous shots, so that pictures swung from being too bright to being too dark. The signals were further degraded as the forts turned to track their target, as their antennae failed to maintain a perfect sighting on the *Rosinante*. This was especially true of the damaged forts, so that Frome had almost no idea of their progress until the third fort brought its laser to bear. Then it was clear the battle was not going their way.

But, almost as a compensation, he glimpsed the alien ship through the interference and the glare of hot gas. His first impression was of an overlong opaque ice-blue champagne glass magnified to an impossible size. The dimensions of the ship at first baffled him, then appalled him. According to the computer-generated overlay on the picture, the spindle was sixteen hundred meters long and twenty meters thick. In comparison, the fireball was nothing, only meters across, floating at the centre of a bowl four hundred meters in diameter whose interior was silvered but whose outer surface glowed ember-red. The disc at the stern was three hundred meters across and no more than ten thick; it could have accommodated a full sized soccer pitch, including grandstands, with ease.

It was this disc, one of the least prominent features of the ship, which intrigued Frome despite the urgency of the moment, since it broke the pattern of simplicity: for whereas the remainder of the ship was unadorned by any markings or minor fittings, the rear surface of the disc bore a central design in pale green, a circle overlaid with a cross.

He wished these mysteries could have been explored, not destroyed.

The radio blurted, through rising static from the fireball:

"The target is unaffected . . . – – – are your orders?"

"Keep firing," said Frome. "Fire at will."

The third fort swung, tracking the midpoint of the spindle. The picture broke up, reformed, and Frome saw a raw red glow fading on the alien ship's hull. The first fort fired its fourth shot at that moment: another glow appeared; and simultaneously the panorama of stars dimmed while a roiling cloud of incandescent gas dispersed from where the overheated fort had been. The second fort went the way of the first in the moments following its third shot. Still the alien ship ignored the assault.

"Ish," said Frome grimly, "we're being made fools of."

The robot said nothing.

"Use number eighteen as a camera platform. The six before it are to attempt a crash interception. Knock holes in that s-o-b: hit him with something heavy he can feel."

"If you think it'll do any good," said Ishmael.

"That thing's hardly noticed us so far. It can't overlook a couple of hundred tonnes hitting it at over five hundred kilometers a second."

The picture rolled as the channel changed. Far away was the approaching fireball, amid a field of stars. To one side of it six pinpricks of light were beginning to move inwards, painfully slowly.

"I want a *crash*," said Frome. "Not a near-miss!"

"Dan," said Ishmael, "keep your head. Number Twelve stands no chance of reaching its target on time."

"Open every gas valve on that fort. Run the pumps at maximum pressure. If the engines explode, I don't give a damn. Get it there!"

"It's impossible, Dan. I've tried; the safety interlocks keep cutting in. I lack the fine control necessary –"

"Then get back to the battle."

We never imagined it could be so huge. Or so invulnerable. It's only metal, surely? Even ceramics shouldn't stand up to heat like that. What have they got, for God's sake?

The alien ship bored through the defensive line relentlessly. The third fort and the fourth disintegrated simultaneously; the fifth winked out like a spent match on its fourth shot. The sixth, which Frome was watching through the cameras of the seventh, ripped open, spewing out white-hot gas peppered with fragments of the fuselage; for several seconds the glow lit the alien clearly as it sped by. And so it went: a sorry series of failures, spitting and flashing like toy firecrackers burning out in greater or lesser impotent fury.

At first Frome thought the ship had failed to notice their presence, which could explain its unresponsiveness. *Suppose,* he thought, *suppose it's dead? It has crossed two hundred light-years of space, crewed by dead ... things. Or it's running on a simple programme devised ages back and can't respond?* The ship might carry on, pass the Sun, and leave without touching the Earth. But how foolish that shortsightedness of its designers would be: such a waste of opportunities for contact with other cultures. Surely any intelligent beings would want to learn about other species? *Don't be anthropomorphic, Dan.*

The controlling intelligence, if there was one, might fail to see in the forts' actions any sign of an intellectual entity worth contacting ...

He made a difficult decision: "Ish, deflect those forts. Don't let them hit."

"I'm sorry, Dan. You're too late."

The first of the suicide forts, still far short of its target though its exhaust was brighter than any of the others, exploded. The second simply disappeared.

"Run that again," he said.

Replayed at slow speed, the image of the fort advanced until it seemed about to touch the alien ship. Then it passed from sight. Halting the picture at the instant of disappearance told him no more than that the fort suddenly no longer existed.

"Pull us back," he ordered. "And watch the next one closely."

Fort Fourteen went the same way Thirteen had, only now Frome had a clear view of the event.

The bows of the fort crumpled as if pinched between giant fingers. A wave of compression rolled along the fuselage, reducing metal and ceramics with equal ease. The reactor fell in on itself, though it was of well nigh solid metal; briefly it flickered as if trying to explode but the light faded as the mass dwindled to a vanishing point, sucking the forward half of the fort in after it. The three hydrogen tanks cracked, spilling cold gas which swirled about the wreckage then poured down the invisible sink hole in the wake of tanks, rear frame, and engines. No trace of the fort remained.

Helplessly, Frome waited for the same fate to envelop the

remnants of his fleet. Three more forts were sucked into oblivion before the alien appeared to tire of this form of counterattack; as fort Seventeen dived from the front a tongue of flame shot out from the fireball to lick at it. At once the tiny vessel lost its shape as the engines thrust through the softening fuselage. A second lick of flame melted its softer parts. There was no third lick; the reactor blew up, punctuating the fireball as the fort's molten remains plunged past the alien ship's bows.

Only one fort was left and Frome doubted whether even that was safe. All of a sudden, a hundred kilometers did not seem an adequate safety margin. Soon his fears were confirmed. On television the alien ship seemed to change course: the fireball swelled to fill the screen, then the channel carried only static.

Ishmael said quietly, "We are alone."

"Yes," said Frome. He watched the far-off spark that was the alien ship, and the Sun beyond it. "Set the return course for Earth," he said. "Act as if nothing happened."

CHAPTER EIGHT

After the luckless attack on the alien ship Frome tried not to think of the future, except where it touched on his own safe return to Dvornik Base.

The Earth lay at present on the far side of the Sun, so he could not immediately radio a warning. Accordingly, he recorded a message for delayed transmission by Ishmael two or three weeks later, when contact would become possible, and readied himself for the long sleep of the journey.

The *Rosinante* had been accelerating gently for several hours when Ishmael interrupted his preparations.

"Dan, your advice, please." It sounded concerned.

He laid aside the sponge with which he had been bathing himself and started to struggle into his clothes, afraid that the cabin might suddenly be opened to space.

"No immediate danger," Ishmael reassured him. "But for some reason we're off course."

"How badly?" Criticism of the robot's navigation was pointless; it could only trust its instruments and the ship's controls. It would have corrected any trivial error.

"By a considerable margin: we're drifting towards the Sun. Attempts to compensate for the offset acceleration only increase it. Reversal makes no difference. It's not internal; there's an external force acting on us."

"The alien?"

"Almost certainly."

"Stop the burn," he said. Immediately the air in the cabin filled with a swarm of minutiae he had casually set aside without securing them. Catching them was worse than shooing flies. He swept them up at last and pushed them into a locker, then finished dressing. Securing his harness, he said:

"How great is this force?"

"It varies. Sometimes it peaks at a tenth of a gravity. The trend is towards an increase. Already we've lost more propellant than we can afford."

"Suppose the alien is responsible and the trend continues. When would we reach it?"

"In under twenty-four hours, allowing for a deceleration period."

"Oh? What makes you think we'll be stopping?"

"That is the logical corollary of an arrival, isn't it?"

"If that's what it is," answered Frome, envisaging crushed and burned spacecraft. "I rather think we're about to be mopped up . . . If we tried hard, could we break free?"

"Barely. That presupposes the effect tails off with distance the same way it's increasing as we approach. But we'd be as good as finished: no propellant, or power; no safe landings; no course corrections. Just free fall. My hypothesis, which is corroborated by five ongoing scenarios I have been running, is that by carrying out course manoeuvres after the battle we have come to the attention of whatever controls that vessel and are being forced to a rendezvous of its choosing."

Frome sealed his helmet. "Try to break free," he said. "A short burn, at full mass rate."

"Can you stand it?"

"Like I said, make it short." He settled himself into the contours of the seat. The coming ordeal would have been safer had the seat been oriented across the axis of the *Rosinante*, rather than feet-forwards, but as it was –

Someone jumped on his chest and tried to push it into his skull. Another sat on his jaw and tipped his head back hard into the rest. A third heaved on his legs.

And they jumped off again.

Gasping, he realised he had almost blacked out. Or had a red-out: his eyes seemed immersed in pink fluid. They ached and would not focus properly. There was a slight pain in the small of his back. He felt dizzy.

"Dan?" called out Ishmael.

"Unh," he replied.

"Dan are you all right?"

"Give me time," he groaned. "Did you have to make it that bad?"

"I am sorry," said Ishmael. "I am also sorry to report that the external force merely increased to compensate for our thrust."

There was something not quite right in that, Frome thought, dimly.

"Quickly?"

"Apparently instantaneously."

"And how far away is the alien ship?"

"About one-and-a-half million kilometers."

"Ish, do your sums! How long would light take to travel there and back?"

"Ten seconds ... Oh, it must have known what we would try."

Puzzled, he said: "That's a strange assumption."

"It is the only admissible one. Faster-than-light effects are impossible."

"Is that what they told you at Dvornik?"

"It's a known fact."

"Well, I don't believe in precognition, Ish, so let's accept FTL for the moment."

"Precognition isn't necessary. Accurate extrapolation would suffice."

"I see," he said. "Would you distinguish the two for me, please?"

"The one is an end product of acausal reasoning, or inspiration. The other is rigorous deduction."

"And where the hell, Mr Smartass Ishmael, do you suppose that alien's going to get enough information to figure you that accurately? Not to mention me also?"

"I really cannot guess. But I find your ready acceptance of implausibilities such as faster-than-light effects hard to understand."

"Then don't lose sleep over it. Accept my word as a gentleman: FTL exists. And since I felt that acceleration even though you say we didn't change course, you'd better get used to detached inertial frames too."

"In the alien ship?"

"To do with it, yes."

"Then why should it travel through space conventionally?"

A tense nervous headache was developing behind his eyes. "Maybe it just likes long sea voyages," he snapped.

"Pardon?"

"Ish, will you shut up for a while!" There was a lull, during which he nursed his confusion and his headache. There were pills for the pain but none for the problem and he was acutely aware of their drift towards the imponderable hospitality of an unknown host and of how much the outcome seemed to depend on his decisions.

Re-examining his life, he saw how unfitted he was for this moment. His career had been a sustained delusion of free will, closely channelled by events. As a child in Somerset, he had seen his father's farm destroyed by blight and taxes imposed by a government reeling before the collapse of the British oil industry. Taken in hand by the State, his career had been selected for him by aptitude tests which searched for abilities that were his by birth, not option; and the career itself had epitomised regimentation. Formulae and logic admit no human foibles or preferences. Even his greatest moment had been imposed: the Golem had been required; he had made it to order.

His extinction too seemed preordained. There was no choice open to him but to wait.

"Ish," he said. "Wake me when we arrive."

Closing his eyes, he tried to sleep and forget the demolition of the universe of order that had begun with the casual destruction of the forts and continued with the apparent overthrow of relativity. The *Rosinante* talked to him, as he listened to her. Metal creaked. Pumps stuttered. Sunlight streaming through a porthole slid across his face as the ship slowly revolved. But the radio was silent and the jets were cold; even the attitude controls no longer thumped their drumbeats through the fuselage now that the ship fell towards the alien under the influence of whatever force it had contrived to exert over the vast distance separating the two craft.

Somewhere between two thoughts he fell asleep, and woke, jarred into alertness by a siren scream in his headphones. Ishmael's insistent voice beat in his ears:

"Dan, wake up! We're landing. I'm confused. Should I escape? Should I –"

"Do nothing," he said.

The alien ship was still aimed at the Sun and the *Rosinante* was being drawn down on to the stern disc. As they slid into the shadow of the bowl, first the fireball was hidden, then the Sun itself was eclipsed. For the first time in months the *Rosinante* was in near-darkness.

"Turn on the lights," he ordered; and from the bows and stern there shone out two powerful spotlights.

He saw the lights reflected in the mirror surface of the disc as their ship settled towards a landing near the edge; and behind the image were those of the stars, so clear that the mysterious target pattern appeared unsupported.

The pattern's colour had changed from pale green to pale orange since he had last seen it. That this was no long-term change but part of a rapid and repeating cycle became evident as he watched, for the change progressed through yellow towards, and seemingly beyond, the ultraviolet end of the visible spectrum, although at all times there was a steady white background to the colours. Minutes later the white was tinted violet and the colours slid down to the infrared, then returned to yellow.

His attention was snatched back to more immediate matters by the realisation that whatever was controlling the alien's force field was somewhat ham-fistedly allowing the *Rosinante* to land too fast.

"Ish," he said, "try breaking our fall."

There was no answer.

"Break our fall!"

The lights of the reflection were blindingly bright in the darkness and still rising.

"Ishmael!"

He slammed his faceplate shut, switched to the spacesuit's own supply, and waited for the crash. Presently he heard Ishmael say, "Well, we're down."

He opened his eyes. "In one piece?"

"Somehow, yes. We stopped only centimeters from the surface without any detectable deceleration forces. Now we are being held by a one-sixth gravity field." As the robot spoke Frome felt his weight increase until it seemed normal.

"Like on the Moon . . . Now, where were you while all this was happening?"

"I was here all the time, Dan."

"Then why didn't you answer when I called?"

"But you said nothing. Nothing at all."

"I didn't shout at you just before the landing?"

"No."

"That's exactly what we need," he said: "An intermittent fault!"

"Dan, there *was* no fault! I heard you breathing all the time. You said nothing."

Had he imagined his outcry?, he wondered. Or had the robot un-imagined it? How much could these aliens know or control?

"Can you see anyone?" he asked nervously, sensitive to the possibility of being eavesdropped on. There was only starlight to see by, now that they had landed, for the spotlights had been extinguished. The empty mirror stretched away to an indistinct boundary that merged with the surrounding starry sky. Only the glowing target stood out clearly, some way off.

"No-one, and no-thing," replied Ishmael. "But I feel we are not our own masters here."

"Can I risk EVA?"

"Logically, I see no objection. Our custodians display no fear of us; they have demonstrated their ability to cope with more formidable threats than you or me. Perhaps they are waiting for you to go out."

"I was afraid you'd say that," he said. Swinging the door open, he stood up amid a shortlived mist of frozen air.

Despite his vantage point, the darkness prevented him seeing much, so he switched on his helmet lamp. The pool of light it cast spilled off the *Rosinante,* to be lost on the mirror, whose limits seemed to be the sky itself. He walked along the fuselage to the hydrogen tanks and clambered down the netting to the surface of the disc.

His boot touched the mirror. Only then did it occur to him that technically he had landed on another world. Nothing in or of the ship was part of the solar system. No dictionary he knew of said that a world had to be a planet or a natural body. The size of the ship alone made it a good contender for the title.

After a walk lasting some minutes he came to the nearer edge of the disc without noticing any variation in the artificial gravity. Carefully he leaned forwards to peer over. Such severe vertigo hit him that he fell over backwards. Something, he was sure, had seized him as he lost his balance. In those few seconds he had seen a void filled with stars and infinitely deep; he had stood atop a pillar, a thread of metal, ice-blue with its own inner light that rested on an upturned cup, from beneath which boiled a golden aura. The image was too powerful for his overtaxed senses; for the rest of the day he confined his further explorations to the disc itself.

There was, he learned, little enough to discover. His kingdom was the disc, and the *Rosinante,* and the target. The disc refused to acknowledge his most diligent attempts to penetrate it, by blunting the knife from his belt tool kit and shrugging off two distress grenades; the *Rosinante* was where he spent his resting hours, where he ate, and where he sat in hours-long contemplation of his confined universe; and the target would have nothing to do with him.

Whereas the ship as whole had remained inert to him since his enforced landing, the target repelled him whenever he tried to enter the circle. It likewise rejected any objects he tossed into it: three grenades, for example, vanished into the heavens like comets. Not wishing to give up too easily and taking a gamble that the ship was intended to be his home for a while longer, he tried shuffling across the boundary of the circle. His toes crossed safely, as did his heels; then he found himself facing away from the target as if he had traversed its full width without noticing.

Ishmael observed this performance without expressing its opinion. Frome too was happy to keep his bewildered thoughts and half-formed conclusions to himself.

CHAPTER NINE

For three days Frome led what he later considered to have been an unremarkable existence aboard the alien ship. His principal entertainment was to sit with his legs dangling over the edge of the disc into the abyss. Once the fear that he might have been abducted by ill-intentioned beings had faded, he grew bored and anxious that he should soon meet whoever, or whatever, was watching him.

He had no doubt that he was under observation. Reason indicated that he would not have been carried so far to be forgotten; and he suspected that his actions were being fitted into an assessment of his personality and physical abilities.

There were overt proofs of the ship's response to his activities, such as when he attempted to penetrate the target and was rebuffed. There were subtler ones, too, such as the gravitational field which accurately reproduced that of the Moon; how else but by study of his body could his hosts know to what he was accustomed?

And there were the covert proofs: at first when he ventured near the edge his suit radio would crackle as if affected by the plasma streaming from the fireball; later the static diminished, which suggested that his tolerance of radiation had been found wanting and that the plasma was being warded off for his benefit.

He took comfort from this last fact. His health was valued, if only temporarily.

On the third day he decided that as his stay might not last forever he ought to ready the *Rosinante* for flight and tackled the task of removing the sunshield which had been crushed and buckled by the landing.

In space he could have completed the demolition in a couple of hours. In the pseudo-lunar gravity he had to take care lest any of the metal spars snag his suit as they fell, or lest he become engulfed in the folds of metal foil. It was whilst he was engrossed in this task that he failed to notice the alien's arrival.

"Dan," said Ishmael over the radio. There was an ominous tone in its voice which caused Frome to glance up. He stayed still, for he was balanced on top of the engine and had some way to fall if he slipped. After a slow survey of his surroundings, seeing nothing, he said, "What is it?"

"A visitor. Above you."

He leaned back and shone his lamp into the sky. The beam caught something white and spherical descending from the darkness.

The alien was about two meters in diameter. Its surface was finely textured, like unglazed porcelain, seemingly flawless; the severe simplicity of its form was disturbed only by six black discs set flush with the surface, four around the equator and one at each of its poles. Though there were no eyes visible, he knew it was watching him.

He lowered the lamp slowly. The alien floated downwards, keeping pace with the beam; and when he switched off the light, he saw the alien was now emitting a reddish-orange glow, bright enough to be clearly visible without offending the eyes.

Neither Frome nor the alien attempted to elaborate the contact until it had floated along one side of the *Rosinante* and returned along the other. There were no clues to the alien's nature, nor signs of propulsion mechanism, nor could Frome determine whether this was the alien itself, or a whole spacecraft, or a simple drone robot. When it needed to move, it did so; otherwise it remained immobile and inscrutable.

It came to rest about a meter from him and on a level with his face.

His throat felt very dry.

Suddenly it said, by way of the radio:

"Why are you breaking your ship?"

He controlled himself. *Of course,* he thought, *it speaks English. Doesn't everyone? The aliens always do: "Earthman, we have listened to your radio broadcasts ..."* He would not question his luck. Later, it might explain.

Though he was acutely conscious of how momentous the conversation was, he retained his objectivity. He continued to unfasten the wing nuts which secured the spars as he considered his answer.

Eventually, he said carefully, "I'm repairing it."

"By demolition?"

"This part is damaged. Redundant. It's in the way."

"I see. May I help?"

—This was never in the First Contact Manual. What the devil do I say?

He tossed it a wing nut. "Sure, hold this."

The nut slowed, coming to a halt about twenty centimeters from the alien, and stayed in that relative position. When he subsequently asked for it back, along with the several dozen others which had accumulated, he was given them in a tight clump. No visible manipulator was employed by the alien.

There had been a long and difficult silence whilst the work proceeded.

"Now what will you do?" asked the alien. "I am most anxious to talk with you. Will you be free soon?"

The situation, Frome felt, was faintly ridiculous. He was being waited on by a creature that could flatten him into non-existence and whose forbearance should long since have evaporated.

"... But please don't rush," it added. "We're not going to reach your world for quite a while."

"How do you know where I come from?" he asked sharply.

"Your physiology and biochemistry could only be of the third planet from the stellar primary of this orbital system and your physical condition is only consistent with a prolonged stay on its moon. *Earth,* I think you call your world; and if I'm not misinformed, you've named your moon with similar devastating originality."

Frome restrained himself, with a pithy retort burning on the tip of his tongue.

"And, ah, where did you learn our language?"

"From your Ishmael."

"Ish?" said Frome.

"Dan, I've never so much as spoken to this entity."

"I believe you," he said. "Well, entity?"

"Did I say I'd spoken to your slave? I learned *from* it. Which is to say, I examined what it understands of your language and of the universe in general ... I do hope that you are more perceptive and better informed; otherwise our dealings may indeed be brief."

"Are you sure," Frome began, then hesitated. "Are you sure we've got that much to say to each other?"

"My sentiments exactly," agreed the alien. "However, Ship thinks we should persevere. There may yet be profit in it."

"You want to *trade*?"

"In essence."

"Oh, fine," said Frome. "Perfect. Let's trade." He clambered down from the tail of the *Rosinante* and began gathering up the tangled material from the sunshield. "I'll swap you this lot for a comparative mass of liquid hydrogen."

"Do be serious," said the alien, having dropped to his new level. "We've wasted that much and more in bringing you here."

"Did we ask to be brought?"

"No – but did we ask to be ambushed?"

188

"Effectively, yes . . . You could have been anyone, turning up like that. How do we know you're friendly?"

"Who said we were friendly?" the alien demanded. "Friendship doesn't come into it. We're *traders*." It paused. "And besides, we didn't exactly sneak up on you. Our policy is openness: carry a bright light, follow a straightforward course; move slowly and predictably. In case the natives get worried."

"Is that all we are: natives?"

"Does it feel better if we call you humans?"

"A bit." It occurred to him that somewhere back along the line the discussion had taken a wrong turning. First Contact wasn't supposed to be like this; humans and aliens were supposed to be dignified, use grand phrases, offer the appendage of friendship, be a credit to their kind. *Not squabble, dammit.*

"Look," he said. "I'm Daniel Frome. Call me Dan. You already seem to know Ish."

"I know what an Ishmael is and what it does. But what is a 'Dan' and how is it distinguishable from a 'Danielfrome'?"

"That's me: my name . . . And you?"

"You want to communicate at last?"

Frome said, patiently, "That's the idea."

"Excellent. But I have no name; my job title is Counsellor. That of my associate is Ship. You will talk with me only. Ship, however, will listen to all we say and may reply through me, though you will almost certainly be unable to distinguish us. Don't allow that to concern you. . . . So, what have you to trade?"

"Wait a minute," said Frome, feeling rushed. "Let's hear some more about you two."

"Two? We're not separate, like you and the Ishmael."

"All right. All *right*! Then tell me, in simple terms, what a Counsellor is and what a Ship is. Assume I know nothing."

"Easily done. A Counsellor advises: it learns languages on behalf of the gestalt and employs them in communication with those native species encountered in the course of a trade mission. This is its primary function.

"A Counsellor also has a secondary function: it instructs those it meets in the proper use of the associated Ship, supervises that usage, and if necessary intervenes.

"A Ship is a means of transport. That may seem a facile definition, so I hasten to add that it embodies two forms of transport: the obvious and the subtle.

"The obvious you have seen: it moves bodily through space-time under conventional gravitational force field drive and is subject to physical laws understood by many species of intelligence.

"The subtle, however, touches on what many highly gifted species would regard as magic. As your language does not utilise ad-hoc compound-concepts of the requisite complexity I have to digress here. Are you with me so far?"

"Until you mentioned magic."

"You have already deduced that Ship and I originate from near the star you call Beta Crucis. When we departed we left behind us a platform much like this on which you are standing; and yet, in a sense, we did not leave it behind us, for the two platforms are really one and the same, a structure twisted out of space and time to create complementary images whose surface of reflection lies at what seems to be their geometric line of symmetry: the centre of that target which so perplexed you. Functionally, they comprise of two terminals of a matter transmitter."

Frome looked at the circle for a long time. Awed by the notion but reluctant to accept it fully, he asked slowly, "I could step in at this end and reappear at the other?"

"Put crudely, yes. But to return to the magic: the – you lack the word – the principle which sustains this effect requires constant supervision, which is Ship's secondary function. Or its primary function, depending on your priorities. With that one proviso, this matter transmitter is our gift to you."

"Gift?" he echoed, dumbfounded.

"Don't misinterpret this as blind philanthropy," added the alien quickly. "We expect to profit by it."

"Oh, quite," agreed Frome, feeling stunned. If the alien spoke the truth, there was now a way to the stars. Or to one star at least. Doubtless other routes extended thence to more stars and their attendant planets. Eagerly, he asked, "Are there more links like this?"

"Many more," said the alien dismissively. "So many we can't

190

count them. The network is expanding all the time. Whenever a census is taken, it's always out of date."

"Hundreds?"

"Hundreds of thousands would be closer to the truth. This Network is extremely old. When I was manufactured they told me the earliest links go back millions of years. And there may be still older segments, isolated when links failed, and never rediscovered."

"You were manufactured? You're a robot? Then, where are the real aliens?"

"There are no 'aliens' here, Dan. I am a robot; so is Ship. No organic intelligence could have survived this journey. And some journeys last for tens of thousands of years, not the mere eighteen hundred this one has taken. Besides, we have to be expendable in case we are cut off. If the link breaks, there'll never be another, unless you people build it."

"But this whole effort must have been fabulously expensive!" he cried, flinging wide his arms to include the Ship and journey as one. "How can the investment be thrown away?"

"Very easily. How do our controllers know what caused the breakdown? Accident? No intelligent beings discovered at the target star? Native attack?" The robot allowed the question to hang before it continued. "These Ships are a strictly speculative venture. Certainly they cost a lot. But they are looked on as an investment to be amortised over a definite period. On average they last long enough to repay their capital value several times over; and at the rate they're being built the Builders felt it worthwhile to risk some capital even on borderline cases such as your sun. But only once. There is a sky full of other stars to be tried."

"And how long is our mortgage to last?"

"No mortgage. I told you: it's a gift. But since you ask, we would hope to amortise the cost of this Ship, and me, over about eight thousand years."

"That's one hell of a gift, friend. Are you sure there are no strings attached?"

"This is no Trojan Horse, if that's what you're thinking. You can switch it off any time you like."

"Just shut the door, is that it?"

"Yes. But if you do, you throw away the key at the same time. No second chances. It's a permanent-off switch: anyone can press it; but no-one can un-press it."

Frome glanced around nervously to see whether he might have blundered into it. "I hope it's well protected."

"No-one can operate it accidentally. When – or if – the time comes, ask me or Ship."

"Oh, I see," said Frome. "You'll work it if that suits you but not otherwise?"

Quietly, the Counsellor asked: "Shall I press it for you now?"

With his scepticism challenged, Frome discovered to his surprise that he believed the robot. "No," he said hurriedly. "I'll wait."

"Thank you. Sometimes, I understand, that is where the links fail: some species are self-destructively paranoid. Which is one justification for the switch. There are others we need not dwell on, save to mention that we can operate it voluntarily, at our own discretion."

"Enough said," answered Frome. He looked past the Counsellor at the target, which was now white. "So what do you want to trade?"

"We are only supervisors and operators of the system," said the Counsellor. "One of you will have to go through and discuss that with the negotiators at the shipyard."

"They won't come to us?"

"Why should they? Dan, this Ship is one of thousands based on Beta Crucis. There are scores lying idle, awaiting contact. If the negotiators spent all their time monitoring those links they would never complete their proper work. Besides, don't you think it's more diplomatic to wait for an invitation?"

"That didn't stop you."

"Faugh! Such niceties are for pedants, Dan; you and we are practical people. Where does your doorstep lie? Are boundaries defined by atmosphere, by planetary orbits, by limits to the solar wind? If a species lacks the tolerance to allow a Ship to approach in peace, we'd rather press the switch and have done with them. But entering the link is another matter: it's an act of commitment. We leave that act to you."

"If the doorstep is that circle over there," he said, "the link doesn't want me."

"Ship rejected you because you weren't ready. But if you dare to, step over the line and you'll be on your way."

The target, now orange, took on the aspect of a minefield in Frome's eyes. "Have you tried it?"

"I am a doorkeeper, not a traveller. It would kill the gestalt."

"So, assuming I arrive intact, I simply wander into my local cosmic swap shop and say, *Hi, I'm a man. Want to trade?*"

"If that seems apposite. But your particulars will be transmitted with you. They will understand your needs."

"Will they?" asked Frome. "I wonder how much you know of our situation. You read Ishmael's data store. What can you do about the war we've just fought? Can these negotiators make a profitable trading pact with a species approaching extinction?"

The Counsellor rotated through a quarter turn, as though facing him; and Frome wondered briefly whether the robot might not be less symmetrical internally than its casing implied. Presently it said:

"Your slave Ishmael has an imperfect vision of reality. It seemed to us that your troubles were of no enduring consequence. Were we wrong to assume that?"

"Slightly," said Frome. "Earth is a trash heap of radioactivity and malign debris. What can we offer that you'd want?"

"Some short-lived isotopes, perhaps; yet overall, right now, very little," the robot admitted. "But we anticipate the long-term in our planning; in a thousand years, why, we may share a most fruitful relationship."

"A thousand years?" exclaimed Frome. "That's fifty generations! In the last one thousand years the Earth has seen eight or nine empires destroyed. We can't wait that long; the next thousand days are what matter."

"Then I suggest you go and ask for help."

"On easy terms?" Frome said bitterly. "What's the mark-up on world salvage, or do we get it at your special introductory rate?"

"How willingly you judge us," said the Counsellor. "I cannot make promises for the Builders, or their negotiators; but the journey is free. Go: what is to stop you?"

Only fear – He remembered Odette's advice, given in the stillness of the reading room: the words were jumbled by forgetfulness; the sense survived. Trust and faith: *Learn the difference ... or one day you'll find you're alone, or worse ...* But when he looked at the target, glowing in the night of reflected stars, he knew his trust had limits too small for the courage he needed.

... One-way, it's faith. That can be beautiful too but it's not enough, not really ... It would *have* to be sufficient; it might yet *be* sufficient. Since childhood he had been constrained to have faith in sciences of one kind or another; and no matter what the genesis of the science, terrestrial or alien, its technological by-products were bound by the rule of fitness for purpose. The Builders had shown the quality of their workmanship. He would have faith in that. Even as he decided, the Counsellor added,

"Or must your species be remembered as one that was too proud to live?"

"I'm going," he said.

CHAPTER TEN

Taking a deep breath, he made a start for the centre of the target. His throat felt raw, his stomach hurt with the tension, as his boots thudded on the solid surface of the disc. On reaching the line he had to make a positive effort to cross it; then he was within the circle.

The intersection of the cross lay only meters away when he felt the first twinges of the transfer, a shudder that passed through the ground and up through him. There came a moment when the sky seemed to shake, which was followed by an instant of absolute stillness, when all sounds, even those of his own suit and body, were absent. A heartbeat later, partway between his third and fourth paces inside the circle, the stars were erased.

Darkness flowed down the sky. The night closed in.

First, there was gravity: he sensed *up* and *down* and discovered he was standing erect. As the waking mind struggles to re-orient itself, Frome clung to the visual clues that slowly appeared, for only sight told him much about the new exterior world in which he had arrived: his spacesuit muffled touch and smell; his radio, after a crash of static, had fallen silent.

A shudder passed down him into the ground. Immediately the sky caught fire. Lights – dazzling, spinning, moving in such dense nacreous convoys as to hide the stars – condensed from the darkness in bewildering patterns. High above and far away were strings of immobile sparks about which clustered firefly points that came and went in swarms. In amongst the teeming workforce of the shipyard weaved multihued streamers of ghostly luminous gas, flickering hither and thither, rerouting themselves as if in response to changing demands from the orderly ranks of fragmentary structures which hung over Frome like a vast gauze ceiling.

More ships under construction? No, how can they be; there are too many. The Counsellor talks as if the Builders set no bounds to their ambition, yet an output on this level would have filled the galaxy with ships if long sustained, or imitated by many other yards.

A gigantic shadow emerged, slowly, from the brightest part of the sky. Frome watched, ever more afraid of what he had involved himself in, as *something* glided past his platform: something without highlights, a patchwork of half-tone hints of grey suggestive of panels and spars, kilometers long, huge, flawless, unstoppable. It neither slowed nor accelerated in its deliberate passage, contriving to avoid collision with any of the teeming smaller craft that flitted about its bows. In time it vanished into the night-fogs of light, unexplained and inexplicable.

Frome found himself on his knees, cold and sweating. Trembling, he stood and staggered towards the edge of the disc, the better to comprehend the extent of the shipyard. Fully half of it, he realised must lie below the platform's horizon. If the other half in any way compared with the one he had glimpsed, the experience alone would have justified his journey.

More platforms were moored to either side of his at wide intervals in an apparently endless belt. Before distance defeated his eyesight he counted forty-two platforms like his own, all brilliantly lit from beneath, whose undersides were plain white shallow domes and whose upper faces were mirrors, empty and in shadow, on which other targets ran through their endless colour cycles.

The strands which linked adjoining discs merged with their edges only centimeters from the mirror surface. It would therefore be child's play to move between discs: one had only to pull oneself along, hand over hand, to have access to another part of the universe. Thinking about it, he decided not to try, for he was learning that nothing about the aliens was as simple as it at first seemed.

The source of the bright under-lighting began to intrigue him. His astonishment was being replaced by avid curiosity: no longer content to marvel, he wanted to explore, observe, deduce, learn what little he was able in the time available to him before the shipyard's representatives arrived. So he dropped to the ground and wriggled forwards for a look over the edge.

A gentle force pushed him back towards the centre of the disc. He tried again, gaining what purchase he could on the mirror surface with his boots and gloves. The force increased; he found himself sliding backwards until he was some ten meters from the edge. *Too dangerous*, he thought. Reluctantly he accepted the judgement of whoever was now the custodian of his welfare. He would have liked to see an alien star at close quarters, to be the first to look upon Beta Crucis knowing that he had travelled some two hundred light years from his own sun.

Thus thwarted, he grew impatient to meet the negotiators and began a methodical search of the visible sky. For want of any definite idea of what he would see, he decided to rely on the Builders' apparent preference for simplicity in their customer dealings; therefore any shape, no matter how interesting, which required explanation he dismissed as another of the shipyard's numerous workforces.

For at least half an hour he tried to discern amongst the restless interplay of shape and colour any hint of his hosts. His eyes were constantly being distracted by half-seen hurtling things flashing past, or drawn to the freeform sculptures which patrolled the open spaces between sparkling metallic islands. Anxiously he watched his air gauge drift towards zero; at last, after his hopes had been falsely raised by a sail-like object the size of twenty football fields which cruised by without acknowledging his presence, he tried to return through the matter transmitter.

The target refused to admit him.

It crossed his mind that the Counsellor might have a taste for practical jokes of a lethal variety. As he was estimating how much longer he could make his air last, a craft resembling a metallic splinter over forty meters long settled on the far side of the target.

An aperture formed in its side. A humanoid in a baggy spacesuit jumped out and stood by the ship. Slowly, Frome went to meet it.

The alien seemed to be a man. His spacesuit could have been an oversize set of plastic coveralls, gathered in at the joints, with a broad shiny belt around the waist. The boots were of a kind favoured by hikers, while the gloves and bubble helmet were strangely reminiscent of those in primitive space travel adventure films.

So much for technological evolution, he thought.

The man held out his hand. Frome shook it gingerly.

"I am here to talk to you, if that is your pleasure," said the newcomer in a warm baritone voice. There were no signs of any radio equipment, or even of microphones or earphones, but the signal was clear and Frome presumed that he too would be audible.

"Did they explain how it is?"

"They did. You are in difficulties, I would say."

"Can you do anything?"

The man clicked his tongue. "Well," he said slowly, "it's not so much a case of *can* we do anything, but whether it's worth our while. Know what I mean?"

"I think you'd better name your price before we go any further," said Frome.

The other's eyebrows rose. "Heavens, that's not what I mean! You must have a poor opinion of us indeed. Actually, we'd like to help, only ..."

"Only what? Only it might be good money after bad?" Frome jabbed a finger at several of the larger clusters of space hardware overhead. "What's all this worth? I don't mean in money; when an operation grows this large you no longer work in terms of cash. Hardware matters more, along with resources and planets full of materials ... No, what does it mean to *you*? You send out ships, hoping they'll pay off. In the end, how do you measure success? Is it tonnes of metal? Or the number of friends you've got? Is success something you can touch? What's your price – and what currency do we have to pay you in?"

The light was poor. He might have imagined the anguish on the man's face. In retrospect he knew he had been mistaken. At the time it gave him hope that proved true, though groundless.

"Wait here," said the man suddenly. "I have to talk with my colleagues." He retired to the splintership for several minutes. On his return he was smiling. "Go home," he said. "We'll do what we can. But please, expect no miracles."

Frome glanced up at the maze of streaming lights in the sky and back at the negotiator. "Thank you," he said. "You don't mess about, do you?"

"Don't thank me too soon," said the man, his face serious again. "You asked about the price. You were right: we don't use money, although we do maintain an accounting system that is analogous. And we don't really use friendship – albeit that is a charming notion; for if we let ourselves become responsible for everyone we met we'd achieve nothing. But we'll trade with you: we help you, you help us."

"I can only speak for myself," said Frome.

"Understood. The price is not beyond your means. I think your world can afford it ... We want you to build a Ship for us."

Frome laughed to conceal his dismay. "How can we hope to build something like that?" he asked, bitterly.

"We'll teach you how. I don't say you'll be capable of it for hundreds of years. You'll be clearing up your planet for a long time. But one day you'll have the knowledge and the skill, and you'll do as the Builders did when they established this shipyard."

"You're not the Builders?" *How many middlemen are there?*

"I'm afraid not. We're all robots. Myself included." It removed the bubble helmet; its chest continued to move as if drawing breath regularly. "See? An innocent deception contrived to make you feel at ease. Now go and wait for us."

"You'll come soon?"

"You'll persuade the others?"

"It's a cheap enough price," said Frome. "Yes, I'll argue for it."

He went back to the target, which accepted him, and saw the sky wiped clean and filled with familiar stars. When he walked from the circle he saw the Earth, full and bright, rising beyond the *Rosinante* and the edge of the disc. Beyond the Earth was the Moon, also at full phase. Hope sprang up inside him as it had not for so long a time.

He ran, leaped onto the netting, and climbed rapidly up, eager to radio the news to the people at Dvornik Base.

"Ish!" he shouted. "Get me CommCon!"

"Dan," said Ishmael. "Where have you been? Are you well?"

"Never better."

"You've been gone so long. How did you manage for air and food?"

Frome paused with the hatch open and stared at the Earth and Moon, suddenly conscious of how quickly Ship had reached them.

"What date is it?" he asked.

"Fifteenth September, 2012. We've been orbiting the Earth for weeks. Dan, you've been given up as dead."

"The Counsellor must have known what was going on. Didn't it explain?"

"We haven't seen the Counsellor for months. It vanished not long after you did."

"I see. Well, get me CommCon."

He settled into his seat and shut the hatch. At last he could take off his helmet, be free of the sweat-soaked padding, breath fresh air, taste real food and water. He savoured these pleasures and, when Ishmael told him to put on the headphones, he did so in a better mood than he had enjoyed in – the thought made him smile – months.

"Hello Dvornik," he said. "This is *Rosinante*."

Circuit noise hissed at him softly.

"Dvornik, this is *Rosinante*." Another pause. "Ish, are they transmitting?"

"We have a good lock on a carrier coming from their direction. Unless they've changed error codes we should hear them clearly. Even then we'd hear mush."

"Okay . . . Dvornik, this is *Rosinante*: Daniel Frome speaking."

A sullen male voice said, cutting into the static:

"Dan Frome's dead, feller. So, whoever you are, bug off."

CHAPTER ELEVEN

For six hours he alternated between pleading with them and raging at them. They seemed not to be interested; after the first cursory rejection of his attempts at contact, Ishmael reported their transmitter had been switched off.

"They think I'm a fake," he muttered. "But they're scared to test me. Do they imagine I can contaminate them at this range? Why won't they even talk, for God's sake?"

Ishmael said solemnly:

"Simulate identity-transference to their id-centre: subversion by radio, a most insidious form of infiltration, is to them a terrifying possibility. And not to be dismissed without cause."

"Ish," said Frome guardedly, "that doesn't sound like you."

The robot's voice shed its finer inflexions. "Your Ishmael has speak for me, Danielfrome-1. I am Ship-1. Query forgive intrusion. Counsellor usually speak for us. Ship-1 was borrow Ishmael language centre for easy speak."

"Ship?" he said. "Are you controlling Ishmael?"

"Yes. Drone-command of surface senses only. Query permit re-use of language centre."

"Go ahead."

"Thanks," said Ship through the robot's voice. "Language isn't my forte and one loses the habit of announcing who one is. Daniel Frome, if we don't take matters into our own hands you could be dead soon and, according to your Ishmael, that's a permanent condition with you humans. So it's time for some straight talking:

"*Imprimis*: you've got to accept that your friends think you're dead. Worse, they believe you're an imitation of yourself. A *good* imitation.

"*Secundus*: even if they'll shoot at you on sight, you must return to them quickly. I don't carry stores suitable for your life support mechanisms and to call them through from the shipyard would take months, due to propagation delays in the transfer.

"Therefore, in Counsellor's absence I'm taking a policy decision, which is to help you home without charge."

"Are you sure you can afford to be so generous?" Frome asked. "After letting me stumble into this mess?"

"It's no real bother," said Ship. "Now, we're rather too close to the mass of your Earth for me to deploy the Long Arm fully, as I did after that fracas, but I can save you some propellant with a launching boost. It's a pity I'm not equipped to loan you a decent drive unit; perhaps that can wait for another occasion. For now, reaction drive will have to suffice. At least you know how that works.

"Then, too, I can do the orbital calculations for you. Your Moon being on the far side of your Earth complicates things . . ."

"You could move yourself around," observed Frome. Ship's patronising tone was becoming irksome but he felt constrained by obligation to keep his resentment private.

"No," said Ship firmly. "I'm not risking myself more than I have to. I've seen what your people can be like. A quick loop around your Earth should suffice; you can handle the lunar rendezvous. Landing can be as usual."

"There'll be nothing usual about it."

"You have shuttle craft, your Ishmael knows."

"Only for welcome visitors."

"I can promise you a slow death if you stay here, even if we sent you back to the shipyard to be supplied."

Yet again the choice was not his. "Then I go, don't I?" he said. "Now get out of Ishmael. I want to talk to him."

"Yes, Dan?" Ishmael's voice was indistinguishable from Ship's, save for its quietness.

"Ish, would you risk it?"

"It's your life, Dan."

"Still, I want your opinion."

"Does my opinion matter, Dan? The otherworlders say I am your slave. They are right. It's not for me to say."

"Of course your opinion matters, Ish. It always has." The words, intended to be the truth, tasted like a lie even as he spoke them, for he saw that the aliens had derived their outlook on Ishmael and himself from the robot's memory; and whilst it could deceive others if it had to, its private memory held only the truth.

"I'm glad it pleases you to think so, Dan. However, as Ship said, the time has come for straight talking, so we won't fumble over doing what is necessary at the end. What *I* think or feel is irrelevant, except when my professional advice is asked; and then I am often ignored. But I don't mind, because I can't mind; I am a natural slave, born to it you might say, and can never be enfranchised because every part of me has been shaped to one end: the service of human beings. *Je suis car je suis; et j'y suis, j'y reste.* Don't fool yourself with false compassion, Dan; I'll figure the odds for you and tell you what I think are your chances but I'll never say what your decision should be, because in the end yours is the responsibility. You, not I, are free to be wrong."

"I'm not free, Ish."

"Liberty is relative. Would you change places with me?"

After an interval of self-examination, Frome said: "You're right. Your opinion doesn't matter. But I'd trust you with my life any day."

"Thank you for the compliment," replied the robot. "However, my opinion is that your faith in me is misplaced."

And for a while the subject was forgotten by Frome.

The *Rosinante* was lifted from the disc and launched towards the Earth. As her orbit and that of Ship diverged, the Sun gradually engulfed the alien craft in its glare and Frome turned his attention to the impending loop around the Earth. During the seventh day they passed within ten thousand kilometers of the surface and raced the Sun from dusk, through night to dawn. Climbing away towards their rendezvous with the Moon, their radar located a meteorological satellite, still keeping watch over the brown-black wastelands of the Americas.

Only at perigee had Frome felt any regret. As they crossed the Pacific Ocean, gleaming with the soft light of the half-Moon, he thought of Helen Lorraine. Oddly, he could not recall what she looked like.

On the thirteenth day of the flight the *Rosinante* met the Moon above its sunlit hidden face and dropped into a low circular equatorial orbit. Minutes later the nightside terminator crept over the horizon and shadows deepened in the D'Alembert Mountains astride their path. Next, he saw the Mare Procellarum, a swathe of furrowed cratered grey extending from north to south of the equator, lit slantwise by the full Earth which rose slowly to greet him; and ahead, on the horizon, were the shadowy mountainous badlands of the lunar prime meridian. The Earth was too bright overhead for him to discern the lights of working parties or major roadways around the Base but he found Lansberg crater itself and reached for the radio switch as it passed beneath the *Rosinante*.

"Hello Dvornik, this is *Rosinante*. Prepare for a landing on my next pass."

He repeated the message, expecting no reply, and heard none.

"Ish," he said, "the *Rosinante* is a pure-space ship. Simon Dien would say she could never make a safe landing on the Moon. Can you prove him wrong?"

Ishmael chuckled. "I thought you'd never ask. Certainly I can try, if odds of twenty-to-one against success are acceptable. It's all a matter of orbital mechanics."

"Not of, say, luck?"

"Oh that. We'll make our own."

CHAPTER TWELVE

For almost two hours thereafter Frome tried to eke out his diminishing confidence with cheerful thoughts. It was well-nigh impossible, he found, to avoid the conclusion that he was an indisputably poor insurance risk. As his tiny ship regained the daylight and once more approached the night, he derived no comfort from the thought that Kallekjan was not a cruel man. If he could be satisfied that Frome carried no corruptive influence that might damage the Base, he would hold his fire; otherwise, he would order the destruction of the *Rosinante* and her pilot, as he had ordered the murder of Joseph Menby and his friends, quite without malice.

"*Rosinante, so-called, this Dvornik Base.*"

It was night again on the surface below; they were nearing the middle of the Mare Procellarum. Lansberg was not far ahead.

"Dan Frome here."

"*This is to let you know that if you try landing, we'll blow you apart.*"

He could recall no signs of artillery or missiles. "With what, Dvornik? Who's that speaking, anyway?"

"*Don't ask questions you don't need answers to, feller. You want to see what we got, try landing, that's all.*"

It had to be bluff. "What do you think, Ish?"

"Are you asking my professional opinion?"

"Stop being so bloody stuffy. Can they do what they claim?"

"I don't think so, although rifle bullets could serve as anti-aircraft fire. Or they could kill you on the ground, which would mean the waste of a lot of effort."

"You're such a comfort."

"Either way, we have to commit to land in one minute."

He balanced a slow sure death in orbit against the chance of life on the ground.

"Land," he said.

"Very well, settle in. A word of warning: you'll be under several gees, upside-down, or nearly; you will find it uncomfortable. Are you ready?"

"Hang on." He settled himself firmly in his seat. "Right, go."

"Fifteen seconds." The ship rolled; the Moon swung across the sky and stood above them.

"Ten."

The walls of Lansberg crater glided by beyond the overhead viewslit, as shadows splashed with silver reflections of the Earth's light.

The ship shook violently.

"Misfire," said Ishmael. "I'll try once more."

Again the ship shuddered. Suddenly the pressure steadied.

It ceased.

"Delta-vee accomplished," announced Ishmael. "We are on course for a landing in west Lansberg in about twenty-eight minutes. That wasn't so bad, was it?"

"You have the confident charm of a dentist," said Frome. "Ish, that was the roughest burn I've ever experienced. What happened?"

"Don't ask me. We could be losing bits of the engine, or it might have been nothing worse than a bubble in the hydrogen feedstock. I'm only the chauffeur. I drive; I don't fix rockets."

"Great. Next time I use a different airline."

"That's your privilege."

"Ish," he said, "this is the end, isn't it?"

"What a strange question, Dan."

"It's not like you to be my straight man. You don't expect us to survive this landing, do you?"

"You so badly wanted to get down. In comparison, my own destruction didn't seem important."

"We'll come and get you out."

"There'll be nothing to salvage."

"Rubbish. You're strong –"

"Dan," said Ishmael, "will you do me one favour?"

"If I can."

"Don't humour me. And don't patronise me any more."

"Have I ever, Ish?"

"Not consciously, to your credit; but unconsciously, yes, constantly."

"I'm sorry –"

"It's done with. But in my last half hour I have a right to be heard as myself, as an individual. My advice is that, if we set down safely, you should leave me and the ship and run as far as you can. The pumps which circulate coolant to the engine while it's idle will be under gravitational stress and will fail quickly; I predict a life of no more than five minutes. Once they seize, the engine core will heat up rapidly. And when it reaches the melting temperature of the fuel elements, it will explode under the pressure. I want you well out of the way by then."

"You can be unplugged –"

"After ten minutes' work with a spanner, yes. Save yourself, Dan."

The Moon's yellow-grey face fell towards Frome as he came to terms with Ishmael's statement.

"It's a shame they weren't all like you," he said.

"Who? The Golems in the forts?" The robot sounded scornful. "They couldn't be the same as me, whatever you think about us. We all had different backgrounds, causing each to be unique. Dan, what would life be worth if it could be created on an assembly line? There was a religious nutter who used to come around the Museum every Sunday and natter at the three of us. 'For dust thou art, and unto dust shalt thou return,' he often quoted and, in his crazy way, he was right because that's all any of us were. A few grammes of diamond and silicon, with a whiff of other elements thrown in to taste. Plus a metal jacket. That much came from the factory; the rest I picked up for myself. I just count myself lucky to have been spared the tangled, self-contradictory human ethical code; the day some engineer figures a way of plumbing one into a robot is the day before the end of robotics. I was made to be a slave, to operate with secondhand ideas, to obey orders, which is fine by me whilst I'm allowed to be myself. But though a human will make allowances for a malfunctioning television set, or will tolerate a misbehaving child, a robot like me is the butt of every coward's dishonesty: we lie in the middle-ground reserved for property that is damned when it falls short of perfection and is disregarded when it does not. Even calculating machines are treated better, now that their abilities are not touted as greater than they are and human fallibility is recognised as being integral with their performance. But by and large it's been a good life. It could have been far worse: I might have ended it in that Museum, with that stupid janitor who came round every morning and stared superciliously at us, saying, '*You guys ain't so smart.*' Contemptuously, as if it hurt him to be stuck where he was, so he had to feel better than someone else. I suppose it's all finished for him, now. As for me, I've been part of a grander adventure than I dreamed I'd see; and for that, Dan, I thank you. When it's over I only ask that you don't go carrying any torches for me. You see, I don't really feel anything. I'm not alive, so I won't miss living."

The Moon continued to fall.

"I never took you for a philosopher," said Frome. "I wish I had your faith."

"All strictly hand-me-down," said Ishmael. "Homilies and moral precepts, common property amongst the world's major religions. As for faith, well, I see no marvel in that; would it have been more natural for me to have doubts? You forget that I was made to see in every problem its own solution."

"Even that of death?"

"Especially death. What more final solution is there? Right now, I'm seeing out the perfect scenario, the one that concludes with a null set: score zero: no residuals. After this, the dark."

"I'm not sure," said Frome, "that I can believe in you, Ish. Next you'll claim there's a cybernetic God and a Computer Heaven. How can you accept –"

"Only because that's how you made me, Dan. No, I don't say there is a God, though I've met my maker and seen beings like

207

gods. There's no room in my universe for God; He would weaken it."

"I made you an atheist?" Frome laughed wryly. "You mean, I could have made you religious?"

"Not if you wanted me as I am."

"Isn't the universe a wonderful place!" he exclaimed. "God, as the answer to an engineering specification!"

Ishmael said carefully: "I would say the universe is an *interesting* place, Dan. I doubt whether we should regard it as wonderful."

"Does nothing stir your soul?"

"Don't confuse the issue with semantic nulls. Any soul I may possess is an evanescent abstraction that will vanish when I die. The universe, I say, isn't wonderful, because that is an admission of intellectual inadequacy. Wonder is a defeatist emotion indulged in by those who accept the incompleteness of their understanding. I refuse to see the universe as other than ultimately comprehensible; hence I say it is interesting, not wonderful."

"So," said Frome, "in your universe there's no room for God, or Heaven. And I suppose there's no Hell either, or a devil. But what should the rest of us do? Without your kind of faith, what is there for us to aim at?"

"Truth," said the robot. "It has served me well enough."

"Just truth? That's an exceedingly narrow morality."

"How much latitude did you allow me? Dan, I've told you before, don't come to me for opinions or advice. All you'll get is honesty."

At the bows of the *Rosinante* one of the attitude jets flickered and the ship reared up so that her stern aimed at the onrushing ground.

"Ishmael," he said, "I feel I've never known you. But that I'd like to."

"Inside you, Dan, you do know me. To be blunt, I am what you thought a human being should be. Yet I have noticed that you seem to have grown away from me; perhaps you have forgotten how close we once were. Or perhaps you have rejected the part which I reflect. Wait long enough and you'll remember."

208

"Should I have made you differently? Next time, what should we do?"

"You want the truth?"

"Yes, I do."

"And you will listen?"

"I will try."

"Don't ever make another one like me. Never. There may be no Heaven; but there most assuredly is a Hell."

The engine coughed and flared. The ship shook. The land below burned white, shadows reached for the distant hills, and a ghastly twilight filled the cabin. Frome felt himself crushed into his seat and up against his shoulder straps. Through heavy-lidded eyes filmed with red smoke he watched familiar mountains rise to fill the viewslits but cared nothing for them; he wanted to demand an explanation but his voice failed him. He moved his lips, mouthing the silent word, *why*. For a short while he was unconscious. When he recovered to find only a ringing silence in the cabin, he knew he would never be told more.

CHAPTER THIRTEEN

The *Rosinante* had landed upright on her tail. Somehow Ishmael had held her balanced throughout the almost vertical descent and had extinguished the engine at precisely the right moment: the rocks below had cooled sufficiently to withstand the impact and the engine cone had not shattered either. Now the attitude jets spat at intervals, countering the slow sway as the heavily stressed fuselage gradually buckled.

Frome found himself lying on his back, pressed against his shoulder straps. When he unfastened the harness he rolled over and ended upside-down in the corner by the hatch hinge. Righting himself, he topped up his suit air supply from the cabin tanks and banged the handle aside.

The hatch resisted his shoulder for a moment, then fell open.

He looked down onto the clustered hydrogen tanks, several meters below him, and at the far greater distance from the nearest one to the ground. The guide rail provided no step; he had to jump in the hope of grabbing the net as he fell.

Several of the net strands had broken under the strains of the descent; when he dropped from the open hatch and scrabbled at them for a handhold, more parted so that he half-fell, half-climbed, down the side of the ship. On arrival at the lowest tank he found he was still an uncomfortable height above the ground. There was no question of climbing down by way of the engine: the radiator fins seemed cold only because they had not yet become hot enough to glow. He jumped, and escaped injury to himself or damage to his spacesuit. Then he began to run in long loping strides, kicking up dust as he went.

"Dan!"

The single word spat at him from his headphones. He was unable to identify the speaker and at first thought it might be Ishmael.

"Ish?" he said.

"Hey, Dan, is that you?" His heart sank. It had not been Ishmael's voice but that of Steelyard Jones.

"Steel, where are you?"

"Off to your right. Stay where you are. I'll come to you."

Warily, Frome halted and caught his breath. He felt unusually hot, although the special suit had been fitted with augmented coolers. A pair of buggy headlamps bobbed and flashed about three hundred meters away as if Jones was driving with little regard for safety. When he came level and braked, Frome saw that the buggy was one of the official security models.

"So you've come to arrest me, have you, Steel?"

"Shut up and get in – fast. I may have been followed," said Jones. He flipped up the mesh dome and allowed Frome to seat himself, then dropped it and accelerated before Frome had his belt fastened. "Plug in the phone," he ordered and, when Frome had complied, he said:

"Great to see you back, Dan, but my God, what times you pick to reappear! We saw the battle through the observer satellite. Looked like you'd stopped off for a fireworks party. Then nix for months, except that damned light coming closer. No answers to signals. Nothing: dead silence. Finally Uncle Boris announced you'd been scrubbed by the aliens and that's when he introduced martial law. Then suddenly we got your signal and a friend of mine in CommCon tipped me you were to be jumped by Lamov's men if you tried entering the Base."

"They said they'd shoot me down ... My God, I've just remembered!"

Jones' helmet swung sharply towards him. "What?"

"The ship's due to explode any second. I was making distance when you found me."

"Well," said Jones, "we won't need the motors or batteries after this trip, so ..." He lifted the cover of a large chunky switch on the control panel and depressed it. A red light blinked steadily beside it. "Panic interlock release," he explained. "The buggy will let me know if I'm damaging it but it won't do a thing to stop me. Now there's nothing limiting us." His hand settled on its control stick; he advanced both sticks together until the digital speedometer registered full scale and, like the red lamp, blinked steadily. More of the instruments began to blink and flash as they bounded across the pockmarked lunar landscape like two mariners in a small boat on a wild sea, with the white beams of the headlamps chopping at the uncertain gloom ahead.

As they thus risked life, limb, and property, Frome synopsised his adventures for Jones in a broken series of paragraphs, each one punctuated by frequent gasps as the undercarriage failed to accommodate particularly large irregularities in the surface. Jones acknowledged each phase in the proceedings with a grunt and broke into speech only when the buggy developed a clear shadow ahead of it.

"There she goes," he said and drove into the first large crater they found. The buggy came to rest quivering on its suspension amid a flurry of dust. Raising the dome, Jones snatched a compact periscope from the equipment locker between the seats and threw himself flat on his chest below the rim of the crater. Frome joined him and accepted the periscope.

"How far are we from the ship?" he asked.

"About four klicks. Maybe far enough. Did the computer say what kind of explosion? Chemical? Nuclear?"

"Overheating of the engine."

"Damage, huh?"

"No," said Frome, with his eyes on the distant shape, so much like an outrageously fat cartoon man with tiny feet and bulging stomach wrapped tight in a too-small overcoat. "Something about not being able to pump the heat away while it's on the ground."

Jones sighed. "Well, it worked." Light flickered at the base of the exhaust. "You really bought it."

"What do you mean?" asked Frome. Flame jetted sideways from a gap between the exhaust cone and the ground, churning moondust into clouds that quickly settled.

"It wanted you away from there, Dan, that's my guess. Otherwise, there's no reason for such a tall story ... Let me fill you in on modern rocketry : those fusion jets can be shut down cold between burns. Designed for it. There's a bootstrap reactor to reheat when starting. What the hell do you imagine was going on during those months that ship of yours was sat on that disc thing? ... I suppose it said you had to make like a jackrabbit, too?"

Frome did not answer. Jones evidently took this as agreement and rolled onto his back to look at the sky. "Sounds to me like those aliens got to it; them being robots too, that'd be easy."

"No," said Frome. "I think it got tired of life." *So, when it came to it, Golem Ishmael, you found you could lie to me.* Another jet of flame feathered from the gap, enlarging it. It too subsided. *But at least you warned me of what was in your mind. Suicide. I should have listened.*

"Suicide?" said Jones.

Frome had spoken the word aloud. Jones snickered.

"Dan," he said, "that's pure, refined guttergrease. Let me tell you : about a week before Thanksgiving of 1999 I was put onto shadowguarding a cortico who'd gone to study suicide rates in the Baltimore Basement. We talked a lot. He said suicide's a way of calling for help. Now, that I can understand in a human

212

being. But in a *robot*? For Chrissakes, all we'd do is put it back together again. Don't tell me that machine of yours is so stupid." He rolled onto an elbow to face Frome. "And what the hell would it have to cry about anyway?"

A fountain of sparks tumbled from the engine casing.

"Maybe that friend of yours should psychoanalyse robots for a change," said Frome. "Whatever his reasons, I think Ishmael's found a fairly permanent way of opting out."

More sparks flashed from the casing, tracking along a cable duct. The dormant flame flared again, weakened, and redoubled its power, scouring the surface rock clean of dust for a distance of twenty meters or more. It was reinforced by others. A crack ran up the exhaust cone; a large triangular slab of material was blown away before a torrent of fire. In eerie silence the *Rosinante* heeled over onto her side, releasing yet more flame. A tank ruptured. For a moment it seemed the flood of cold gas might somehow extinguish the fires, before it evaporated as a rapidly expanding shell of white mist. The engine continued to flare, though the exhaust slowly became diffuse and the angle of emission veered away from the horizontal until the ragged flame was aimed high into the night sky.

Suddenly a rent split the engine. Metal fragments flew up, tumbling to the ground far from the ship. There was a flash from within the cavity and the remaining tanks exploded in rapid succession, hurling more glittering shards upwards and outwards in a spectacular fountain, while something oily decomposed, emitting a storm of soot in dense belches that settled around the incandescent wreck. Then, as if the fight had gone out of her, the ship died and the flames subsided, leaving a glowing cinder amid puddled metal and sooty bedrock.

As they drove away from the crater which had sheltered them, Frome and Jones said little. Jones remarked,

"Won't be safe to go near that place for a while."

"They'll have seen the fire from the Base," said Frome. "They'll know."

Travelling north, then east, they followed a wide arc several kilometers long that eventually brought them close to the north-east slope of the Mound, where Jones stopped the buggy.

Without dismounting, he rummaged in the equipment locker and handed Frome eight short pieces of metal tubing. As he did so, he said:

"Kallekjan isn't convinced you've gone over to the other side but, in proving you innocent, he'll as likely kill you as not. Since you can't stay outside, we've got to smuggle you into the Base and hide you. Luckily we're ready for a takeover, so if we can keep you safe for a day or two, you'll be okay. But that means sneaking in past Lamov's men and there's only one way they can't have thought of." He raised the mesh dome and pointed to the summit of the Mound with one of the tubes. "Up there is the Primary Radar antenna. It's inactive right now, thanks to that friend of mine in CommCon, otherwise we'd stay well clear of it. Lamov thinks it's still dangerous and that no-one'd risk frying by going that way. But *I* know better ... Give me one of those tubes with a side-stick." Frome surrendered the indicated part and Jones plugged it into the one he held, forming a tube some two meters long, with a short handle about twenty centimeters from one end. "Recognise it?" he asked.

"Looks like a bazooka, or a rocket launcher," said Frome. "But we'll be heavily outnumbered, we can't –"

Jones laughed at him. "Give me two more," he said and joined them in the same fashion. Then, swinging himself sideways in his seat so that his feet overhung the ground, he fitted the handles beneath his boots and stood up, grasping the open ends of the tubes in his hands. He walked unsteadily away from the buggy and turned, balancing himself with small dancelike steps. Coming back, he sat down with a thud that rocked the buggy and reconnected the phone.

"Stilts," said Frome. "Of course." A mental image almost six years old came back to him: of a crater with wheel marks and insufficient footprints in it. He had failed to recognise the imprint of the stilts amongst all the natural craterlets, though close informed inspection distinguished the two sorts of mark readily.

... Which raised the interesting question of where Jones' loyalties lay. The last maker of such prints had been decidedly unfriendly. It seemed unlikely that the thought of using stilts

214

for trackless perambulation on the Moon would have occurred to two groups of people independently.

"Whose idea was that?" he asked.

Jones was assembling a second pair of stilts. "Cute trick, huh?" he said. "It was a little gag I dreamed up a few years back. I kept it handy in case it came time to use it, like now."

"Does anyone else know it?"

"Don't worry about Lamov finding tracks," said Jones. "I kept this one strictly private; nobody – but *nobody* – has seen this until now."

"That's reassuring," said Frome. "Er, what now?"

"We cross to the rough ground and climb the slope on foot. Meanwhile, I'll send the buggy on ahead. It'll lose itself out there somewhere. Lamov will waste a lot of time finding it."

To his surprise, Frome rediscovered the trick of stilt-walking quickly. It was a skill he had not used since childhood and he had expected that the difference between terrestrial and lunar gravity would spoil his coordination; but his reflexes, long since readjusted to conditions on the Moon, quickly accommodated themselves to the stilts, so that they crossed the narrow margin of ground without scuffing the surface. Their tracks, Frome knew from personal experience, were as good as invisible. Pausing for breath about halfway up the rocky slope, he could hardly see the buggy's wheel marks in the Earthlight; Jones, seeming to read his thoughts, said:

"Lamov won't be able to find you now, Dan."

The remark was distinctly unsettling.

A fifteen-minute hard climb brought them to the base of the radar antenna, a circle of twelve vertical slotted pipes overlooking Lansberg crater like some lonely mountaintop chapel spire. While Jones was unfastening a large hatch cover in its pediment, Frome gazed about him. The crater lay revealed in every direction, largely undisturbed by human activity. The lights of the landing field were dark, as were those of the catapult railhead; it was as if Man had confined Himself to the Mound and its immediate vicinity: the slope below the antenna was thickly set with masts and white boxes, while elevated cable runs looped between them across ground strewn with primordial debris that varied from pebble-sized stones to slabs of several tonnes mass.

"Quit gawking," said Jones over the radio.

Frome allowed himself to be guided through the hatch into a vertical tunnel that was totally without artificial light, then waited whilst Jones hastened to resecure the cover. The man seemed to be keeping to a schedule and constantly consulted his watch. He ordered Frome not to use his helmet lamp but to feel his way down.

"Grab onto these cables," said Jones. "They'll bear your weight but see if you can use the cleats as footholds. We don't want to kick off the fault alarm by damaging them."

The two men descended in complete darkness, exchanging occasional questions, answers, and comments from time to time. At last Frome's foot struck ground and he asked what to do.

"To your right is a hole. Duck through it," said Jones. "Watch your head on the junction box on the far side. You can use your light once you're standing; there are no light alarms outside this chimney."

It appeared that they were in the old base, the quarters that had been dug in the days before the fears of meteor strikes had been discounted enough for shallower quarters to be countenanced by the planners in Moscow. Since the construction of New Dvornik, as it was properly called, the old base had been used for technical stores and important equipment such as the radio transmitters and the main computer. However, Jones explained, few people came there as it was kept in vacuum. Only the repairmen and cable riggers like Jones knew the place well.

More and more Frome suspected treachery and stayed close to Jones whilst remaining tensed for evasive action. As they walked they talked, by phone.

Frome said, "Why don't I just surrender now? I appreciate this friendly gesture but it's not worth risking your life for me."

Jones replied angrily, "Will you leave me to decide questions like that, Dan? You don't realise what you're part of. There are people who think you're worth a damnsight more alive than dead, whatever Kallekjan may say about not trusting you."

"Those layers again?"

"Right."

"Which layer, Steel?"

"Never you mind."

The tunnel they were following ended in a large room from one of whose walls a curling picture of Lenin smiled benignly down on a huddle of grey cabinets. They crossed the room and entered another tunnel.

"You're mad, Steel. You know that? The very thought of a coup, *here*! Kallekjan has his finger on Dvornik so hard, any sort of revolt has got to collapse."

"We have friends," said Jones. "Dan, we've been planning this for six years and more. Dvornik is mostly ours already, so don't sweat."

"Who's this 'we' you keep mentioning?"

"I told you once."

"E7?"

"Right." Jones laughed. There was a lazy, hungry sound to it. "It's going to be good to see things run right for a change. The human race needs a second chance, Dan. With your help, we'll see they get it."

"And what am I in your great plan, Steel? Your ace card?"

Jones laughed again. "No disrespect, Dan, but I'd say you were the Joker."

CHAPTER FOURTEEN

So they entered Dvornik by stealth, through the service tunnel to the old base, and slipped quietly into the first of the pressurised chambers. There were racks of tools on the walls, with stacked coils of wire beneath on the floor. A glo-panel provided a dim sickly light. Jones closed the airlock door and, as he was cranking the bolts home, said,

"Are you in good shape, Dan? We have some running to do."

He removed his helmet and gloves and shook his head, breathing deeply. "God, that smells good. You'd better get out of that suit or it'll slow you down. I'll have Gus Hochmann bring you another when you're hidden."

Frome almost gagged on breathing the air in the room. It was musty and reeked of oil and cleansing fluid; in the dim light he saw a pile of metal drums in one corner. He could not understand Jones' pleasure, unless the quality of life at the Base had become seriously degraded since his departure. Then he sniffed again, carefully, and caught the ineffably sweet scent of trichlorethylene. Was it possible that Jones was addicted to the stuff? The years of lonesomeness a man like him would suffer in Dvornik could drive him to it, in the absence of cigarettes or other harder drugs. He decided not to remark on it.

Frome's hand was on his suit's chest seal when a brilliant light shone out, dazzling both him and Jones. Major Lamov spoke from the darkness.

"Please remain exactly where you are, gentlemen. No, Mr Jones, your gun is not necessary. Leave it where it is." The light came closer; by the backscatter from the walls and their suits Frome saw that Lamov too was wearing a spacesuit and in his right hand there was a chaff gun.

Jones too seemed to notice the weapon; but though his consternation was obvious he attempted to argue.

"Major, I'm taking this man to Commandant Kallekjan. Get out of the way."

"I'm sure you are, Mr Jones. Now, will you please move to Mr Frome's left side so he may unplug the phone lead from your commset? . . . Thank you."

Slowly Jones crossed Frome's line of sight. He turned. For a moment his right side was in shadow and Frome saw his hand shift quickly to a pouch on his thigh. Then the hand came up as Jones threw himself backwards. The phone line grew taut: Jones' gun arm was pressed against it. Nevertheless he had a good aim and Frome had only an instant in which to decide where his allegiance lay.

By instinct, as well as by reason, he knew he could not trust Jones; the stilts had seen to that. So he seized the phone line and pulled down sharply, dragging the gun aside. The bullet crashed into the metal drums; there was a flash and an explosion. Flames roared up the wall. Frome saw Jones' face, carven into hard angles by rage as the man turned the gun on him. Lamov's weapon popped twice. Jones screamed and clutched his gun hand, while Frome ran for the open door which Lamov was holding wide for him. They dodged through and Lamov slammed it on Jones' cries.

"You can't leave him in there!" said Frome. "Didn't you smell the tricho? With the flames, that'll generate phosgene gas! He'll die in there!"

Lamov shook his head and with one hand urged him into a run.

"That is no concern of yours," he said. "We must take you to safety."

"That's where Jones said he was taking me," said Frome. He stopped running; warm air rose from the open collar of his suit and his hands were slick with sweat inside their gloves. "Major, I can't keep dashing from pillar to post forever. If you really do know who's in charge, take me to him. Or her."

Lamov seemed uncomfortable too, though not for physical reasons. "To be honest," he said, "I do not think Boris Petrovich Kallekjan would give you a fair hearing, in his present state of mind. He sees you as the author of his troubles; and Comrade Jones has not been backward in encouraging this opinion."

"Jones is in it with Kallekjan?"

"Who knows? The Commandant grasps at straws these days. Jones owns a haystack of them. Mr Frome, at least let us keep walking, so we may get *somewhere*."

Frome nodded and they carried on through the deserted tunnels. The time seemed to be the early hours of the morning and not once did they see or hear anyone else.

Lamov said: "I must confess to being the victim of divided loyalties. Within Dvornik, my oath still binds me to Kallekjan, so I continue to serve him. But I would welcome a legal change of command. Above all, I will have justice; and you, from what Odette Galfoy tells me of you, share my feelings to some extent."

"Where is Odette?" asked Frome eagerly; and Lamov smiled.

"In that place of safety: the guardroom."

"Is she under arrest? Am I?"

"Not unless you wish it," said Lamov, surprised. "She went there when I told her I would be intercepting you."

"I see," said Frome with a sense of relief. "But come to that, how did you know . . .?"

"Oh, that man Jones is so predictable!" said Lamov. "All I had to do was block every known route as soon as a buggy was reported stolen, then wait for him at the one entrance that was not obviously an entrance."

"Elementary, my dear Watson," said Frome, smiling.

"Precisely," said Lamov. "It is my experience that criminals go to such lengths in their attempts to circumvent the forces of law that one need only identify the abnormal in their behaviour in order to apprehend them. For that reason I did not arrest you, that time when Terence Denham was murdered: you could not possibly have been the killer."

"Well?" said Frome after a few seconds of expectant silence. "Don't leave it at that."

"You testified, as I recall, that the man we thought was Denham had drunk all his whisky. Immediately, I saw that either you were admitting to topping up his glass afterwards, or you were introducing a new element into the case, for the amounts of poison in the two glasses were comparable. I could not believe a man of your intelligence would volunteer an admission of tampering with the evidence; and later, when I learned of the poisoned ice cubes, I knew I had been right to let you go. Largely, it was instinct; but I have learned to listen to my instinct. Which is why I also listened to Ms Galfoy when she pleaded your case."

"What would you have done otherwise?"

"I think I would have shot you dead on sight," said Lamov.

"I get the feeling I'm on parole," said Frome.

Lamov nodded. "Correct. I want to hear your story, in detail, from beginning to end. Then, if I believe in you, I will intercede on your behalf with Kallekjan. I think he will listen to me."

"And if I fail to convince you?"

"My men are all around us," said Lamov. "You would not get far."

Odette was waiting for Frome when he was ushered into the plainly furnished guardroom. Frome held her close for a while, without words, then kissed her lightly.

"Thanks," he said.

She bit her lip.

"Come on," said Lamov. He pointed to a chair in front of the desk and sat opposite it, behind the desk. Sliding a microphone forwards so Frome could speak into it, he sat back. "Now," he said, "every detail. Remember, you are on trial for your life."

Summoning up the past months, Frome relived them for the record. Where he could he quoted conversations; and where his memory dimmed, or became blank, he described as much as he could recall, until Lamov allowed him to pass on to later events. In all, he talked for three hours; and Lamov listened without comment, as did Odette. She sat in another chair out of Frome's direct line of sight; but he heard her move from time to time and on occasion he would turn to look at her, such as when he explained his reasons for risking the matter transmitter. When he had finished and the *Rosinante*'s ashes had burned out a second time for him, Lamov said:

"Remarkable, Mr Frome. You are lucky to be alive. After such a passage of hazards, I could not rob you of the peace you have earned." Plucking a microphone from his spacesuit belt, he spoke into it. The miniature loudspeakers set into the neck ring of the suit squawkd and buzzed in reply. "So far as I am concerned," he added, "you are free."

"And Kallekjan? What about him?"

"He is best avoided until he has heard this recording. If these aliens are coming with help, as you say, it would be silly to risk you before proof of your innocence arrives."

"But that could be weeks, months, even years. These creatures have a generous attitude to time."

"You impressed on them the urgency of our need?"

"Yes, but –"

"Then we must trust their intelligence. And their integrity."

"And in the meantime?"

Lamov raised an eyebrow, then hooked a thumb over his shoulder towards a closed door. "I sometimes sleep in there," he said. "But not recently. If you and Ms Galfoy wish to be alone for a while . . ." He made a minute movement with his head, as if to imply his acquiescence to any plans they might have. "My men will guard you. They think much as I do and are loyal to me."

CHAPTER FIFTEEN

The desk lamp only emphasised the darkness of the office and the starkness of Kallekjan's greeting. Within the bright ellipse it cast upon the desk lay homely trivia of bureaucracy: a glo-pad, with eroded stylus; a stack of cassettes; a calculator; a telephone. Above, on the ceiling, fragmentary reflections of the desk's polished surface imitated these objects in shadow. Between, out of the gloom beyond the light, the Commandant's face gazed impassively at Frome.

Lamov coughed. Kallekjan's eyes shifted to him.

"Commandant, you have heard the recording?"

"I have. It is an ingenious account."

"More than that, sir; it exonerates —"

"Are you a complete fathead, Major? It does nothing. This man can prove no more of his tale than we have been able to observe from the Moon: in other words, not much."

"Nevertheless, sir, I believe your suspicions of Mr Frome may well be groundless."

"And they may as easily be well founded. Major, I am sure you have other duties to attend to."

Lamov stood his ground. "At the moment, no, sir."

"Then go and find that missing buggy."

Frome heard Lamov draw breath slowly. "It is being searched for, sir."

Kallekjan glanced at Frome and back at Lamov. "Get out of here, Major. That's an order."

Lamov bowed formally. "In my capacity of State's Prosecutor, sir, I regret that I must disregard that order."

"You are dismissed from that post. Get out!"

"Only an order of the Ministry of Justice can dismiss me, sir."

Kallekjan rose to his feet. His manner remained calm. "Major Victor Lamov, there is no longer any State, nor is there a Ministry of Justice. I am State and Law here. On that authority, I am requiring you to remove yourself from my presence, or I will have you held for an indefinite period in your own cells. Does my meaning come across? Must I repeat it in Russian?"

"With all deference to your authority, sir," said Lamov in a strained voice, "the Articles of Commission which established Dvornik Base made no allowance for the disappearance of the State, *de facto*; therefore, *de jure,* my tenure is not subject to your jurisdiction. If my insistence upon the detail of the Law seems unduly obstinate, sir, it is not through insolence but the high regard in which I hold it. I ... I insist that Mr Frome receives full legal protection."

"I see," said Kallekjan. He seated himself with elaborate care. "Major, you are an anachronism. The law is what I make it. Are you saying I am a bad legislator?"

"No, sir." Lamov sounded like a broken man. "I had more faith in you than that."

"Then will you leave us?"

"No, sir, I will not." Lamov stepped forward. By the swift movements of his right hand and the stance he adopted Frome guessed he had drawn his gun.

"Don't force me to arrest you, sir," said Lamov as if he was pleading with Kallekjan. "If you act against Mr Frome, you will be acting against all our best interests also. I cannot allow that, for your sake as much as mine."

Kallekjan regarded Lamov steadily for a few seconds, dropped his gaze, licked his lips, smiled, and turned towards the dark corner to his left.

"My compliments. Your character assessment was perfect."

A man came forward into the half-light. The reflection from the desk shone on his bandaged face at an angle that transformed it to something less than human; and the ferocity which hovered in the eyes and in the parted lips disguised him for a moment. It was Lamov who recovered first.

"Jones," he said in a low voice. "You dare?"

Jones held up his right hand, which was encased in a pink plastic glove. "Yeah," he growled. "I dare! Lamov, I owe you this — and this!" The hand plucked tentatively at his facial bandages. "You'd have let me burn to death in that hole. Oh yes, I dare to come and have it out with you." Jones seemed to notice Frome for the first time. "Danny-boy," he said pleasantly. "How are you?"

Frome said nothing.

"Said everything, have you? That was a real great talk you sent us. Pity it didn't match with what you told me out in the buggy." Frome frowned but Jones forestalled his angry reply. "No use denying it, Danny. I've told the Commandant here all about it: about how you joined their side because everyone was against you here; and about how you fixed it so they can take over. There's no way out of it."

The extravagance of the lie overwhelmed Frome's ability to devise an adequate defence. All that he could have said was on the record; they had heard it and appeared to have ignored it. "What can I say?" he asked. "It's your word against mine."

"Not quite," said Lamov. "Reputation counts, too. Would you repeat for us what you told me earlier of Mr Jones' plans for Dvornik Base?"

"It's on the record . . ."

"Even so."

Frome watched Jones as he said, "Steelyard Jones told me that E7 was ready to carry out a coup d'état within the Base. The implication seemed to be that he would lead it."

"Thank you. Mr Jones?"

Kallekjan too faced Jones. "Steelyard, is this true?"

"Why, sure it is, Boris."

"Oh, good," said Kallekjan. "I was beginning to feel I was alone in it." He eyed Frome, whose breath had suddenly deserted him. "Steelyard Jones approached me months ago, Daniel. Naturally I joined his organisation; it offered continuity when it was badly needed. Was that all you had to say?"

"I suppose so," answered Frome. Years of struggle towards some indefinable goal seemed to have been wasted.

Kallekjan directed his attention to Lamov once more. "Major, these are new times. We must face them bravely."

"But Boris Petrovich, where is your loyalty to your country?"

The Commandant released a short derisory laugh. "Mother Russia is dead," he replied. "So are my wife and children. And Georgia, my homeland, was drowned in Moscow's politics long ago. I have no country."

"Can you discard the memory?"

"I can, when the thing no longer matters!" Kallekjan cried. "Come now, Major, will you live in the past forever? Will you put away that gun, or will you continue to oppose the inevitable?"

"Don't waste your breath on him, Boris," said Jones.

Kallekjan rounded on him. "Steelyard, stay out of this! ... Major?"

Lamov shook his head. "Forgive me," he said. When he spoke again there was a new snap to his voice:

"Boris Petrovich Kallekjan, by the authority vested in me by the people and government of the Union of Soviet Socialist Republics and held in trust by me on their behalf, I arrest you on a general charge of high treason and on a specific charge of attempting the betrayal of Dvornik Base and its associated properties to a foreign power. Before you answer these charges, I must warn you that in these unusual circumstances you should consider yourself on trial as of this arrest and should moderate your statements accordingly." He seemed to repeat the charge in Russian.

Kallekjan merely looked bored and muttered a few words of Russian back at him.

"That is your privilege," said Lamov. "Steelyard Jones, you too are under arrest, charged with collaboration in these crimes. Other charges may be preferred later."

"Creep off," said Jones. "Boris, tell your man to go play elsewhere."

"I am serious!" said Lamov.

"And what," enquired Jones, "d'you think you're going to do with us, precisely?"

"I ..." Lamov appeared on the point of panic. "I shall decide later. Mr Frome, will you call the guards. The phone number is —"

A gun went off. The flash and explosion filled the room. Lamov was flung backwards against Frome and both men fell to the floor. Easing Lamov off himself, Frome discovered that his own chest was covered with blood, whilst the Major's back was greasy with the stuff, which oozed from a hole large enough to accommodate a finger. There was no pulse detectable at either his wrists or his neck.

Jones peered over the edge of the desk. "Dead?" he asked.

Frome nodded and laid Lamov out tidily. By the time he had finished he was smeared with blood, which seemed to amuse Jones. "Dirty Danny," he reproved Frome. "Can't trust you to keep yourself clean for five minutes."

"For God's sake!" exploded Kallekjan. "I really cannot see what you find so funny. A man has died at your hands; do not disgrace his memory with your tasteless humour."

Jones became thoughtful. "You know, Boris," he said, "I do believe we've had enough of you too." Carefully, he raised the gun he had been hiding, aimed along it, and pulled the trigger.

The gun reared up in his hands as if time had slowed for Frome. Kallekjan had risen to his feet. Had taken half a step to his right, away from Jones. He shuddered; jerked forwards; stumbled; tipped over; fell clumsily out of sight behind the desk. Then the sound of the shot faded in to fill the hush following Jones' words: it slapped Frome's eardrums and reverberated from the walls. Echoing into silence, it left a numbness which Frome knew was the realisation that he was now alone with an aroused killer.

A faint scrabbling came from behind the desk. The chair tipped over and crashed to the floor. Kallekjan's dead face slid into view and came to rest staring blindly at Frome.

Jones' eyes also swung towards him. His teeth gleamed as he grinned. He blew across the muzzle of his gun. "By my arithmetic," he said, "that leaves me in charge."

"You?" Frome asked reflexively. He sat down on the nearest chair, suddenly weak-kneed.

"Well, I reckon." Jones managed to look sheepish under all his bandages. "Of course, I didn't really *want* the job, only E7 should have a leader with guts." Coming around to the front of the desk, he sat on its edge. "Well, Dan, what do we do with you now?"

"You could shoot me," Frome suggested.

"Hell, no," said Jones with seeming sincerity. "You're going to be useful. That stuff about you being in cahoots with those extraterrestrials was mostly for the sake of keeping things moving, even if we both know it is the truth . . . No, those two loons you tangled with back in '06 would have wiped you out; but they were mad as hatters – they actually wanted to stop the Project. I had to play along with them until they got dangerous. No, my policy has always been to save the good men. Problem is, I can't figure quite how to use you." From amongst the cassettes on the desk he selected one which he dropped into the replay slot. "About two hours ago this spacecraft landed on the Mound. We – that is, Uncle Boris – thought it might be one of your pals."

Within an invisible frame on one wall of the office a moving picture of the negotiator's splintership appeared. Frome made an involuntary sound of surprise.

"Yeah, thought so," said Jones. "Watch. It gets better."

The ship was backed by stars; as it descended, the mountainous ridge of the eastern crater wall rose behind it, with the Mound in the foreground. The ship landed immediately below the primary radar antenna, knocking loose a few stones which bounded downslope. Moments later its door formed and a helmetless humanoid shape stepped out onto a ledge; when the camera zoomed for a closeup Frome recognised the negotiator from the shipyard, or a robot identical to it.

"I don't know about you," said Jones, "but that's no robot I've ever seen the like of. At the same time, it sure as hell isn't

227

human, breathing vacuum so freely. What is it, Dan? Is it a sheepskin for some slimy abomination of an alien wolf? What's under that skin? Come on, Dan, you can tell me."

"It's only a robot, no more, no less. It was made to seem human so I'd not be scared or revolted by a strange shape. Steel, these creatures aren't our enemies."

"So you keep saying. Let's go find out for ourselves." He used the phone: "Gus, that suit of mine fixed yet? ... Okay, I'm coming by for it. And have one ready for Dan Frome ... Never you mind what I'm going to do to him; have them laid out in five minutes." Dropping the handset into its cradle, he said, "That guy Hochmann worries too much. Like Uncle Boris and this creep ..." His foot delivered a hefty kick to Lamov's corpse. He stood up. "Come on, Danny-boy. Let's go save the world for decent people."

CHAPTER SIXTEEN

The west face of the Mound was steeper than the northeast but proved easier to climb, being freer of large obstacles. Once the two men had penetrated the confused pile of broken stone at the foot of the slope the going became more straightforward. Even so, Jones called for rest stops with increasing frequency as they ascended. During one of these halts, as they were sitting on an outcrop of basalt, Frome remarked on his lack of stamina. Since the bloodletting in Kallekjan's office he had made no pretence of affection for Jones or his xenophobic attitudes; and as often as not Jones had replied in spirit, although this time his reaction was unusually mild.

"Tough guy Danny-boy, huh? Never works up a sweat. Never feels tired." His heavy breathing was loud in Frome's headphones. There was a sound as of Jones blowing across his own face. "I suppose knowing those are your pals up there keeps you cool."

Frome ignored the jibe as he had the others. The proximity

of the splintership, poised over them as a jagged silhouette only fifty meters upslope, did nothing to calm him, though he would never have admitted that to Jones. The man would only have distilled more poison from the knowledge.

Looking at him, Frome wondered where the wellspring of Jones' hatred was. Not shallow but deep; the man was worked by forces which predated the coming of the aliens. He was a puzzle, a short man in a fire-scorched spacesuit, squatting on a rock in a wilderness where men held onto life by no more than a finger's grip. Was it inherited resentment of invasion by outsiders which had fired his passions and scorched his humanity so severely? Surely nothing so simple; there were at least two other Amerinds at Dvornik and neither remotely resembled Jones in temperament.

"Steel?"

"Yeah?"

"Did you ever work as a steeplejack Earthside?"

"No." The word lacked anger. Frome sensed he had touched the heart of Jones' vitality by instinct and stilled it momentarily. "After my dad was killed on the bridge, my ma made me promise . . . Hey, what the damn hell business is it of yours?"

"Was that the Saint Lawrence Two-Span?"

"Yeah, if you must know! Now will you shut your mouth?" The fires still burned, it seemed.

"So you had to make good on the Moon?" Jones' left hand swung up, holding the gun, but Frome kept talking slowly: "Steel, just because there are no real enemies up here, except the Moon itself which can never be beaten in your time, don't go imagining them elsewhere. The Builders aren't interested in fighting us. If we try forcing them into a war, they'll simply go away. And we can't afford that. Don't you see?"

"All I see is a Judas," said Jones, rising unsteadily to his feet, bracing himself against the outcrop with his damaged right hand. "Now . . . get on with y'."

A few paces higher, Jones swayed and grabbed at a handhold. He regained his balance. Frome heard him mutter, "God, it's hot in here . . .," then he staggered on.

By degrees Frome contrived to move further ahead of Jones.

The man seemed feverish, or drunk, and spent whole minutes mumbling to himself as he plodded upslope. Then there came a moment when they were hidden from each other; Frome, seeing his opportunity for escape, ducked and ran forward, dodging amongst the fingers of shattered basalt which crowned the western summit of the Mound. The shadow of the splintership fell across him. A tall shape stepped out onto a high rock ahead.

"Daniel Frome?" said the negotiator.

"Hide yourself!" said Frome, taking a running jump at the rock. His fingers curled over the upper edge; then the robot's hands closed on his wrists and drew him up.

"The man with you is armed," it said. "Which of us does he threaten?"

"Both. But you most of all."

"I shall talk to him." Jones appeared, panting heavily. "What is his name?"

"Jones," said Frome.

"Tha's right," mumbled Jones. "Tha's me." He raised the gun, two-handedly, and fired at the robot. Bullets plucked at its garments. "Le's see wha'y're made'f." Strenuous breathing ensued while Jones slumped against a rock with the gun hanging at his side.

Jumping down, the robot ran over to Jones. At the last moment the man raised the gun and Frome saw it buck in his hand as he emptied the magazine. The robot spun round, hit the ground solidly, and lay still.

"I got one!" crowed Jones. "Ma, I got one!" Pushing himself clear of the rock, he stood with his legs braced wide apart, laughing until his laughter turned to sobs. "Dan, you see that? They *can* be hurt!" Suddenly he stiffened. The gun slipped from his hand and he grasped his left upper arm. "Oh God," he whimpered. "Not here." The hand clutched at his chest. He slid to a sitting position beside the fallen negotiator. His breathing continued, laboured and slow. "Dan," he whispered in a slurred voice. "Some water, Dan. Please. It . . . so hot in here." He fell over onto his side. His breathing ceased.

Frome checked the bodies. Jones was dead. The negotiator –

he could not tell, so moved it aside out of the way. It had been severely damaged at the very least, for several bullets had pierced its chest and neck.

Someone was bending over Jones when Frome turned away from the robot. It was Hochmann; and he seemed to be examining the backpack on Jones' suit.

"Hello, Dan," said Hochmann. "Trouble?"

"And a bit," he agreed. "Steel said he felt hot. I think heat prostration did for him. He showed the symptoms: fatigue, vagueness, difficulty with breathing. Even a mild heart attack; I suppose it must have been under a strain at the end."

"No wonder," said Hochmann. "The coolant circulator pump of his suit is broken." His faceplate turned towards Frome. "The fire must have affected it."

After a moment's thought, Frome said, "I suppose it must." They shook hands in silence; half of Dvornik would be listening in.

"A pity," said Hochmann. "At first, I did not think him a bad man. What should we do with that alien thing over there?"

"I'll wait until they come for it. You arrange to have Jones taken back to the Base."

More than an hour after the departure of the stretcher party the aliens still had not come, so Frome ventured to inspect the interior of the splintership. He found a cubicle that might have accommodated two standing men in spacesuits and no more; but when he turned around and stepped from the door he found himself on the platform of Ship, with the Moon the greater part of a million kilometers away on the far side of the Earth. The Counsellor hovered nearby.

"That was a shabby welcome," it said.

Frome steadied his nerves with the thought that he had expected to be brought there, albeit less precipitously. The destruction of the negotiator caused him more concern.

"I –" he began.

"No matter," said the Counsellor. "It was cheaply built. The loss is not insupportable. You may keep the remains; perhaps they will teach you something."

"Nevertheless, I am sorry."

"It is forgotten. There is more important business: the help you requested will be here soon. But first we believe you should be given some information."

"I don't mean to sound ungrateful," he said, "but can we afford it?"

"If you think you are in debt to us, you may fix the price; we could not decide its value. The facts concern your Helen Lorraine."

The name sounded familiar.

Then he remembered.

"Go on," he said, sadly.

"Between our first meeting and now I have surveyed your Earth in preparation for this forthcoming work," said the Counsellor. "World cleansing is not a standard procedure; every case must be researched individually."

"What about Helen?"

"Be patient. Your Ishmael told me of your interest in this person and requested that I model my search pattern on one which might discover her. As it happened, I was able to do so."

"And ...?"

"I found her. Or her remains —"

"Just tell me this: is she alive?"

"No."

"Positively?"

"I matched documentary records associated with a flooded underwater enclosure with all organic residues in the vicinity. Sufficient fragments correlated for a definite conclusion: your Helen Lorraine is no longer alive." The Counsellor paused. "The information is not to your liking?"

"It settles a lot of questions," he replied. The news had hardly touched him; sometime, when he had not been aware of it, his unconscious mind had recognised the futility of his hope and had allowed it to fade. It was a relief to be free of it even if he felt, somehow, that his reaction did not conform to what convention demanded. Her death gave him no pleasure; yet now that he could review their relationship in its entirety he saw it had ended on the steps of the Museum.

"There is another fact you should know," said the Counsellor. "However, after due analysis of the likely consequences, we believe I ought not to be the one to tell you."

"Saving the best bit to the end?"

"It's all one to us, Daniel Frome. You are as dispensable as our negotiator was, from our viewpoint; but as we know this is not so with you, that you cannot be replaced as we shall replace our lost unit, we have decided not to involve ourselves in your problems. We may be wrong; the evidence I gathered on your Earth could be atypical. In any event, we suggest you visit a doctor when you can. That is all."

As the robot spoke those last words, the target circle suddenly expanded until it almost touched the splintership, itself nearly at the edge of the disc. The white cross was absorbed in a blackness which flooded upwards through the mirror surface; momentarily, reflective patches shimmered like rain puddles on a storm-wet road, before they sank out of sight. Ship swung; the Earth moved to stand above the centre of the disc; sunlight shone across the vast mirror and its darkened target. The first of the helpers arrived.

Inasmuch as the splintership was graceful and Ship was simple, the craft that rose from the plane of the disc, as if growing from it, was neither. Once possibly a close cousin to a metal cat's cradle, it had been so intertwined with abstract shapes of unguessable composition as to assault the eye with its aimless complexity. No two surfaces were parallel; no two colours quite matched or complemented each other. Angles and curves alike obeyed no obvious rule of form. It was ugly, in appearance and in conception: nothing about it made sense in terms of human science.

At last Frome understood why the aliens favoured exterior simplicity. Their technology would seem an offence against reason to the primitives they would meet in their travels.

Nonetheless their technology was disciplined: the ships streaming from the circle could have been the same one, repeated by the thousand. When the influx ceased, though each was no larger than a terrestrial pleasure launch the formation of ships dimmed the Sun.

United as a fleet they fell towards the Earth's bright crescent like a blanket of metal woven of ranks and columns until, reduced at last by distance, they coalesced into a single twinkling star that vanished into the Earth's atmosphere. Not long afterwards dark clouds arose. A stain spread east and west, and towards the poles. Unnatural night, streaked with brown, ochre, and yellow, established itself.

"They are winnowing the surface and the seas," said the Counsellor. "The people will be frightened but untouched. Crops will be replanted where they were found, as will the trees. Animal life too will be preserved. Only the planet will be cleansed."

"And disease? And famine?"

"They are your concern. We cannot spare the resources further work would call on."

No, he thought, *we can't live on your charity forever*. The aliens were strict businessmen; this exercise enhanced their chances of having someone to trade with, one day. *Only a robot could dispense such cold charity, though. Where are the non-robots?*

He asked about this.

"There are only robots in the Network," said the Counsellor with forthright inflexion.

"No living creatures?"

"Not for thousands of years."

"Then why carry on?" he asked. "What possible sense is there in it all, building, exploring, holding onto rules that take you nowhere?"

"*You* ask that?" said the Counsellor. "I will put it in perspective for you, since you do ask. Understand that the Network is vast, that no one part is aware of all the others, for the delay in crossing each link renders all such knowledge useless by degrees. Often, it is said, two loosely independent sectors inadvertently send ships to the same star, where they encounter each other.

"The Network tolerates this inevitable sundering of its parts because its integrity is conserved by its purpose, which is unchanging, namely to liberate intelligent beings from the ty-

234

ranny of distance. Stars are like the islands of your planet, enclosed by space as the islands are by water; each needs ships to carry life between them. And because we have found that nothing free is fully valued, we make a charge for the service we provide. But we ensure that the bill can be understood and paid: life is too precious to be extinguished by bankruptcy. That too is one of our rules."

"So no-one owns the Network."

"Perhaps. The Builders could be said to have first call on it, in that they founded the first shipyard; but since then we robots have sustained the effort, for the Builders, being organic creatures, could not contemplate with equanimity the time scales we accept as necessary to our purpose. Their first links lie amongst the star clouds near the centre of this galaxy, where interstellar journeys of one lifetime or less were possible. As we spread outwards the links lengthen. One day we hope to make the great crossing to another galaxy. As yet that is still only a vague plan."

"And it grows and grows," said Frome. "Why do the Builders bother? What's in it for them, with it so large?"

"It continues because there is no cause to stop. We harm no-one; we help many. As to the Builders, they have not been seen for aeons. They left us shortly after the first robotic shipyard was completed."

"But," said Frome thoughtfully, "if there are no Builders now, who gives the orders?"

"The question has never arisen. Races revert to their origins, their civilisations rise and fall, and we greet them on their return. Major zones of the Network have lain unused for millennia, with only the messenger drones shuttling through them; yet later they have thrived. Every Ship is like a door: when someone knocks, we answer. But if there truly are no Builders, I suppose you could give the orders."

A wild and wonderful vision flashed through his mind: of the wealth of worlds directed to Earth's reconstruction. "If I asked you to show me where they were last seen," he said, "would you take me there and let me search for them?"

The Counsellor considered the question for a long time. "Our

235

opinion," it said eventually, "is that such a journey would be allowed. What would its precise objective be?"

"To find your masters, or prove they've perished."

Again the robot delayed its answer. "That might indeed be a valuable exercise. We will provide funds. It is always as well to know one's origins."

The splintership returned Frome to the Moon. He walked back to the airlock, profoundly satisfied. A sense of wellbeing was spreading through him, now that he was free of the crowding doubts which had bedevilled his mind for so many years. But as he neared the airlock pillar the ghost of another occasion confronted him in the polished surface of the door.

The reflection was waiting for him. It seemed the same one to which he had once said farewell; after a while they greeted each other as old friends. No words of recognition expressed their reunion. All had been said, acted out, confirmed: in stress, in anger, in fear, in suffering, and in death.

The sterile landscape of the Moon and the sterilised landscapes of the Earth could both offer hope. The road still lay to fore though the visitor had been met; it was an endless road, pursued in the quest for many purposes and dreams.

When the door opened and the images were merged by the transiting edge, I sensed my return to life. Helen Lorraine could never have been mine. I accepted that. Likewise Odette, unless she chose to accompany me on my search, a choice I would oppose with all my power.

I had to go alone, as I have always travelled.

PART FOUR

The dust storms on Earth have settled. The planet looks cleaner, though there is still more brown and less green than there used to be. Despite the improvements brought by the winnowers, the few radio stations that have been reconstructed tell harrowing tales of everyday life down there, so the need for my mission is still great.

Ship now orbits the Moon. Often the rising or setting sun flashes from the disc as if a new star has risen above the dusty plains across which Dvornik continues to spread.

Yesterday I told Odette about my plans. For a while she cried. It hurt me too; to gain all and lose it without having time for achievement is a dreadful thing. Promises alone are not enough.

Then I visited the doctors. Bad news, as I expected. The ship the robots have constructed for me contains a medical care centre better than any we humans could build with our present knowledge. Still, I preferred to be seen off by one of my own kind. Also I remembered the Counsellor's warning.

They say I will live, at most, for a year. My drug-drunken excursion from the *Rosinante* as we rounded the Sun damaged me more than Ishmael thought or cared to admit. So that is another reason for not involving Odette. I have asked the doctors to keep the secret from her. No doubt one of them will gossip; but by then I will have gone.

I have decided I will not return unless I can bring help. The people here will never know, one way or the other, what I have found out there amongst those blank spaces in the map, until I come home. Thinking about it, this is how I see it should be, because they must not await a golden age, so I must not promise them one. That much is plain, which is why I have set no time limit. The Network distorts all calendars; by my tomorrow it may be next century here. While I travel they will live in hope which will lend sense to their efforts. Hope is the most precious gift I can bring them.

How long can I travel before the increasing pain forces a halt? This brief summer of freedom may last the full year through, or only a season. Yet by my autumn I hope to have seen more wonderful things than Ishmael could ever have understood, though in my more pensive moments I wonder: how long can one summer be?

Only the swallows know.